PRAISE FOR

"A rollercoaster of emotions. Absolutely brilliant and beautiful."
—Alex Brown, bestselling author of
*A Postcard from Italy*, for *Statistically Speaking*

"Utterly spellbinding, it sent shock waves through my heart."
—Cathy Bramley, *Sunday Times* best-
selling author, for *Statistically Speaking*

"This book is a triumph."
—*Woman's Own* for *Statistically Speaking*

"Emotional, beautiful, wonderful. Debbie Johnson at her finest."
—Milly Johnson, *Sunday Times* best-
selling author, for *Statistically Speaking*

"Debbie Johnson writes stories that make your heart happy. Her words are wise, funny, and honest: an arm-around-the-shoulders, a smile through tears, and a gentle companion to make sense of life. I adore her books, packed with hope and heart."
—Miranda Dickinson, *Sunday Times* bestselling author

"Jenny James' midlife road trip with a reclusive stranger gave me all sorts of ideas . . . Warm, witty, relatable, poignant—Jenny is a delight!"
—Emma Grey, bestselling author of *The Last Love Note*

"... a love letter to those who have been kicked in the teeth by life but picked themselves up and became better and happier versions of themselves. Life is truly what you make it."

—Julia London, *New York Times* bestselling author, for *Jenny James Is Not a Disaster*

"... a breezy, entertaining, and insightful 'when life gives you lemons' story about second chances and starting over that brims with both humor and heart. Readers will fall for Jenny James's honest and hilarious voice in this winning narrative that explores the themes of love, friendship, and forgiveness. I thoroughly enjoyed this heartwarming and uplifting book and found myself rooting for Jenny from the very first page!"

—Angela Brown, bestselling author of *Olivia Strauss Is Running Out of Time*, for *Jenny James Is Not a Disaster*

"Uplifting, poignant, and very funny."

—Lucy Diamond, *Sunday Times* best-selling author, for *Jenny James Is Not a Disaster*

"Romantic, heartbreaking, and packed with Debbie's trademark warmth and wisdom."

—Catherine Isaac, author of *You Me Everything*, for *Jenny James Is Not a Disaster*

# STATISTICALLY
# SPEAKING

ALSO BY DEBBIE JOHNSON

*Jenny James Is Not a Disaster*

COMFORT FOOD CAFÉ

*A Wedding at the Comfort Food Café*
*A Gift from the Comfort Food Café*
*Sunshine at the Comfort Food Café*
*Coming Home to the Comfort Food Café*
*Christmas at the Comfort Food Café*
*Summer of the Comfort Food Café*

# STATISTICALLY SPEAKING

*A Novel*

DEBBIE JOHNSON

HARPER MUSE

*Statistically Speaking*

Published by Harper Muse, an imprint of HarperCollins Focus LLC.

**Library of Congress Cataloging-in-Publication Data**
Names: Johnson, Debbie (Debbie M.) author.
Title: Statistically speaking : a novel / Debbie Johnson.
Description: [Nashville] : Harper Muse, 2024. | Summary: "When Gemma's anxiety gets the best of her, she opens her sock drawer and starts counting. Lately, she's been counting a lot of socks"—Provided by publisher.
Identifiers: LCCN 2024018862 (print) | LCCN 2024018863 (ebook) |
    ISBN 9781400248049 (paperback) | ISBN 9781400248070 (epub) |
    ISBN 9781400248100
Subjects: LCGFT: Novels.
Classification: LCC PR6110.O42 S73 2024 (print) | LCC PR6110.O42 (ebook)
LC record available at https://lccn.loc.gov/2024018862
LC ebook record available at https://lccn.loc.gov/2024018863

*Printed in the United States of America*

24 25 26 27 28 LBC 5 4 3 2 1

*To Milly Johnson, for just being you.*

# PART I
# THEN

# CHAPTER I

# TEN TINY FINGERS, TEN TINY TOES

*October, eighteen years ago*

**"You're doing great," the midwife** says, glancing up at me from between my trembling, sweat-sheened knees. "Keep going, my love, just keep going."

She is trying to be encouraging, trying to be kind, trying to help me through this. I know that none of this is her fault, but still, I kind of want to punch her in the face.

I ignore her and concentrate on counting my breaths, counting the precious moments of calm between waves of agony.

At my side, Geoff with a G is murmuring words of encouragement while pointedly averting his gaze from the war zone that is my lower half.

"Brilliant, Gemma," he mutters, eyes skittering, his skin pale and waxy. He looks as though he's in so much distress that you'd think he was the one doing this.

None of this is his fault either, but I want to punch him in the face as well.

I grunt and screw up my eyes and push so hard when I am told to that I feel as though I might pass out from lack of oxygen. My fists are scrunched around creased hospital sheets, my hair is stuck to my forehead in damp clumps, and I can taste salt on my otherwise dry lips. I push, and I pant, and I want to give up. Actually, I don't just want to give up; I think I might want to die.

In the background, the music is doing nothing to help. I'd put together some songs, back when I thought listening to them might make a difference, but now that just seems silly. As if Robbie Williams singing about angels could help with this. It's definitely not Robbie's fault, but if he were in the room, and I had the spare energy, his face wouldn't be safe either.

Mainly, I want to punch myself in the face—because this is *my* fault. And it is so much harder than I thought, than I ever could have imagined it would be. It is nothing like it is on television—but then again, neither was the act that started it all. There is nothing magical about any of it, nothing beautiful or perfect. Just pain, and worry, and a weird sense of loneliness.

Your first love and motherhood come with such loaded expectations. They are the moments that are supposed to mean something. To connect you to something bigger than yourself. To make you feel special.

That's all bullshit, I reckon. If losing your virginity and having a baby were sold the way they really are, nobody would ever do either of those things, and the human race would die out. If they were billed as "pain and worry and a weird sense of loneliness," nobody would be in such a rush to do either, would they? We've all been conned.

Life isn't rainbows and unicorns. It's sludge-gray drizzle and feral rats. Then again, I am not in the best of moods.

I am sixteen and I am having a baby. I am pushing a real-life human being out of my lady parts, and it hurts. It hurts a lot, and I left "tired" behind about twelve hours ago—now I am well into "so exhausted I may never leave this bloody bed."

I knew it would be painful, but I wasn't prepared for the exhaustion, the sense of defeat, the feeling of failure—the suspicion that I might not be able to do what millions of women have done for millennia, squatting in deserts and on bathroom floors and in the backs of taxis. I am too crap to even give birth properly.

I want to cry, for so many reasons—but I am too wrung out to spare the tears. I feel another wave of pain and get yelled at to push, and I try, I really do, but I have nothing left to give. All of me has floated away in a cloud of despair and sheer knackeredness.

"I can't do this!" I scream. "Please, just make it stop! Make it stop!" I bite my lip hard, three times, tasting blood on my tongue.

Geoff with a G looks even queasier, but he takes hold of one of my hands, squeezes my fingers, and says: "You're okay, Gemma. You can do this. You know you can."

He doesn't sound very convinced, but it is something to cling to. Kind words, a kind touch. A kind man. It calms me enough that I take in more air, gulping it in greedily.

"Gemma, you're nearly there, love!" says the midwife. I've forgotten her name. Something Irish, I think, even though her accent is pure East London. This is my third midwife—I have gone through a few shift changes now.

"You said that hours ago!" I scream at her. "You were lying! You're a bloody liar!"

The midwife actually laughs out loud at this accusation. It is a strange sound to hear floating up to my ears, a tinkling of amusement as she roots around, as she inspects, as she probes.

"Gemma, I can see her head!" she adds. "And I'm not lying—I can see her head, and she has lovely red hair like you, and she is so ready to come and meet you—come on now, one last big push for me!"

Red hair. Huh. I've always hated mine, but for some reason I feel weirdly pleased that she has it too. Like it's a connection we will always have, no matter what else we lose. A twine of ginger reaching down through the ages. I grip hold of Geoff's hand, tighter than any sane human being would appreciate, and I push, growling out a long stream of air, forcing myself to find that last shred of strength that I need. I lean forward as I do it, squashed up and folded and as concertinaed as my mal-formed body can get.

I hear Geoff and the midwife speaking words that don't register; I feel a flickering sensation behind my eyes, a high-pitched ringing in my ears, the world around me a blanked-out, buzzing void: nothing exists but me and this moment and doing this one thing. The most important thing I have ever done.

I am sixteen and I am having a baby. A baby girl, with red hair. I let out one scream, put all my energy into helping her into the world, and know that I am spent. That I have nothing more to give. If this is not enough, then this is not happening.

It is enough. And it is happening. Head, shoulders, tiny body, slithering into this small room in this busy hospital, like she's in a rush now. She's rushing out of me and into her own life—into a world that I hope treats her well.

I feel disconnected from my own body as she arrives, bur-dened with a sense of physical relief and emotional dread. I stare at the curtains, at the stripes, repeated patterns of three different shades of green. I read somewhere once that green is supposed to be calming. It is not—at least not in this situation.

I blink rapidly as the midwife pulls my baby up and into her solid hands. I wonder how many babies she has delivered with those hands, how many women she has helped. I find that I don't really care, about that or about anything. I am done, I am trembling, I am slick with sweat. It has even caught in my eyelashes, is dripping from my brows. The skin of my face feels sore and stretched over my bones.

I look at the clock on the off-white wall. It is just past midnight on October 3. It is her birthday. She took her sweet time and arrived ten days after she was scheduled to. But she is here, this brand-new thing, this fresh creature, this tiny human. This life waiting to unfold. She is here, and she has been born to the sound of Kelis singing about her milkshake. That doesn't seem right, somehow—but it is done, and I can only hope that she hasn't absorbed it. That she won't grow up to have a weird yearning to lie on tables in diners.

The midwife—she's called Siobhan, I suddenly remember—is cooing and chatting as she cuts the cord, starts to check the baby over. It only takes minutes, but it is enough time for me to lose whatever magic was keeping me upright and present.

I collapse backward, my head banging against the steel of the bed frame. I don't even feel it. I am suddenly bone-deep cold, shivering, in shock. If I'd just finished a marathon, someone would wrap me in a foil sheet and give me a Mars bar.

"Here she is—absolutely perfect! Eight pounds, two ounces, and a lovely length—she's going to be a tall one!" says Siobhan, bringing the tiny form, wrapped in a blanket, toward me. I see one pudgy arm sticking out, fist clenched in bright red fury. Like she's already angry at the world.

"I don't want to hold her!" I say quickly, holding my hands up to ward them away, wishing I could run—not even a marathon, just out of this room. Away from here, away from now.

I cannot run, though. I cannot move. I am trapped, my body still pulsating, my mind spiraling as she approaches.

"It's okay, Gemma," says Geoff with a G. He has stood up, is peering into that blanket, smiling at what he sees.

"You should see her. You should hold her. You'll regret it if you don't." I glare at him, filled with anger—with a bright red fury of my own. I have so many regrets already; what harm could one more possibly do me?

I don't have the energy to argue, though, and I accept the bundle that is passed to me. Part of me knows he is right. That even if this hurts, I must do it, or wake up every single day for the rest of my life wishing I'd been brave enough.

I have held babies before. Some of my foster families also took in tiny ones like this. I have changed nappies and warmed bottles, and wondered what all the fuss is about. Babies are noisy and messy and not very good conversationalists and I never understood why people are so keen on them.

This, though, is different. This is my baby. This is a baby who has lived inside my body for more than nine months. This is a little girl with red hair and a red face, and she is at once a stranger and someone I have known for all of eternity. She is new and she is old and she is everything all at the same time.

She nestles into me, her face turning sideways, rooting and snuffling, one finger flipping up as though she was born knowing how to be rude. She has a bad attitude, I decide, as I peel back the covers and gaze at her face. I like people with a bad attitude.

"Perfect, Gemma," says Siobhan, hovering by my side. "Look at that. Look at what you did, you brave girl. Ten tiny fingers, ten tiny toes."

The midwife is patronizing me, which I can't blame her for. It's hard to argue a case for your maturity and wisdom when you've just given birth to a baby you conceived while you were still in school.

But she is also mistaken, at least about one of those things. The baby might be perfect, but I am not brave. I am not brave at all. I ignore her, lost now in more important things. Like counting those ten tiny fingers, those ten tiny toes, and drinking in that angry, red face. I stroke my baby's hair, damp and gooey still, and she blinks her eyes open and stares up at me. Her eyes are wide and a dark shade that could be either blue or gray, but I know they'll probably change anyway over the next few months. I saw it in one of the books Geoff gave me.

I won't be in her life by then. It is strange to think that I will not be around to see what color eyes she has. It is one of the many things I will never know. The way she looks at me, though, is enough for now.

The way she looks at me, it feels like she understands it all. Like she knows all the stuff, the good and the bad and the boring. It is the stare of someone who sees right through you, who cuts through the bullshit, who knows everything that has ever happened in the universe ever. Minutes old and already the wisest being I've met.

Geoff is blathering. Siobhan is chattering. Kelis has been replaced by Christina Aguilera. None of it matters. It is all surplus to requirements. All that matters is me and my baby—this beautiful-ugly, young-old scrap of a person lying on my chest.

It is me and her and it is the magic. It is the rainbows and the unicorns and the perfect. It is the everything—the anti-lonely, the anti-weird, the anti-fear. It is the best I have ever felt in my life, and it is the worst I have ever felt in my life.

She is perfect, the most beautiful human I have ever seen. I cannot believe she came from me. She is perfect, and now I am going to give her away. I am going to let her be taken out of my arms, out of this room, passed on to strangers. Her real life starts as soon as she is away from me, in a better reality. One where she will be loved and cherished and well fed and well cared for. Where she will have a good home, and people who love her, and an education, and opportunity.

Where she won't have me.

I kiss her red face, and smell her red hair, and try to imprint every detail of this moment, of this creation, into my memory.

"I love you, Baby," I murmur. I don't want to give her a name. That is for her new family to do. The family that Geoff with a G found and vetted and worked with. The family that will give her the life I can't. The family that will give her the awesome world she deserves. To me, she will always be just Baby.

"It's not too late, you know," says Geoff quietly. "Nothing is settled, nothing is definite. You have weeks to decide before anything gets signed. You could keep her until then, see how you feel. We can find ways to help you—you don't have to rush into this."

I don't meet his eyes—my eyes are on my baby, soaking in her wondrousness—but I manage a smile for him. He means well, and I no longer wish to damage his face.

He means well, but he and I both know what that help would look like. I might find a foster family that would take in a teenager and a newborn. I might find a place in an independent living unit. I might even be able to find my own place, if I were very special and very lucky and the Gods of Forgotten Children smiled upon me. There would be assessments and key workers and reports and visits and a grinding sense of benign scrutiny. Every move, every mistake, every choice I made, would be watched.

I've lived in and out of this system for a lot of my life, and I know how it feels to always be watched. Sometimes the system works—I have met good people, had foster parents who helped me, found some stability. Sometimes it doesn't work, and the less said about that the better. But none of it is what I want for this little girl—she shouldn't have to settle for second best, for anything less than perfect.

I don't want her growing up with a mum who is still too young to look after her properly. A mum who can barely make a Pot Noodle without scalding herself. I don't want her growing up with the smell of mold in cheap rooms, or picking up on the secondhand anxiety that I'd be bound to share on endless walks with a pram on endless aimless days, worried about money and safety and what will become of us.

There isn't a smiling grandma with abundant patience; there isn't a long-lost auntie who will take us in. There is just me and well-meaning strangers, and that is not good enough for her. I want to give her the world—but all I can give her is this. The knowledge that I am not ready. That I am not capable, right now, of being what she needs. What she deserves.

Her new family—her real family—is more than ready. They have wanted her for years. They have her nursery painted in yellow and cream, they have tiny sleepsuits all soft and clean, and they have a baby-shaped hole in their hearts that she will fill.

I could love her, but I couldn't give her that world. I love her, so I am giving her away.

I drag my gaze away from hers and look up at Geoff. He looks a bit teary-eyed and I wonder if he is cut out for this job—for being a social worker. He shouldn't even be here, really—he is doing more than his job demands. Going above and beyond, and risking broken finger bones to be here with me.

"It's okay," I say firmly. "I've made up my mind. I've thought about it all, Geoff. It's what is best for her. And probably me. You can take her."

Siobhan is silent for once, nodding when she sees my resolve, silently taking my newborn into her arms.

"They are lovely, Gemma," Geoff replies. "She couldn't ask for better parents. They're so excited about meeting her."

I nod and close my eyes. I am sad and tired and don't want to be conscious anymore. There is a possibility that I may never want to be conscious again.

"Have you got the letter?" I ask.

"I have, and I'll make sure they get it."

"Could I have it back? Just for a minute. And a pen. I need a pen."

Geoff fumbles in the satchel bag he carries everywhere with him, big enough to contain the files that summarize his clients' lives. He pulls out a brown envelope, removes the letter inside it, then rummages some more. I hear him muttering something about how he can never find a bloody pen, and he is saved by Siobhan. She passes one over to him, and he nods gratefully before he brings them both to me.

I wriggle as upright as I can, and feel like my body might split in two. I wince, and Geoff gives me a book to lean on. It is a hardback Tom Clancy novel, which almost makes me laugh—Geoff is the least macho man I have ever met. Perhaps it belongs to his wife.

I screw up my eyes, folding the letter over to the blank bit at the end. I already know there are 1,615 words. Probably too many, maybe not enough—if this is going to be all of me that she has, how could it ever be enough? I wrote that letter over and over, so many times, the floor around me scattered with balled-up sheets and my fingers aching and stained from cheap, leaking pens.

Still, I need to write more. I need to say more. I need to tell her about this moment in time, this perfect, wonderful, terrible moment.

I scrawl a hurried PS. My writing is wrecked, and I am scared of blotting the pages with sweat, but eventually it is done. I pass it over to Geoff, and I fall back onto the bed and back into the cold, numb place that I know will help me survive this. A place I am all too familiar with. Geoff puts the letter back into the envelope and into his bag. He smiles at me and looks as though he is about to speak.

"Don't," I preempt. "There isn't anything else to be said."

He nods decisively, and Siobhan passes him the baby, legs kicking and fists still waving. He accepts this precious bundle and leaves the room. He takes the perfect and the rainbow and the unicorn with him. I am left there with a midwife and a placenta, and the knowledge that doing the right thing doesn't always feel right.

I imagine my own mother, sixteen years ago, in a room like this, riddled with mind-worms and drugs and a life that was swallowing her whole. I wonder if she saw me, a tiny thing with bright red hair, and felt all that pain and glory and potential.

It is too much. It is too hard. I am deflated and empty in every way. I feel my mind fracturing into a million pieces, falling into a dark place that I might never escape from.

I console myself with remembering. With counting. With ten tiny fingers and ten tiny toes.

# CHAPTER 2

# 1,656 WORDS AND WAY TOO MANY FEELINGS

*Dear Baby,*

*This is a weird one to write, and probably a weird one to read. This is, like, version fifty, and I've decided it's the final version, because I'm never going to get it entirely right and because I've got blisters on my pen-holding finger now.*

*Anyway, your real parents have promised they will give this to you when they think you're old enough. That might mean when you're ten or when you're fifty, who knows? I've suggested they give it to you when you're sixteen, which is how old I am now.*

*So—this is me. Your biological mother. As I write this you are still inside me, which is odd, but I think I'll miss it. I'll miss you, and I'll miss knowing that you're safe and well and protected. I can't imagine putting my hand on my tummy and you not being there.*

*If you're reading this, you know that you were adopted, and I hope you have a really good life and that your mum and dad tell you off plenty and set loads of rules for you. It might not feel like it, but that's a good thing, honest—it means they're bothered. So maybe try not to hate them for it, like*

*I see all my mates do—they're always moaning about being controlled and stuff.*

*That's it, by the way—the sum of my life wisdom.*

*I don't have much to share with you on that front, because, like I say, I'm sixteen. I don't regret having you—you were not some terrible mistake—but I would maybe also say on the life wisdom front that vodka and boys don't mix that well, so be careful with that.*

*You're probably wondering why I gave you away, and that's fair, and that's why I'm writing this. I didn't want you to grow up feeling rejected, or crap about yourself, or at least no more than normal. So, here's the thing—I didn't give you away because I didn't love you, or because I didn't want you, or because there was anything wrong with you. I haven't met you in person yet, but I just know you're perfect in every way a baby can be perfect. I can tell.*

*I gave you away because of me, and my life, and what I can't do for you. My mum has a mental illness, and she also does a lot of drugs and drinks too much, and I'm sure that's all kind of bundled up for her in one horrible package. If I was looking at her life from the outside, I'd feel so sorry for her—she tries so hard, and on days when she's her version of normal, she is really funny and kind and good to be with. But on the days when she's not, she's so sad she can't get out of bed, or sometimes she's scary and out of control. Either way, it makes you feel completely freaked out.*

*I know it's not her fault, but I am angry with her anyway. Then I feel guilty for being angry, and it all gets squished up in my head. One of the ways I deal with that is by counting things. Whenever I'm a bit stressed or upset, I count stuff to calm me down. Stupid things, like steps, and windows, and how many Skittles there are in a bag. I started doing that when I was really little, like about seven, I think. Old enough to count, anyway. She told me she was going out to get some chips and would only be five minutes, and I was at home on my own and I was scared. So I started counting because I knew there were sixty seconds in each minute. Every time I got to sixty I made a mark on my coloring book.*

*Eventually the coloring book was pretty full, and I was pretty hungry, and I couldn't even cry anymore because I was so tired. She didn't come home for three days, and I just ate dry cereal out of the box. I even counted how many bits of Coco Pops there were.*

*After that, she went to hospital for a bit. And she gave me away. Then she came home and seemed better and got me back. Then it happened again, and again, until eventually she agreed that she would give me away for a longer time.*

*I didn't want that—even though it was shitty at home with my mum, it was still at home with my mum, which felt less frightening than living with strangers. But that's what happened, and I think now I can understand it a bit better. She didn't just give me away for the reasons I maybe thought at the time—because I was a pain, because I was inconvenient, because she preferred a simpler life without me. Or maybe she did, I don't know—it was all a bit chaotic.*

*But I think maybe she also gave me away because she knew it was better for me. She knew it was unhealthy for me, being with her, and maybe even dangerous. I think she gave me away because she wanted me to be safe and to be able to go to bed at night without having to check she hadn't left toast burning or worrying that she'd spent all our money and that I'd be hungry for the rest of the week.*

*I say maybe, because I don't know—we don't have the kind of relationship where we can talk about it. I don't see her much anymore, and that's both good and bad. Maybe if I'd had a letter like this, I'd know—I'd know she did some of the things she did because she actually loved me. And I think that would have helped—it would have made me feel better.*

*So that's why I am writing this. So you can feel better. So you will always know that I didn't give you away because I didn't love you, or because you did anything wrong. I do love you, more than I've ever loved anyone. It's weird and huge and really unexpected, how much I love you.*

*But I'm also only sixteen. I live in foster care. At the moment I'm with a woman called Audrey and she is really strict and takes no crap, and that is a good thing for me.*

*Audrey makes sure all the boring stuff is taken care of. I have clean clothes and food and a bed—she's good to me, but she doesn't love me, and I feel that a lot. I compare myself to my friends and it makes me feel lonely. I know my mum loves me, but she can't give me any of that other stuff, and that other stuff is important too. If I could mix and match them, that'd be great—but you can't do that with human beings. I can't give you all the bits of me that love you but let someone else do the boring bit that keeps you safe and happy—I have to give all of you away, and hope you'll find the real deal with them. All of the bits you need in one place.*

*If I was older, if my whole universe was different, I would keep you. But this is the reality—I have no other family, I have no money, and I don't have anything to offer you. I don't want you to grow up worried about how many Coco Pops are left in the box. I don't want you to grow up messed up by how messed up I am. I have thought about it such a lot, Baby, I really have—and even if you hate me for it, that's all right. You can. But you are going to have a proper family, and a nice life, and I hope all your worries will be normal ones, like about your mates and your exams and boys (hint: don't worry about any of those things!).*

*I can't tell you much about your bio-dad because I don't know much. I am ashamed to say this, but I don't even know his name—but he was pretty cool, and he was nice to me. If you're good at wheelies, that comes from him. I met him in the park, hanging around, and he was only visiting and disappeared as fast as he arrived. I don't know what all that counts for, but there you go. I don't know my dad either—as legend has it, my mum got pregnant while she was at Glastonbury at the music festival, but I've never known if that was true or just an interesting story she created.*

*It's both scary and wonderful how casually a life can be created. You're drunk or careless or in love and carried away, and suddenly a whole new human person is there, with their own set of dreams and needs and disappointments. I hope you don't have to continue this line of women who give away their children, because it sucks.*

*I'm going to stop now, and I am going to just say this—you are loved, and you are perfect, and you are going to be brilliant. I'm sad I won't be around to see that, how brilliant you'll be, but I think maybe you'll be less brilliant if you get stuck with me as your parent. Having a mum around isn't always for the best if it isn't the right mum.*

*Shine on, lovely Baby. I wish all the awesome for you.*

*Lots of love,*

*Your mum (my name is Gemma, by the way)*

*xxxxx*

*PS—I have met you now. You are amazing. The most beautiful thing I have ever seen, and the best thing I have ever done. You will never be mine, but I will be forever yours.*

# PART 2
# NOW

# CHAPTER 3

# ONE HUNDRED IRON MEN AND ONE BLACK CLOUD

*September, eighteen years later*

**"So,"** I say to Bill as he sprawls next to me on the concrete steps that lead down to the beach, "how did my life get so messy? I've been here for over a year now. I only meant to stay for a few months. I meant to keep it simple. I blame you."

Bill gazes at me with unreadable brown eyes, thuds his skinny tail once, and lets out a fragrant fart.

"Ha. Well, that told me."

I reach out and scratch behind his ears. He's a weird mix, Bill—some lurcher maybe, some collie, perhaps a bit of Lab. He's multicolored, shades of yellow and brown and gray, and has fur that's so long on his back he has a center parting, and so short on his head that he looks almost bald, apart from his massive and super-expressive eyebrows.

He has come from Hungary and probably doesn't understand a word I'm saying. *As opposed to British dogs*, I think, smiling at how silly this internal conversation is. British dogs would be quick to pick up on the subtleties of my emotional turmoil, wouldn't they? Not.

We have just finished our run, and we are sitting for a moment to gather our wits about us. I am, at least—I'm not so sure about Bill. He's the strong, silent type and doesn't say much.

It is 7:30 a.m., and the beach is already busy with dog walkers. Dog walkers, I have come to learn, are a friendly bunch. I know none of their names, and I have never shared mine, but we know each other by our beasts. There is a man with a small pack of corgis, and a lovely lady with a chatty springer spaniel, and a woman with labradoodles called Bugsy and Ronny, and one with an enormous Old English sheepdog called Marvin. I have no idea how they refer to me in their minds: Bill's mum, maybe, or the Ginger One with the Mixed-up Mongrel.

I have made up stories for them all, of course. I have assigned them fictional lives, complete with fictional partners and fictional children and fictional jobs. It comes as quite a shock when I see one of them out of context, and their actual lives don't match up to the ones I've amused myself with. I mean, who'd have thought that I'd see Mr. Smiley Staffy in town one day, and he'd be wearing a policeman's uniform, and be an actual policeman? In my version of events he was a landscape gardener who took his dog to work with him. Weird.

A small border terrier runs over to us and sniffs Bill's bits. Bill doesn't budge, or respond, or give any indication that he is alive. He is utterly inscrutable. It is a ploy that works, and we are soon left alone again.

It's the first week of September, and the sky is a pure pastel blue, cloudless and serene, colliding with sea and sand in lines of perfect color. It is clear enough to see the Welsh hills in the distance across from me, to see the curve of coastline that becomes Lancashire to my right, and the towers and spires of Liverpool to my left.

It is a strange stretch of land, sand dunes and sea creatures and skylarks singing, thistledown and sea holly and marsh orchids and big horizons and ever-shifting views. All this in a marriage of convenience with giant wind turbines and the cranes and gantries of the docks, container ships and cruise liners ghosting past on mist-laden mornings. A perfect point of balance between nature and the city.

It is also home to an art installation called *Another Place*, a hundred cast-iron figures of naked men, by the artist Antony Gormley. Because we all need more naked men in our eyes, right?

The iron men stretch out into the sea, submerged by the tide, sunk into sand, often dressed up in football shirts or given Christmas hats or sunglasses. It's another strange thing about this place, which I like. I have amused myself many times, walking from statue to statue, counting them, never quite managing them all for fear of getting lost at sea or sinking into mud, never to be seen again.

Today, this early, the tide is out, and the men are exposed, pitted and gritted and looking out at the edge of the world, unmoved and calm.

Me, not so much. I am not calm, and I am not unmoved, and I feel as though a cartoon version of me would feature a giant black rain cloud hovering above my head.

I have done everything I usually do to prepare myself for the day that lies in front of me. I have run my usual distance— three miles—which, for me, is just under six thousand steps. I have walked another mile at a slower pace. I have sipped my water. I have played with the dog. I have sat here and watched the world go by, for as long as I can manage. As an extra treat, I have even done some of that 4-7-8 breathing, with Bill looking on in amusement as I huffed and puffed.

None of it has worked. I still feel wired, and tense, and overadrenalized. It makes me want to start running again, and just keep going until I leave everything, especially myself, behind.

Maybe it's because it's the first full day back at the school where I teach after the long summer break. Maybe it's because I'll be meeting new students, probably new colleagues, and greeting old ones. Maybe it's because Margie, the lady who lives in the flat beneath mine and actually owns Bill, keeps trying to find out my whole life story, and I just don't do life-story swapping. Maybe it's because Karim, the admittedly pretty gorgeous head of PE, has asked me out for a drink and I don't feel ready to have a man in my life just now, even on a casual basis. Maybe it's because I've agreed to a longer contract, adding another year on to the length of time I usually spend anywhere. Maybe it's because I am starting to feel settled here, and I find feeling settled very . . . unsettling.

Maybe, I admit to myself as I stand and stretch and start the walk home, it is all of those things and none of those things.

Maybe it is because she is almost eighteen, and might be doing her A-level exams, like most eighteen-year-olds in England. Maybe it is because this year, I could have been her teacher. Maybe it is because after her A levels, if they go well, she might be choosing universities and courses, standing at a crossroads in her life as she looks at careers and maybe even a gap year. She might have a part-time job, and be planning a big party and her first legal drink, and she will be surrounded by friends and love and choices. She is looking at the future, and it is bright.

Of course, I have no clue if any of this is even remotely true—but I like to imagine it is. I imagine it, because I have no other option. I am not a part of her life, and never will be. I acknowledge this, and let the familiar tug of pain have its way with me, and know that I cannot chase it away before it is ready to go. It is a tenacious creature, this particular pain, made up of tentacles and hooks and talons that plunge deep and hold on tight.

I have missed her every single day since she was born. I have dreamed of her, and yearned for her, and never stopped thinking about her. But still, I know that I did the right thing. I repeat this to myself over and over again, until I feel its familiar truth, sad but consoling.

I reach the house by the beach where I live. It is at the end of a small terraced row, tucked between grand Victorian seaside homes with pastel-colored paint jobs and fancy wrought-iron verandas, and more modern mansions made of sheets of glass and sleek wood. Our terrace is homely, small but perfectly formed, gardens and patios edging out onto the marram grass and sand, within hearing of the waves and within sight of the sea. As I approach, I see Margie pottering around her terrace garden in a bright-pink quilted dressing gown, and watch as Bill gambols toward her.

I see the balcony of my own home, above hers, with the small table and just the one chair and the blanket I've left out there so I can sit, alone, in the now-cool nights, looking out to sea and along to the lit-up wonderland of the port.

I know there are fourteen steps to go up, and that I need to shower, and eat, and try to coax myself into a back-to-school state of mind.

I open the glossy white gate at the end of Margie's terrace, and Bill runs to her, nuzzling her gnarled hands as she tries to hoist a full watering can around. Without asking, I take it from her and start to sprinkle the patio pots, the mystery tubs, the fuchsias, the California lilac in terra-cotta. Every corner of her small space is filled with flowers and plants, with life and color, reaching upward and tumbling down and spreading into every nook and cranny.

Margie sinks down onto her cushioned chair and sighs. "Thanks, babe," she says, massaging fingers that are curled with rheumatoid arthritis. She is only in her midsixties, but she suffers in ways I don't even like to think about. "For that, and for walking the hellhound."

"My pleasure," I reply, trying to sound jaunty. Margie doesn't like to need me, and I don't blame her. "It's good for me. What are you up to today?"

Some of the pain she experiences in the morning will ease as the day wears on—some will not. As well as her hands, she suffers from inflammation in her hips, knees, and feet. Her activities are not likely to take her far from home, which is perhaps why she has made her home so extremely welcoming. Inside as well as outside, it is awash with nature, cozy and bright and filled with softness, warmth, and comfort. I normally do not make friends with my neighbors, but Margie has seduced me.

"Oh, Daniel Craig's due round at ten," she says, grinning as Bill settles at her feet. "He's coming by speedboat. I'll be the talk of the town. What's up with you, anyway? You don't look yourself this morning. Something on your mind?"

*Yes,* I think. *The impending adulthood of the daughter I have never known. The low-level anxiety of feeling trapped in my own skin. The ongoing need to present a normal face to the world when I am anything but normal inside. The persistent, nagging, unnamed worry that all of my well-managed eccentricities might*

*not be so well managed one day, and that I will emerge from my*
*chrysalis of coping and become my own mother.*

"Nope, not especially!" I singsong back at her. She narrows
her eyes in a way that implies she is not convinced, and I back
away from her, out of the gate, saying my goodbyes as I jog
down the path that leads to my own front door. It takes Margie
a good few minutes to get out of her chair, so I am safe as long
as I keep moving.

"You forgot my fact for the day!" she shouts, her voice
following me and stopping me in my tracks. I dash back, pop
my head around the side of the wall, and reply: "The Great
Fire of London. Started this day in 1666. Be careful if you
bake today, Margie!"

She cackles in delight, and her laughter is enough to bring
a smile to my face. I have been reluctant to become a part
of Margie's life, a part of anyone's, in fact—but I cannot
deny the pleasure it brings me, this simple connection, this
straightforward sharing of words and routine and affection.

I try to keep that Margie-inspired smile alive as I run up my
fourteen stairs and into my flat. Today is the first day of class at
the school where I teach. Some of my new students will only
be sixteen years old—babies who think they're all grown up.
The same age I was when I gave birth.

The same age I was when I first met Geoff with a G, the
hospital social worker. The same age I was when I said good-
bye on the same day I promised I was forever hers.

I go over to my phone, put my Get Up and Go playlist on
shuffle, hoping to knock myself out of the bittersweet mood
that is haranguing me. No such luck—it hits on The Clash
with "Should I Stay or Should I Go." The story of my life,
and yet another random reminder of the past. I only started

listening to The Clash because of Geoff—the first time I met him, I noticed he was wearing a band badge on his jacket lapel, as if he was trying to cling to the interesting life he had outside the confines of his work.

I'd been sent to the emergency room by my school after fainting and coming to on the classroom floor, the teacher looking concerned and one of the boys whispering that he could see my knickers.

I still vividly remember it now, that entire day. Telling the nurse who was assessing me that there was absolutely positively no way I could be pregnant, outraged that she was making this assumption based on prejudice—that because I was a foster kid, I'd become yet another statistic. That I would be too dumb to even realize if I was pregnant. The sense of horror when it turned out that her assumptions were based on years of medical experience, not on prejudice. That she was right, that I was predictable as well as stupid.

I'd had the urge to tell her that I'd only done it once, that we'd used what was clearly the world's crappiest condom, that my periods were always unreliable, that I thought I was putting on weight because I was eating too many packs of Wotsits to cope with exam stress . . . I said nothing, of course. I'd already learned by that point in life that staying quiet was usually the best course of action.

I was already past the date when "other options" would be available, so I was sent to Geoff. I remember sitting there in front of him, counting the tiles of linoleum on the floor, noting how many pencils and pens he had on his desk. The first thing I asked was whether I'd be able to do my history exams, which I immediately regretted, as it implied I wasn't taking in the full gravity of the situation.

I knew I was under scrutiny—I always was, and I hated it, the way my life was laid bare for the alphabet soup of concerned professionals to poke and prod at. I'd had people ticking boxes about my welfare for a long time, and as my mother was not a woman who was on intimate terms with the real world, I was more aware than other kids of how easy it was to be judged and found wanting.

He was kind, though, Geoff; he promised me he'd do his best to make sure I managed all my exams. He made me a mug of tea, and talked to me about specialist accommodation, and asked whether my mother would be able to help. I snapped at him that she was "off her head," and was washed with a sense of shame for saying that.

She wasn't off her head. Technically, she suffered from rapid-cycling bipolar disorder. I can look back on it more clearly now as an adult—but then it was hard. Impossibly hard. She spun from being hyper and happy to being paralyzed by depression, combined with drug use and a whole lot of drinking, which started when she was much younger and had no idea about bipolar and just needed something to make all the bad stuff go away. Sometimes I felt sorry for her; sometimes I just detested her. But, pretty much, I always avoided being around her when I needed help, because I was scared of stressing her out. Stressing her out never ended well. She'd done her best, but I was in care because everyone thought it was better for me—including her, and including me.

Geoff didn't react to the anger—he was always good like that. Now, as an adult, sitting here on the edge of my bed and getting ready to head out into a fresh day of doing a job I love, I can calm myself. I can surround myself with a sense of security, with privacy, with protection. Back then, I was one enormous exposed nerve. I sat there in his cubbyhole office, my hands against my belly, still shocked by the idea of there being another living creature in there. I didn't know if I saw it as a parasite, or a cool and beautiful thing I'd done by accident. Part of me wanted to imagine that I'd create my own little family, that I could love it so much that nothing else would matter—that I would never feel alone again.

Part of me thought it'd be a disaster, that I'd pass on all my own messed-up genes and I'd end up resenting us both, and she'd end up hating me.

It was when Geoff started talking about mother-and-baby placements and family support teams and doing a pre-birth assessment that reality started to take hold. I was so sick of being defined by other people back then, by their assessments and acronyms: I was a "looked after child," I had an "independent reviewing officer," and I was surrounded by jargon—*at risk, safeguarding issues, lack of suitable care within the parental environment*. I felt like I was nothing but a giant file, and I didn't want that for any child of mine.

I felt everything closing in on me, my whole life mapped out and swallowed up by this one mistake. I knew I could love a baby—but I also knew that my mother loved me, and in the real world, babies need more than love.

I look around at my lovely little flat, with its pretty balcony, and views across the sea, and nice schools nearby. I think about my job, and my perfectly adequate bank balance, and the sense of stability I've worked hard to build. If I'd had any of this back then, things would have been different—but, of course, I didn't, and as I haven't yet invented a time machine, there is little point imagining that alternate universe.

I close down my thoughts and, instead, open my sock drawer. I have almost an hour before I need to be at work, and nothing calms my mind more than counting socks.

This is a new academic year. It is the year when I could be her teacher. It is the year when I need to start letting go.

## CHAPTER 4

# TWO ENGAGEMENTS, EIGHTY-TWO STUDENTS, AND ONE BRINGER OF JOY

**I carry a little photo** around with me in my purse, folded up and creased and faded now. It's from over a decade ago, when I graduated from university with a degree in history and education.

These days, it looks like an exhibit from a museum, an actual photo on an actual piece of photo paper, and I have taken copies of it digitally as well, in case my bag is ever hit by lightning or stolen by a magpie or, you know, I just lose it.

It is only a photo, a moment frozen in time, but for me it is an essential part of the puzzle of self: I am smiling, a real smile full of joy and, that rarest of beasts, pride. I had achieved what nobody expected me to achieve, including myself, and it felt good. I was wearing that cap and that gown with complete confidence because I knew I'd earned them.

At one side of me is Geoff with a G, grinning almost as much as I am. I stayed in touch with him for a few years after Baby was born, even though we both knew it was maybe a bit weird, and certainly not what he would normally do. But Geoff, I realized then and even more so now, was not normal—he was much better than that. He stuck by me for as long as I needed him; he encouraged me; he was my cheerleader. But, thankfully, without the little skirt and pom-poms.

On the other side of me is my mother, much shorter than me, made entirely of bone and sharp angles. Her hair is scraped from her face into a ponytail. She is attempting to smile, but simply looks frightened. One of her hands is blurred, and I remember her habit of constantly clenching and unclenching her fists, the way she used to dig her nails into the skin of her palm when she felt unstable. A patchwork of tiny half-moon-shaped scars was left on the creased flesh, a testament to her struggles.

She had been in prison for six months before my graduation—not her first time, but the longest spell, and it had clearly taken its toll on her in many different ways.

That day was the last time I ever saw my mum in person, which was more her choice than mine. We spoke a few times afterward, but I always got the feeling that I worried her, un-settled her somehow. I reminded her of things she didn't want to be reminded of. It's complicated, and sad, and sometimes I think we should start again, but I'm not even sure where she's living now. The last time I tried to call her, the line was dead. Her illness and her addictions were so twisted up in each other that things got tougher as I got older. It was as though once she knew I was safe with Audrey, she could give herself permission to stop fighting her demons and descend into her own personal hell. I always sensed that she was relieved to stop even trying, to stop failing, to stop despairing and just to accept who and what she was.

Working with teenagers now, I see the importance of support—of having someone at home who makes sure that the clothes are washed and the food is on the table and the Wi-Fi works; that all the niggling problems of being are taken care of. The million mundane things that go on in the background of a child's existence to ensure that they have the luxury of a boring life—the things that allow them to come into school refreshed and ready to learn.

Not everyone is lucky enough to have that, and it doesn't always come in the traditional shapes and sizes. For some, it isn't a mum or a dad; it's a granny, an aunt, a sibling, or even the parents of their friends.

For me, it came from a variety of places—and I couldn't have gotten my degree without it. Without teachers who believed in me, without Geoff, without Audrey, whom I lived with from the age of fourteen until I was eighteen, without my case worker. I got the feeling I was something of a gold star for them—a planned and completely unmessy adoption, getting through all my exams while I was the size of a house, staying in education, going to university. Afterward, I used my leaving care grant to set myself up in my own small flat and became a model citizen. I know it wasn't the usual narrative they had to deal with.

I was proud of myself, but I also knew I owed a lot to others—and that's one of the reasons this small, creased photograph is so precious to me. It reminds me of what I have gained, what I have lost, what I have managed to become and how. It also reminds me of why I do what I do.

It was not easy, studying for exams while I was pregnant. It was not easy enduring the whispers and the rumors and the mockery; the way my friends backed away from me as though my mistake might be contagious. The way their parents reacted; the stares as I walked to school in my elasticated skirt.

It was not easy in the aftermath of the birth, when I was unable and unwilling to open up to anybody about it, as I lay in my small single bed in the attic of Audrey's home, a room I shared with two other children, crying myself to sleep every night and waking up every morning with stinging eyes and a low-hanging depression that was rivaled only by my determination that this would not be the end of my story.

It was not easy going to university and trying to fit in with the other students, fresh from their gap years and summer holidays and dropped off every term by loving parents in Volvos, left with hugs and cash and home-baked cakes in tins. Their lives had been lived in a reality that was a million miles away from mine, and navigating those distances was hard. I never accepted an invitation to stay with any of them during the holidays because I could never return the invitation. I couldn't join in with their nights out at the pub or communal dinners in Italian restaurants or vacation trips to Ibiza because I had no spare cash.

I stayed in college accommodation all year round, haunting the empty corridors and filling my time with a job in a skirt factory, where my main responsibility was pulling stray strands of nylon off sewn-up fabric.

It wasn't easy forming friendships that were nourishing enough to be real but shallow enough not to cause these worlds to collide. I'm sure I could have done it all better. I'm sure many of the people I met there would have been understanding— but I was too scared of being an object of pity, the token *poor thing* among a crowd of beloved sons and daughters. I kept my distance just enough to not stand out.

It wasn't easy, but I did it. And every year, especially when I start somewhere new, I look at that photo and it fills me up—with hope, with validation, with the sure and certain knowledge that no matter how hard it might feel sometimes, teaching is an important job.

It reminds me that I have the opportunity to make an impact on young people's lives. You never know who might need that extra help; who will carry the memory of this time on into their future with fondness and relief. Who might find our classroom a safe space in a dangerous universe; who might be inspired when they were ready to give up; who might need a distraction from painful truths.

Making a difference in someone's life doesn't have to be all hearts and roses and outpourings of love—I lost touch with Audrey once I moved out, apart from the odd Christmas card. It wasn't exactly a deep, emotional relationship—but it mattered. It counted, and it helped, and it enabled me to get where I am today. Who knows which of the kids walking into this building need more than they are willing to ask for?

It is good to have it, this photo, this talisman, this reminder of why what I do matters so much. I am lucky. Some teachers, I have learned over the years, have been worn down. Eroded by the grind of ever-moving goalposts, under-resourcing, over-work, politics (both national and school level) and paperwork; it's easy to lose sight of how important it is. Why they went into it in the first place; the way they felt when they were newly qualified and still idealistic.

But all of them—even the most battered, the most cynical, the most committed to hating it—will always have the occasional bright spark that makes them smile inside. The quiet kid who eventually opens up; the one who struggles who finally has a lightbulb moment; the difficult pupil who changes completely when you hit upon something that actually interests them.

It's not exactly like living in one of those American high school movies, where the inspirational teacher saves a teenager from a life of gang-related crime because of their hidden love of algebra—but there are, undeniably, moments of absolute genius. Moments that bring you real, honest joy, a feeling of satisfaction so pure it is almost embarrassing.

I actually love my job, but I'm not immune to the stuff that drags either. Some of it is frustrating, a lot of it is tedious, and the hours are long. But I never, ever get fed up with the kids—and I never forget how important education is, even if they don't agree with me.

So as I sit here in the staff room, with its familiar smells of toast and tea and its familiar sounds of chatter and scraping chairs, I fold my photo up once more and slip it, safe and secure, inside my purse again. It has given me the turbo boost I needed. I was in a strangely melancholy state of mind this morning, captured by the past, but today is all about new beginnings.

Some of us have been in to work for mornings or afternoons before today—those of us with limited social lives and no families of our own even more so—but this is the first proper day of class, when we are all together again. It has the strange feel of a boarding school somehow, perhaps because a lot of the teachers seem to be women in their middle years. In the forty-fifth grade at Malory Towers.

Hellos have been exchanged, how-are-yous have been asked, holiday tales swapped, suntans and new haircuts admired. There is an air of both desperation and muted excitement. Soon this will all feel normal again, but right now, it is a hubbub of coming together.

I am sitting alone in one corner, smiling but not joining in with the conversations. My default setting.

They are an active lot, these teachers. The long summer has been filled with rock climbing, camping, tours of the Louvre, island hopping in Greece, and long drives through Tuscany. They have managed their own children, looked after in-laws, stayed with relatives, planted herb gardens, been on open-top bus tours of Liverpool with visitors, adopted kittens, eaten pizza in pop-up restaurants at the waterfront, and, in two cases, been proposed to and gotten engaged.

One of the proposees in question, Miss Shannon—or Hannah to us grown-ups—is showing off her diamond ring to a keen circle of colleagues, who are all reacting in a suitably impressed oohing and aahing way. She looks really, really happy.

I have already congratulated her, and I've had a brief chat with everyone I needed to; I'm now hoping for a few minutes alone before I head into my classroom. I read through my notes in the hope that it will discourage anyone from joining me.

No such luck. Karim places two mugs of coffee on the table in front of me, presumably one for me and one for him, and throws himself down into the squishy chair at my side.

"Isn't it weird," he says, frowning slightly as he looks at Hannah and the small crowd around her, "how most of those women spend all their time moaning about being married and slagging off their husbands, but as soon as there's a wedding on the horizon, they go all mushy-eyed and romantic about it?"

"Maybe it reminds them of the good old days. Or maybe they're not actually as unhappy as they make out, they just like having a moan. It's cathartic to have a moan."

"You can't use big words like that on me," he says, flashing me a toothy grin. "I'm only a humble PE teacher."

I raise my eyebrows at him, and he laughs. We both know that he understands the word *cathartic*, and many others besides—he just likes to pretend to be dumber than he is, for some reason. I think it amuses him.

He has hooked his legs over the side of the chair, as though glorying in the fact that he gets to wear a tracksuit to work—it looks new, dark gray with a white stripe down the sides. His black hair has been trimmed on top, shaved at the sides, and he looks great. Fit, relaxed, comfortable just being himself. I hate that I notice so much about him. I hate that I can't stop looking at him when he's in the room, and often find myself gazing at him from behind book covers, pretending I'm not.

"So, you dodged me all summer," he says, the very slightest twang of the Midlands where he grew up left in his voice.

"No I didn't. I saw you at the Parkrun by the beach."

"That was by accident, so it doesn't count. What I mean is that you avoided going out for a drink with me. I realize that doesn't make me special, because you avoided going out for a drink with anyone from here, but still . . . you broke my heart just a little bit."

He holds up his fingers, gesturing exactly how much heart-break had occurred. It doesn't look like anything fatal.

I stare at him for a moment, realizing that even after all these years, my early and unintentional technique of ignoring boys is still working—I was pretty much the only girl at the fateful teenage house party where I managed to get pregnant who ignored the new boy. D, he was called—Daniel or David or Dumbledore, who knows? I never found out, and I never paid him any attention while the other girls were flirting and hair flicking. It wasn't because I didn't like him; it was because I assumed he wouldn't be interested in me. Apparently, blanking men seems to make you fascinating.

It's not like it worked out that well then, though—or, in fact, anytime since. I have had three serious relationships in my life so far, and none of them have succeeded, obviously. I have been told, at different times and by different men, that I am "closed off," that I "won't allow myself to need anyone," and that I am "an emotional cripple who makes me feel used." That last one was especially harsh, I thought—but not so harsh that maybe a bit of me didn't agree with him. That was eighteen months ago, and my emotionally crippled hobble to the finish line of my relationship with James was one of the reasons I moved jobs. Again.

I've reached the stage where logic tells me to give up. To stay single, because it clearly suits me better. I know that makes the most sense—but I am a human being, and try as I might, I don't always feel sensible. Karim, especially, makes me feel a bit giddy, with his combination of charm and humor and that big smile of his. And any man who makes me feel a bit giddy is usually the absolute last man I will ever show that to.

"I suspect your heart is made of tougher stuff, Karim," I respond. "You're only interested in me because I'm a challenge, and because your sisters will hate me."

Karim has four sisters, all of them older than him, all of them keen to see him settled down, married to a nice girl and producing some offspring. I am 100 percent sure that I am neither nice, nor girlish, nor interested in having babies.

"My sisters wouldn't hate you," he says quickly, stretching his arms overhead in a way that shows off his arms and torso. I suspect it was a move planned to do exactly that. I notice, but I don't react—at least not on the outside. "But you are a challenge, I'll give you that. Is it just me, or don't you date at all?"

"I'm on some dating websites," I say evasively.

"Okay. Well, I buy lottery tickets but I never win. How many people have you actually met up with from these dating sites?"

"Not a lot," I admit. "Less than ten, I'd say."

In reality, the answer is zero—but I'm not lying, because zero is most definitely less than ten.

"Are you worried in case they turn out to be creepy stalkers?"

"No," I reply. "I'm worried they might turn out to be PE teachers."

"Ha! Point to you, Miss Jones. Well, the offer is there if ever you want to take me up on it. I'm not proposing marriage, although we'd get a lot of attention in here if I did. I'm just proposing a drink, a chat, perhaps a walk on the beach followed by wild, uninhibited, and totally excellent sex."

That last part makes me snort coffee out of my mouth in laughter, and he looks delighted with himself as I use a napkin to wipe my face clean.

"Anyway. Something to think on, yes?"

He stands up and strides away, leaving me staring after him and still damp. From the coffee. He seems to know I'm watching, and I swear he gives his tracksuit-clad backside an extra little wiggle. He is making my deliberately celibate lifestyle very difficult to be satisfied with. Being with Karim is like having a box of chocolates open on the kitchen table while you eat celery sticks.

It's been a long, long time since I found a man as attractive as I find him—but for the time being, I am determined to stay solo. I tend to lose the people I get close to, and I'd rather have him on the periphery as an amusing flirtation than added to the list of those I've lost.

I shake my head and look up at the big round institutional clock on the staff room wall. There are twenty minutes to go until my first lesson of the term—second-year A level history. I am scheduled to teach a total of eighty-two students today, first and second years, across four lesson periods. We will range recklessly through time, leaping from tsarist Russia to the Tudors to the birth of the USA—though not all in one day, obviously. I am looking forward to seeing the familiar faces, at least most of them, and to meeting the first years, and to welcoming a new second-year student I know will be arriving today. Kathryn, goes by Katie, Bell is joining us from a school in Middlesex. I don't have a form group so I don't know much about her as yet.

I gather up my bag and head down the corridors to X12, where I will reside for most of the teaching day. This is a bustling inner-city place, offering arts and vocational courses as well as the usual range of A levels. The student common room is a mix of hormones, noise, and a lot of just-about-controlled chaos, painted in varying shades of awesome.

I chose to specialize in further education when I did my teacher training, and I've worked in it ever since, mainly with teenagers but sometimes with adults in the community. I told myself I liked A levels because all the kids doing them had chosen to, and nobody, in theory, should hate the subject. There's always a bit of shuffling around at the start of term, when some pupils realize they've chosen three sciences but actually want to be a musical theater star or vice versa, but on the whole, these are young people who are here willingly, and that makes a difference in their commitment levels.

But if I am grindingly honest, I also chose to teach A levels because it was as far away as I could get from teaching a class that my own given-up baby girl could be in.

Not that I ever thought she'd show up in one—I've moved around a lot, including an early dart to Scotland—but it felt strange, all the time, in those early days. It still does feel strange, if I let it, but I've become better at managing it. At hiding it.

Back then, being without her was so raw that I couldn't hide it. I'd see mums in the shops with babies in strollers and find myself staring into them so intently that I often set off parental alarm bells before I slunk away, stinging with tears and with humiliation. As my own child grew, I became more interested in toddlers—watching two-year-olds in the park, hanging around when it was kicking-out time at the local indoor playground.

By the time I got to teacher training, I knew that she would be in primary school—and the thought of going through that "I wonder what she's like now" torture every single day was too much for me. Teaching young adults didn't stop me from thinking about her—but it did mean I was able to get through my workday without having a meltdown.

At least it did until last year. I'd had to be tough with myself and focus only on the pupils in my classes—it wasn't fair to see them all as surrogates for the daughter I'd willingly given up for adoption. This term, I think it will be even harder—and that is perhaps why I was in such a bleak mood this morning.

After this term, she will be out in the world, out of even my imaginary orbit. I mean, I could be totally wrong about her doing A levels—but Geoff with a G had told me that her new parents were wonderful, supportive, skilled people themselves. That allowed me to fictionalize her life at least this far.

Next year, who knows? I'm sure I'll come up with something new and exciting—but at least I won't be surrounded by people of exactly the same age, day after day after day. I just have to get through this next birthday—she arrived in the world on October 3—and this next year of teaching, and then—well, who knows what? Probably more of the same. Maybe I'll start hanging around on the university campus, in case she chose Liverpool. Maybe I'll go on a gap year, in case I bump into her in New Zealand.

But that's the future, and this is now, and I have a busy day. It takes me five minutes to walk to the classroom—the building is huge, a vast warren that was originally Victorian, and still retains a pretty facade with red brick and ivy and an air of learned antiquity. It's been added on to over the decades, each extension bringing its own architectural horror.

The block that holds the history department, along with English, religious education, philosophy, politics, and general studies, was created in the 1970s—which probably tells you all you need to know about how pretty it is. My room is five doors along on the corridor, and even though I know this for certain, I still count them every single day.

The floor is a deep green linoleum decorated with scuff marks from countless shuffling feet, and the walls are lined with noticeboards that will soon be displaying posters about relevant subjects, clubs, and trips. They're pretty bare right now but will blossom as the week goes on.

It's still very quiet, still almost spookily serene in comparison to the vortex of sound that will descend once the bell goes
and the students swirl in from the gardens, the car park, and
the common room, filling the empty spaces and the silence
with their conversations and backpacks and laughter, their
screams and shouts, their pushing and shoving and flirting and
the tumultuous sense of excitement at simply being young and
alive.

I pause outside the door to my room, noticing that it is
already open, and gently push my way through. I have walked
over to my desk and started to pull wads of papers out of my
bag before I notice that I am not alone.

I give a small internal jump, which I hope she doesn't notice, and smile as the girl sitting quietly at the back of the room
gives me a finger wave. She stands up, and I see that she is tall
and lean and has light auburn hair done in Dutch plaits down
the sides of her face. She's wearing a Guns N' Roses T-shirt,
denim shorts over torn fishnet tights, and a pair of battered
cherry-red Doc Marten boots. A single black stud is in one ear,
a hoop in the other.

"Hi!" I say as she walks toward me, exuding a kind of cool-
girl confidence I could only ever aspire to at her age—or, in
fact, even now.

"You must be Katie," I add as she reaches my desk.

She smiles at me, and it is a tremendous smile—big and
warm and amused, whether at herself or me or the world in
general, I don't really know. All I do know is that it's impossible
not to smile back.

"I am! So I'm guessing you must be Miss Jones?"

I nod and carry on preparing, lining up my pens and stack-
ing my papers while we talk. I prefer to stack paper in piles of

ten, for some reason unbeknownst to me. It just rests easier with my mindset, weirdo that I am. I also like to have my pens in groups of three.

It's not a compulsion—I've known students with OCD, and it can be a destructive and life-bending condition. For me, it's not something that I need to do, but something I just prefer to do. I don't have rituals I have to complete before I leave the house, and I don't feel threatened if one of my pens goes missing.

I can function perfectly well without knowing how many steps it will take me to walk across the class to open a window, or how many roundabouts I will need to navigate on a trip to the supermarket, or how many identical white mugs there are in the cupboards of the staff room. I just function better if I do know those things. I still find numbers comforting, and still enjoy the strangeness of trying to estimate how many coffees I've consumed in my life (currently at around thirty-one thousand, amazingly), or how many bottles of wine I've drunk (that number is best kept between me and my conscience). I find it relaxing to remember dates, to figure out ages, to add up the ships in the Spanish Armada with the ships in Nelson's fleet at Trafalgar, to list Christmas Number Ones and how many copies they sold. I am an absolute titan at a pub quiz.

So, as an offshoot of that, my papers are stacked in tens, and my pens are lined up as triplets, and my new student is staring at my desk with genuine curiosity.

"What happens if you leave a pen at home by mistake?" she asks.

"Absolutely nothing. My head doesn't explode or anything, I promise."

"Good," she replies, laughing, "because I left my pencil case in my mum's car, and I was trying to figure out how to broach the subject of borrowing one."

I hand her a black ballpoint, wincing very slightly inside as I leave twins behind, and say, "There you go, Katie. Keep it— call it a 'welcome to my class' gift. I believe you've moved up from Middlesex recently?"

"Yep," she says, her green eyes skittering off to the side, as though she is uncomfortable discussing it. I, of course, could choose at this very moment to say something like "I used to live in London," and use that to bond with her, two southerners living in the north. But I don't, because I'm uncomfortable discussing that as well.

"My dad died," she says abruptly, "and my mum was a lawyer down there and after that she had to work loads of hours, and we never saw each other. It was a bit rubbish, so we sold the house and moved up here so we could live like millionaires and she could work less."

I smile, knowing she is joking, knowing that this is hard for her and joking is helping her get through it.

"Well, maybe not millionaires," I say gently, "but it's definitely cheaper to live here than down south. Why Liverpool?"

"Mum went to uni here and she always liked it. Plus she—we—needed a fresh start, you know? Our old house was too full of him. Full of him when he was ill, anyway, and neither of us wanted to remember him like that. We wanted to remember him how he was when he was the kind of bloke who cycled twenty miles to the pub at the weekend and went wild swimming and built me a tree house for my fourteenth birthday so I could have some privacy. So, we used to live in a big new house that felt haunted, and now we live in a small old house that feels brand new—if that makes any sense?"

"Perfect sense," I respond. "Where are you living?"

"Waterloo," she says, "in a terrace, with a bright purple front door and lavender in pots and a green gate. It's really nice. We only arrived a few weeks ago, so it's been a bit hectic. I got here early today because I wanted to just chill a bit before everyone else arrived." Weirdly, I think I know exactly the house she's talking about—it's maybe a fifteen-minute walk away from my flat, and quite distinct because of its paint job. I don't mention that, though, as nobody likes to think their teachers have a life, or even exist, outside the classroom. Kids are always surprised if they see me in the shop or a café, like part of them thinks I just hook myself up to some batteries and recharge in a cupboard when they're not around.

"Well, it's a pretty nice bunch in here," I tell her. "I'm sure you'll make friends really quickly; there's no need to be nervous."

She nods, and the plaits bob, and she doesn't actually look at all nervous, I realize. She is bright and bubbly and also cool as a proverbial cucumber. At least now she's not talking about her dad.

"Yeah, I'm sure I will. I'm looking forward to meeting people my own age. My mum's great and we get on really well, but she *is* my mum, you know? I'm eighteen soon, and it'd be nice if I could have actual young people to go for a drink with . . . Is there a history club, anything after school or at lunch or whatever? I know it sounds lame, but I do love history."

"I don't know what kind of teachers you've had before, Katie, but on the whole I don't tend to think people who love history are lame. Because, you know, I'm a history teacher?

And yes, there is a club—I'll put the details up on the notice-board later. We'd love to have you come along. We can talk through your coursework as well. Sometimes, though, I warn you—we dress up. Just for extra-lame fun."

"Excellent! I'll root out my suffragette costume!" she replies, holding up her palm for a high five. Unorthodox, but fine—I briefly slap her palm with mine, and she laughs out loud, like it was the funniest thing ever. I don't know if she's laughing at me or with me, but it makes me join in either way.

She retreats back to her desk at the end of the room and starts to write in her notepad with the pen I gave her.

Katie Bell, I think, is going to be one of those students—the ones who give us teachers the bright spark that makes us smile inside. She will be a bringer of life, and light, and moments of joy.

The bell rings and I stand up, half an eye on Katie, the other half on the door as I wait for the rest of the class to arrive.

I sneak another pen out of my bag and add it to the twins to make triplets.

This, I tell myself, is going to be a good year.

# CHAPTER 5

# TWO SAD WOMEN, SIXTEEN TRUFFLES, AND ONE RATHER MAGNIFICENT MR. DARCY

**"And this new girl, Katie,** she actually turned up in an old-world dress and a fancy hat?" asks Margie, curled up in amusement, a faux-fur blanket over her lap.

"Yep. A big hat with ostrich feathers, full suffrage colors, and bright red lipstick."

I'm telling her, and Bill, the story of the year's first history club meeting, which took place in X12 after school today.

We are in Margie's pretty terraced garden, on a dry but cold evening, watching the sun set over the sea and sipping mugs of tea, steam clouding up into the air. Bill doesn't have any tea because he's really rubbish at holding mugs.

"I wouldn't have thought bright red lippie was much of a feminist symbol," says Margie, "but I'm glad if it is. I used to love a bit of red lippie, me."

"Weirdly, it was," I explain, trying not to sound like a teacher but probably failing. "The suffragettes took a lot of care with their appearance—they wanted to appear feminine and powerful, rather than like they were trying to be men. There's a great story—possibly fictional—that the woman who founded Elizabeth Arden in New York left her office in 1912 to hand out tubes of red lipstick to women who were marching for votes."

"And how many tubes of lipstick did she hand out?" Margie asks mischievously.

"Even I don't know that—but now you've asked, I'll try to find out!"

She lets out one of her cackles, and Bill thumps his tail in response. Party animal.

Margie has crept into my life and now takes up quite a lot of space in it. When I first moved into the flat upstairs, she gave me a cactus in a pot. Told me it would be impossible to kill (she was wrong). I thanked her politely and fully intended to remain on nodding terms only—it had worked with neighbors thus far in life and I didn't see why this would be any different.

That changed the first time I saw her struggling to bring her milk in. She had it delivered, but as I went down for my run one morning, I spotted her in obvious pain attempting to pick it up with her poor twisted hands. I had no idea what was wrong with her then, but knew I couldn't walk by without helping.

Taking in the milk resulted in my being shown her garden, and being convinced to have a cuppa, and hearing pretty much all of Margie's life story. She is sixty-six, Liverpool born and bred, divorced with one grown-up son who lives in Surrey, and has two young grandchildren she only gets to see at Christmas. The love of her life, she told me, is Bill, her rescue dog.

The next morning, as I tried to tiptoe around to the beach path unnoticed, Bill spotted me. He actually jumped up, massive paws resting on top of the fence, and I swear he spoke to me with his eyes. Liquid brown yearning buried beneath tufts of shaggy fur.

Margie had appeared, told me to take no notice of him, she'd let him out for a trot later, but somehow the words just came out of my mouth: Would he like to come for a run with me?

He would, it turned out—and he's been my regular running partner ever since. Margie has been my regular hot-beverage maker, and I have been her regular morning assistant. I do a few bits of shopping for her when she needs it, and she makes me casseroles and bowls of Scouse stew, the local culinary specialty, when she's feeling up to it. She's stopped giving me plants now, because she knows she's just condemning them to an early grave.

It is a strange friendship, but one, reluctantly, I value. I say "reluctantly" because I'm not generally brilliant at keeping friendships going. I'm fine up to a point, but I like to keep it shallow. I'm not a hermit; I enjoy going out, but I like my friends to be of the casual-chat-in-the-pub variety. I don't think I need a psychologist to explain why that is, given my history, but it's not something I really want to fix—I'm happy as I am. Or, at the very least, not unhappy.

Margie often has other ideas and is basically a very nosy person. Maybe it's because her own life has been made smaller in recent years; maybe she has always been like this.

I know she loves these chats, where I tell her about my day and she tells me about the goings-on at the beach, and I do too. When we're talking about stuff like this and not about me, anyway.

"She sounds like a blast, Katie does," she adds. "I wish I could meet her. I'd love to be the sort of person who turns up in fancy dress even when nobody else does."

"I know," I reply, "me too! She just breezed right in, with her hat and her handmade placard demanding votes for women, and didn't give a damn when everyone stared at her.

It was brilliant. Within seconds, everyone was laughing, and she was the center of attention, and everyone knew her name and had told her theirs, and they were all planning what they were going to wear for the next session."

"Some people have that knack, don't they, love? That confidence that makes people want to be around them. I used to have it myself, back in my younger days."

"You still do, Margie. I can't keep away."

"Well, that's just the pulling power of a good dog, that is, Gem. Bill is irresistible to all. So what are you up to tonight? Netflix and chill? Grading? Hot date with that PE teacher fella?"

I'd mentioned Karim to her over the summer, when a text from him had landed while I was picking some of her home-grown strawberries and raspberries. She'd been like Bill with a bone ever since, determined that it was about time I "saw some action."

*"Gorgeous young thing like you,"* she'd said, grinning, *"you need to be out there. If you don't use it, you'll lose it, you know?"*

*"You just want to live vicariously through me,"* I'd replied, not wanting to ponder exactly what it was she thought I might lose—I didn't want to ask, because she doesn't shy away from naming body parts. *"And if that's the case, you're in for a dull time."*

She's asked about him a lot since then, and even made me show her his profile picture on Facebook. I don't really use Facebook, but I am on it, and I do enjoy looking at other people's lives—maybe I'm just as bad as Margie.

*"Ooh, he's lovely,"* she'd said, staring at the screen. *"I'd give him ten out of ten on Dick Advisor!"*

Every now and then, Margie says something so funny and so rude that I can easily imagine her all those years ago, center stage in a life that was full of fun and laughter. She's still center stage really—it's just that she has a much-reduced audience.

This evening, as we sit together, she seems slightly less bubbly than usual. There are tones of regret in her voice, in the way she talks about Katie, and about her own past life.

I can tell already, without her saying anything, that she doesn't want me to leave. I'm not quite sure when this happened but, sneakily, I have started to care about that a lot—I can't bear the thought of going upstairs and imagining her down here, sad and alone.

I'd been planning on a quick visit, in and out to check up on her, but something in the way she is behaving has me on low-level alert.

"I was going to go to the new yoga class at the leisure center," I reply, "but I'm not sure I can be bothered now I'm sitting still. It's been a busy day, and I'm thinking Bill is the only downward dog I need tonight."

She looks at me, her eyes narrowing slightly as though she's searching for evidence of a lie. I manage to hide any regret I might have been feeling, and we sit quietly together, listening to the shrieks of the gulls and the sound of the sea as the tide comes in. It's peaceful here, as the light fades and the remnants of the day slip into the far horizon. A few dog walkers, the occasional cyclist, nothing more.

"So, our Matty called me this afternoon," she says after a while. Matty is her son, who does something complicated in shipping that neither of us understands.

"Oh, right—how is he? The kids okay?"

"Great, yes. But he wanted to tell me they're going away for Christmas this year—Barbados, I think he said. It'll be lovely, I'm sure."

It will be lovely, I think—for Matt and his family. Not for Margie, who looks forward to Christmas with the enthusiasm of a toddler because she gets the chance to see them all. Matty usually drives up to collect her and she spends a week down south, gets to see his twins, Lucy and Luke—six years old now—open their presents, gets to have her Christmas dinner in their big house, and gets to be at the heart of family life for a little while. Having that taken away from her will have been a huge blow, and explains why she seems so deflated.

"I see. How do you feel about that?"

There is a bit of a breeze rolling in from the waterfront, and it whips her wispy gray-blond hair up into a flurry. She swipes at it with her fingers, and I notice they are red and swollen.

"Won't lie, hon, I'm a bit disappointed. He said they'll organize something else, maybe bring me down for the twins' birthdays in January instead. So that'll be nice. I just—well. I'm feeling a bit sorry for myself, I suppose."

"I think you're allowed," I say, reaching out to touch her shoulder. I'm not one of life's natural caregivers, but Margie has a place in my heart—somewhere between mother and friend—and I am sad to see her so down.

"I'm letting myself off, just for tonight. I have a lot to be grateful for, I know that. Matty and his family are all healthy. I have Bill. I have my garden. I even have this mysterious red-head who lives upstairs and spends time with this silly old woman when she should be out having fun."

"Hey, this is my idea of fun! And why don't we make it even more fun and crack open the whisky?"

Her eyes go big and round, and she nods enthusiastically. She starts to struggle to her feet, but I tell her to rest and go fetch the bottle myself. She keeps it in what she calls her "naughty cupboard," and I bring out a box of Thorntons chocolates at the same time.

I splash us both a generous dollop of booze into our tea and put the box on the little tile-topped table that sits between us.

I raise my mug and we clink, both exclaiming, "Cheers!" and laughing.

I don't try to distract her or make her talk it through—Margie doesn't need any encouraging on that front, I've learned, and she will speak when she is ready. Instead, we watch the changing light filtering through the clouds, the first hint of the moon shining on the water.

"I've been thinking about life," she says eventually, after our tea has cooled and the box has been raided. There were sixteen truffles to start with, and only ten remain.

"Oh no—should I call an ambulance?" I say, making her smile.

"Get away with you, cheeky mare," she snaps back. "I'm serious. Almost."

"Go on, then—what are your revelations for the day?"

"Well, I was thinking about all the roles we play. We start off as somebody's child. Then maybe we become somebody's wife, somebody's mother. Somebody's grandmother. Somebody's father, or brother, or best friend. We define ourselves so much by our relationships, don't we? Then when it all gets stripped away—when there's a divorce, or a death, or people just move on—we're left bare. Left as the scraps. And sometimes that feels hard, seeing yourself as the scraps. As the leftover bits of other people's lives, the bits they don't need anymore."

A seagull, white and plump, has come to land on the fence, and Bill lets out a low growl that sees it flap away. Margie is looking at me, waiting for a reply. I have no idea what to say to her—how to make her feel better. How to make myself feel better, as a black cloak of discontent falls soft and cloying around my shoulders.

I realize that some of what she says is true, and I realize that I am none of the things on her list, not really. I have been within touching distance of those roles but never really filled them. It's all been very messed up, and I have had to create my own role. I am me, I am Gemma, and I have always told myself that that is enough. Perhaps, truthfully, I have always simply believed that that is all I deserve.

As I ponder Margie's words, an edge of doubt creeps in— doubt that makes me wonder if I'm actually an understudy in my own life story. If my own fears and regrets—about giving up my baby, about never having any more children, about seeing even a date with Karim as dangerous, and ultimately about eventually turning into my own mother—add up to more than the rest of me. If the things I haven't had, haven't been, equal more than the things I do have and am. It is a horrible thought.

"I don't know, Margie," I say sadly. "I suppose I just try not to think about things too hard. Being deep and meaningful never ends well for me. All I can say is that I don't see you as scraps, not at all. And, anyway, the leftovers are sometimes the very best part of a meal."

I look down at the tile-topped table. It's a mosaic of blues and greens, swirled with patterns of seashells. I start to count the individual squares and reach seventeen before I lose track and have to start again. I can't believe I've sat here so many times and never done this before—I must be slipping.

"You're probably right, love," she says, patting my hand. "Bubble and squeak is made from leftover cabbage and spuds, and it's one of my favorite ever meals! Ignore me. I'm just a silly old moo tonight. Let's have another drink, and raise a toast to the moon, and look forward to the return of the sun."

There is a touch of the pagan to Margie, I've always thought.

We raise our toast, drink some cold tea and whisky, and I wonder how to lift our mood of melancholia. I realize most people would share, would tell their own story, would parcel out that sadness in order to make it smaller and more manageable.

But I also realize that I am not capable of such sharing. That I hoard my story, keep it close to keep me safe. I am not capable of reaching out, and I am not capable, right now, of a pep talk. So, instead, I dig inside my always-crowded brain and find something I am capable of.

"Margie, did you know," I ask, "that on this day in 1960, the actor Colin Firth was born?"

"I did not know that. We should mark that joyous occasion though, shouldn't we? Colin Firth has brought a lot of pleasure into my life over the years."

"Mine too. Shall we go inside, finish these chocolates, and see if we can find *Pride and Prejudice* to watch? I'm no doctor, but I firmly believe that there are very few ills that can't be cured by the sight of Mr. Darcy in his sopping-wet britches. We might be scraps, Margie, but we're scraps with taste!"

# CHAPTER 6

# EIGHTEEN DOWNWARD DOGS AND ONE ENORMOUS SHOCK

**A few days later, I** finally make it to a yoga class, and I have enjoyed it. I like yoga—it is physical enough to distract me, but calming enough to relax me.

The only part I struggle with is this—the bit at the end where we all lie on our mats in corpse pose, and the instructor starts to take us through a mind journey to complete stillness. She is talking about a flower-lined path leading to a tiny cottage, and I let her get on with it while I add up how many arms and legs there are in the room. We all have our own ways to relax.

As the teacher progresses to the front door of the cottage, and admires the lilac wisteria winding around the frame and the red roses cascading toward her, the woman on the mat next to me lets out an enormous fart. And I mean enormous. Absolutely rip-roaring.

It seems to go on for minutes, and is loud enough to shatter eardrums. There is a communal intake of horrified breath in response. The gasps are followed by a shocked silence as people are brought out of their various states of Zen and into the more familiar state of embarrassed English people not knowing how to react to something slightly rude.

The teacher, Olivia, quickly regains her composure and encourages us to reach out and open the door to the cottage. I'm not sure what we're expected to find inside—the lost Ark of the Covenant? The Holy Grail? A great big cake? I suppose it might be different for everyone.

I don't make it through the cottage door. I was probably never going to, but after that extraordinary breaking of wind, I'm definitely going to be doing nothing but choking on my own laughter.

I try to suck it in, to squash it down, to tell myself to be mature—but it feels impossible. I am not mature. I am, apparently, a fifteen-year-old boy. The more I try to stifle it, the worse it gets, and I am soon choking on my own glee. It doesn't help that I glance over to the woman next to me, the perpetrator of this foul deed, and see that her eyes are over-flowing with tears of amusement.

We look at each other, and it's suddenly uncontrollable—we both start giggling. We're trying to keep it quiet, but it's like some kind of runaway train, getting louder and louder and more out of control by the second. I've seen this happen with groups of students, when I talk about someone called Dick or Fanny or have to use the number sixty-nine in a date, but I hadn't realized quite how difficult it is to suppress.

I hold my hands over my mouth, pressing the laughter back in, not aided at all by the fact that she starts making wafting gestures over her own torso and holding her own nose.

I hear a few other sniggers spreading around the room, and know that we have infected our fellow classmates with our hysteria. We are bad, bad yogis.

Olivia wraps up her imaging session perhaps a little faster than usual, and finishes with a slightly resigned-sounding "Namaste."

I don't think I've ever seen a yoga class pack up so quickly. It's mainly women, but there are a few men, and they are all up and rolling their mats or hanging them back on pegs as quick as a flash. A few walk past us, and those who were in the immediate vicinity cast quick glances at my neighbor.

"Yes! It was me!" she announces. "I am Fart Woman!"

There are some laughs, some smiles, some looks of horror as the rest of the class streams past us.

I am taking my time, avoiding the crush, and we end up alone in the room. Fart Woman and I.

"So," she says, grinning, "that was quite funny, wasn't it? I mean, it can't be the first time it's happened . . ."

She is a tiny human being, possibly just about scraping five foot, but possibly not. She has white-blond hair and pale skin and vivid blue eyes, and looks like a pixie out of a Norse legend. The kind of creature you'd encounter hiding behind a waterfall in a fjord, or offering you magic beans. I am five foot eight, so we make quite the odd sight.

"It was possibly the funniest thing that has ever happened in the entire history of time," I reply, tucking my rolled mat under my arm. "And no, it can't be the first time—you can't put your body in all these weird positions and then tell it to relax and not expect the odd squeak to emerge."

"I wouldn't have minded a squeak," she says, seeming both delighted and mortified with it all, "but that was more of a . . . what, an earthquake? A train crash?"

"An explosion, maybe. Or that big boom that planes make when they break the sound barrier."

"Yeah. Well. What's done is done. My bodily functions have shamed me. I'm Erin, by the way. Or Farty McFartFace, if you prefer."

"I'm Gemma," I reply, as we make our way out. "Nice to meet you."

"Gemma . . . would you fancy a coffee? No pressure. I know I'm now a social pariah and you might not want to be seen with me, but—well, I'm new here, and I feel a bit shaken up, and I really feel like I need a mocha to calm my nerves."

She has a point. Nothing quite says, "Everything will be fine," like chocolaty coffee. I glance at my watch and then wonder why. It's a Saturday, and I have nowhere else to be. My social diary is less than packed.

I agree, and we find seats in the café. Most of the yoga class has dispersed, but there are still plenty of people—mums and grandparents watching their kids do swimming classes through the big glass window, a group of older ladies wearing varying shades of Lycra, a muscle-bound man with no visible neck reading a battered paperback copy of *Wuthering Heights*.

Erin goes to the counter and returns with two big mugs and a wad of napkins.

"I am a disaster zone," she announces as she lowers them all to the table. "I have never once in my life not spilled coffee. It's like it's in my DNA."

Sure enough, she sloshes the drinks over the side of the mugs and quickly soaks it all up with the napkins.

"But you have adapted," I reply. "You have evolved into a person who not only spills coffee but is always prepared to clean it up."

"Yes. I'm a miracle of nature. Anyway, isn't it weird that the gym bunny is reading *Wuthering Heights*?"

She says the last part in a whisper, leaning toward me, her pixie eyes wide. I find it impossible to guess an age for her—she could be anywhere between twenty and fifty.

"It is weird, but maybe that says more about us than him? Making assumptions based on the way he looks?"

"You're totally right!"

She stands up and walks briskly over to the man in question. I see her chat with him, radiating friendly energy, and wonder how it must feel to be her—to be so open and confident and willing to engage with the world.

"It's his daughter's," she announces when she returns. "She read it while she was doing her A levels, and he's trying to stay close to her. Isn't that sweet?"

It really is, and I find myself smiling. At her, at him, at this pleasant discovery.

"So," Erin says, after a sip of her coffee, "do you come here often?"

I laugh and reply, "This was my first time at the class, but I do come to the leisure center quite a lot. I live nearby. I can walk here."

I don't add in how many steps it takes—we've only just met, and she's probably not ready for that level of weird.

"Right. Nice. Like I said, I've only recently moved up here. I don't have little kids or anything, which always seems to be a way to meet people in a community, so I thought I'd sneak in this way—though I think I've farted myself out of any chances there. What about you—do you have kids? Actually, no, forget I asked—I'm annoyed with myself. Why do women always get asked that?"

I've had this internal dialogue with myself quite a few times, and there are no easy answers. They range from "lots of women do have kids and it gives them a shared experience to bond over" through to "because we haven't as yet smashed the patriarchy." For me, of course, it's always a slightly loaded question—loaded with regret, with a faint edge of pain, with the smooth lie that it always procures.

"I don't, no," I say, smiling to let her know I'm not offended. I don't add "yet," like I've heard a lot of women do, because I don't really think it's in the stars for me. Another of Margie's "roles in life" that feels out of reach. "I do have part shares in a rescue dog, though."

"Ha! I have a teenager, and sometimes a rescue dog sounds very appealing in comparison! She's meeting me here in a bit, actually. So have you always lived in Liverpool? You don't sound like it . . ."

"No," I reply, "I've only been here for just over a year. I was born down south but I've moved around a lot, and my accent's just got a bit mashed up."

I am used to obfuscating, to clouding the truth, to hiding behind a mist of omissions. But as I look at Erin, at her somehow-innocent face, I feel an urge to dash out into the sunlight.

"London," I say quickly, before I can change my mind. "I'm from London originally. I left after I got my teaching qualification and moved to Scotland. Then there were lots of other places—York, Sheffield, Bath, Cornwall, Essex, the Midlands—doing supply teaching mainly, and now here."

Erin nods and replies, "That sounds really interesting. Have you ever taken your wanderlust abroad?"

I've never thought of it as "interesting," and I have never called it "wanderlust." I find that I like it—*wanderlust* sounds sparkly and fun, as opposed to "too dysfunctional to lay down roots." Wanderlust feels better; it makes me seem mysterious and adventurous rather than a bit broken. Even thinking of myself like that gives me a little boost deep inside. Maybe all that visualization the yoga teacher was talking about works after all.

"Not so far," I answer. "But I suppose it's always an option."

"It is! I know people who've moved all over the world to teach—Japan, Europe, Canada, Australia. You could spend the rest of your life having coffee in different places!"

"Maybe so. But I think I might miss my dog too much."

I realize as I say it that it is true. That I would miss Bill, and I would miss Margie, and I would miss my little flat and its little balcony and its not-so-little views across the edge of the world. I'd even miss Karim and his flirting, and the little pops and sparks I feel when he stands close to me.

I seem to have accidentally laid down the teeniest of roots here already, which is nothing I'd ever planned. Perhaps I'm getting old and don't have the energy to run anymore. Or perhaps, I tell myself, I should visualize this differently as well—perhaps I am becoming more settled and more willing to tolerate complications. Perhaps, one day, I won't even refer to adult relationships as "complications."

"Oh! She's here! Don't say anything!" whispers Erin, gazing over my shoulder. Without any further explanation, she disappears from sight and hides under the table. I can feel her head nudging my calves and have no idea what's going on. She's very small, but one sneaker-clad foot is peeking out.

"Mum, I can see you!" says a voice from behind me. "You're rubbish at this!"

I twist around and see a familiar figure approaching. I am momentarily confused before my brain processes the fact that it is Katie—Katie the Suffragette. Katie my new star pupil. Katie, who has called my new friend Erin "Mum."

"Miss Jones!" she exclaims, looking genuinely pleased to see me. "It's me, Katie—weird when you see people out of context, isn't it? What are you doing with my insane mother?"

I say hello as Erin clambers out from her ineffective hiding spot, laughing as she gives Katie a hug. As she wraps her arms around her, Katie remains a good head and shoulders taller, rolling her eyes at me.

"Sorry," Erin says as they disengage and both sit down. "Playing hide-and-seek is just a silly thing we do. I can't believe you're Katie's teacher—what a weird coincidence!"

It really is, I think—although not in the same scope as meeting your long-lost cousin on Machu Picchu or anything. We do, after all, live in the same neighborhood, served by just this one leisure center.

"To be correct, Mum," Katie replies, "hide-and-seek is a silly thing *you* do. I wouldn't have much luck hiding anywhere."

I glance from one to the other, and I have to agree. Where Erin is petite and pocket-sized, Katie is long and lean, slightly taller than I am, with deep red hair. She usually wears it in plaits at school, but today it is wild and free and framing her face in a wilderness of curls. It is glorious, but I know from experience that she probably hates it.

"I know," says Erin, seeing me stare at them both. "We're practically twins, aren't we?"

There is literally no family resemblance at all—in fact, they couldn't look more different, which leads me to assume that Katie must take after her dad—the dad who died. Erin hasn't mentioned this, which is fine; in fact I'm grateful. It might have been a bit heavy for a first coffee date. It does, though, leave me with a sense of wonder, that she can seem so carefree, so spontaneous, when she is carrying the heaviest of burdens around with her. It takes a lot of strength to be so silly, I suspect.

Katie looks at me, obviously following my mental musings, and says: "Don't worry. She likes to mess with people's heads. I don't look anything like the evil elf that is my mother because I'm adopted. From a long line of Amazonian gingers."

She steals her mum's coffee, and the two of them start to chat about their plans for the rest of the day.

I nod and smile but am having some kind of out-of-body experience; the world suddenly shifts a little. My vision hazes over, and the background sounds—the kids in the swimming pool, the chattering ladies, the spluttering of the coffee machine—become white noise. Time seems to drag slightly, and I watch the man reading *Wuthering Heights* turn a page as though he is in slow motion.

It is a very strange feeling—as though I have been lifted out of time and reality and placed in a bubble, an alternate world.

A world where my logical brain is overruled. Where my normally fact-based fixations fizzle out. Where my grip on what is probable is dissolved by what is possible. The first day we met, Katie told me she would be eighteen "soon." My baby will be eighteen next month. Katie is tall and slim and has red hair. I am tall and slim and have red hair. My baby had my hair, and the midwife said she was long. Katie is adopted. I gave my baby up for adoption.

After spending my whole life running away from what happened to me that year, that night, could it be that it has finally caught up with me?

Could it be that Katie—this vibrant, happy, confident girl—is the daughter I couldn't keep but never stopped loving?

Bumping into a student at a local venue is a coincidence. This would be something much bigger. So big, it could swallow me whole.

# CHAPTER 7

# NINETY-SIX POINTS IN A PUB QUIZ, THREE GLASSES OF DRY WHITE WINE, AND ONE UNANSWERABLE QUESTION

**The rest of that Saturday** passes in something of a fever dream. I do the things I have to do—I run Margie to the shops to get her "bits," and I sit out with her while we have a cuppa and laugh at the rogue corgi who likes to run up to people for a stroke and then pee on their feet. I do my laundry, obsessively folding and storing random fabric items with no idea what they are or why I have them.

I try to do some lesson planning but find that my concentration simply will not hold that far. I substitute some admin for actual work, organizing papers and Word documents and sourcing some useful online references. I usually find lining up my different-colored highlighter pens very calming, but even that doesn't work.

I try to watch a TV show called *The Bridge*, which everyone at work tells me I will enjoy, but I struggle to keep up with the subtitles. I do, however, deduce that the female lead character is a clever but prickly woman who has issues with social interaction, and the paranoid corner of my brain wonders if that's why my work colleagues suggested I'd enjoy it—because they thought I'd identify with her somehow.

Eventually, I go through my herb and spice shelf and make a list of which ones need refreshing. Once I reach the point where I am checking the use-by dates on small jars of cumin, I have to acknowledge that the displacement activities aren't working. All my tried-and-tested methods are failing me.

In a wild and reckless moment, I simply decide to put all the jars and packets back without bothering to examine them for the tiny printed dates. Lord help me, I might one day die from using expired turmeric, and it will be all that I deserve.

By 8:00 p.m., I give up. I allow myself to collapse onto my big bed in my pajamas, freshly showered, my wet hair streaming across the pillow in a way I know I will regret later. I make an attempt at self-care, lighting a jasmine-scented candle that Margie gave me, putting a Florence and the Machine album on, closing all the curtains so the last of the sunlight is blocked.

I hate being alone and sad while the sun is still shining outside. I think it's a childhood thing. In my younger years, I was often indoors and isolated—either because I was worried about my mum, or because she had "friends" over and I was scared of them, or because in foster care I often wanted to hide myself away from any potential threats, even when they didn't actually exist.

Long summer nights could be torture as I lay there fretting, listening to the sounds of the parallel universe going on around me: the yells of other kids playing, traffic, people having parties, footballs thudding against curbs. The sound of other people existing in a world that I couldn't quite reach, the strange mix of wanting to join in and not feeling able to.

So I have learned to manage that sensation, to close the curtains against their world, to create my own. My bed is soft and comfortable, my duvet cover smells fresh and clean, the room is dark and the music cocoons me. I try to give myself the very best chance to be okay—but tonight it is going to be hard. Tonight, I am powerless to stop myself from thinking about what has happened, and about what it has triggered in my mind. The facts are simple. Katie Bell is a soon-to-be eighteen-year-old girl who is adopted. She has a birth date potentially near that of my own child; she is from Middlesex, which is not a million miles away from London; and she shares certain physical characteristics with me in terms of hair and build.

There are other facts, too, and I feel them crowding in, waving their hands in my face and looking for attention. Like the fact that I don't know her exact birthday, even though I can find it out easily enough once I'm back at school on Monday.

But even if it is the same date, almost one thousand nine hundred babies were born in the UK on that day anyway. Another fact is that thousands of children are adopted every year. And the science tells me that all gingers are not actually genetically related.

The second set of facts should override the first set; I see that very plainly. I see that this would be a huge and insane coincidence, statistically improbable, that the numbers do not back up the likelihood of that kind of occurrence.

But for once in my life, the numbers aren't helping. I am casting them aside, discarding them, throwing them to the wind. It feels terrifying, and even though I am lying flat on my bed, I have a sense of instability that is so strong it is almost physical.

I try yet another of my techniques and go through a list of Other Things That Happened on October 3. Iraq gains independence from Great Britain in 1932. The space shuttle *Atlantis* is launched in 1985. East and West Germany are re-unified in 1990. Saint Francis of Assisi dies in 1226.

On and on I go, trying to put that one day into perspective—except I can't. For me, the only thing that mattered on that day was the birth of my daughter. The soft nuzzle of her face nestled into my skin. The downy red hair beneath my fingertips. The way I felt when she left the room—like all the air, all the joy, left with her. Now I am gripped with this creeping certainty that I have found her again. No matter how much I try to talk myself out of it, how much I try to logic my way through the maze, I simply can't—I feel like it could be true. That it might be true. That it *is* true.

And if it is, it doesn't just bring joy. It brings a whole world of other questions. If she is mine, do I even want her to know? Am I ready for that, and more importantly, is she? And how would it make Erin feel, after the tumultuous year of loss and upheaval she's suffered? We have swapped phone numbers, made noises about meeting up again, could become friends. How would "Hey, just wondering, is your adopted daughter actually the biological fruit of my loins?" fold into that? Do I even deserve to be in my daughter's life at all, as anything more than a teacher, a mentor, possibly a family friend?

These are big questions, and I know I am foolish to even be racing ahead and considering them when I don't have the relevant facts in place. I like facts. I like numbers. There is safety in numbers, and I like to be safe. Now, for some reason, I seem to be deliberately unraveling myself.

Underlying this mishmash of conflicting emotions, there is one that is so much bigger than the others: relief.

Relief because, if Katie is mine, she has had an amazing life. Yes, there has been sadness recently, but she is clearly a loved and cherished young woman, the product of a caring and devoted family unit. She has wanted for nothing, and she is astonishing in every way. She is clever and confident and comfortable in her own skin.

There was always part of me that wondered, part of me that dreaded finding out that she hadn't been happy. That being adopted had messed her up, left her with a feeling of rejection. That her new parents might not have been as wonderful as I'd been told. That she could have ended up, despite my best intentions, with a life of pain and struggle.

Maybe, I tell myself, that's why my nonlogical side is so desperate for Katie to be the one—because if she is, I made the right decision. I never could have raised a girl as clued-up as Katie. I was only a child myself, and I just know I'd have messed it all up in a million different ways. If Katie is mine, then giving her up for adoption was the best thing I ever could have done for her.

Am I actually just looking for a way to let myself off a hook that I've been dangling from for so many years now?

I am exhausted from examining this thing from all angles. From going over and over it and still getting no further. From this frantic rollercoaster of thoughts. I wish I was the kind of person who had sleeping pills, so I could just knock myself out for a while. Or the kind of person who might drink herself into oblivion. I am not, sadly—because that always takes me too far into the territory that my mum lived in, and that is a far-off land I am happy never to visit.

I have shown no signs thus far of developing my mother's condition, but I have my counting, and I have my strict protocols for maintaining order, and I am always a tiny bit scared of what might happen to me if those things stop working. If something big comes along and knocks me off course, like a rogue asteroid heading for earth. Something exactly like this. Could this be my extinction-level event?

I am soon wandering through the solar system, distracting myself with counting each planet's moons, when my phone rings.

My hand slaps along the duvet until I find it, and I see Karim's name bright on the screen. My first instinct is to ignore it; I am barely fit company for myself, let alone anyone else—but some lingering sense of politeness, or perhaps, more truthfully, a need to be taken out of my own mental whirlpool, leads me to answer.

"Gemma! Pub quiz, near yours—come, please, we need you!"

I can hear the noise of glasses clinking and background chatter as he speaks, and it is like a soundscape from a different reality.

"Sorry, I'm busy," I lie.

"No you're not. You're always a month ahead of everything, and I came past earlier and saw your car in the drive."

"That sounds a bit creepy, you know. Maybe not some-thing you should admit to. Anyway, my car could be there because I got a taxi, or because I'm away for the weekend, or because I'm on a road trip with Hell's Angels."

"You're in bed already, aren't you? I can hear Florence and the Machine. That's going-to-bed music. Come on—it's Saturday night. Live a little."

"You only want me for my superior knowledge base," I reply, smiling against all odds. It is another huge relief—to be talking to someone other than myself. To be talking to someone who affects body parts other than my poor swollen brain.

"Well, that and your superior everything else—but please do come. One of my sisters is up for the weekend and I have to prove to her that I have a life."

I glance at the screen and see that it is, in fact, only 8:22 p.m. I can still hear kids playing on the beach and the sound of dogs barking. It is still early, and I am still sad, and there is way too much evening left to fill. I might actually explode if I stay in all night, trying to figure this stuff out.

I ask Karim where he is and get off the phone. This isn't a date, but it is Saturday night, and I can't go out looking like a bag lady. I find some skinny jeans and a pair of heels, and a soft cashmere sweater in pale green. My hair is irredeemable, half wet and huge, so I just give it a quick pass with the dryer and pile it up into a messy bun. A dab of mascara, and I'm pretty much as good as I can get.

I knock at Margie's before I leave, just to let her know I'll be out. When she opens the door, Bill ambles out to lean against my legs, which is one of the many ways he shows his canine love. Margie makes a "give us a twirl" motion and says, "Ooh la la!"

"I'm just out to a quiz night," I say simply. "At the pub."

"I can see that," she replies, her eyes crinkling in amusement, "and I'm glad. Here was me, assuming you might already be in your pj's and tucked up in bed!"

"As if!" I reply, laughing, because we both know that's exactly what I was doing. She gives me a big hug, which I tolerate better than usual, and I make my way to the busy street that forms the heart of our small town.

Moving my feet helps me to move my mindset, and it's easier to distract myself once I'm active. Even if I don't make it all the way to the pub quiz, it is good to be outside. Good to see things, hear things, smell things. Good to remind myself that life is going on all around me.

The road is lined with bars and restaurants, some with tables and chairs outside, with takeaway places, an ice-cream parlor, and coffee shops. It's always buzzing, and tonight is no exception. The pub is called the Hornet, and it is painted in black and yellow. A small crowd of smokers stand outside, and I recognize a few local faces as I make my way inside.

The place is packed, and I have a moment of almost panic, where I consider simply turning tail and going home again. Then I remind myself that the only thing waiting for me at the flat is an endless night of fevered speculation, of tossing and turning and trying to sleep when my brain is trying to solve unsolvable problems. I don't have answers to a lot of the questions about my life—but here, at a pub quiz, I will be positively awash with answers.

I spot Karim sitting at a corner table with an older woman, who I presume is his sister. Her dark hair is cut into a thick bob, and she is a round human—even when she is sitting I can tell that she is short, that there is plenty of her, and that her face is a perfect circle. She smiles as I walk over, and the smile tells me she has no issues with her weight at all—she is one of those women who owns everything that she is, and has the confidence to carry it all.

Karim stands up in a weirdly chivalrous move while I sit down, and says: "Gemma, this is my sister Asha. She's my oldest sibling, which makes her about seventy-four."

Asha reaches out and swats his arm in a move that has the familiarity of one she's made many times before. "I only feel that old when I'm around you, baby brother," she replies. "You are responsible for every wrinkle on my face."

He grins at her, and I feel their warmth. Their bond. That sense of family that is taken for granted by so many, and which I have never really experienced. It is good to be around such positive energy, and I am glad that I forced myself out of my pit of solitude to take a mini-break into someone else's life.

"Nice to meet you, Asha," I say, as Karim goes off to get us drinks. "Are you in town for long?"

"No, I'm going back to Birmingham tomorrow. I was up here to give a talk at a conference at the university, and I booked a hotel near Karim so I could nag him for a day or so."

"Oh, a conference—that sounds interesting!"

"Believe me, it's not—unless you're fascinated by pediatric dentistry, and not many people are."

I nod and accede the point. It's a tough one to disagree with.

"So, Karim tells me you're the cleverest girl in the entire world," she says, smiling. Her eyes are deep brown and focused intently on me. I can almost feel her examining me, maybe trying to estimate my age, wondering if I'm a suitable match for the only unmarried member of her tribe. *I'm not*, I want to say, to save her the trouble.

"I'm not sure about the entire world," I reply, looking around, "but it is possible that I will know more random crap than most of the people in here."

"Even that team that's brought their own clipboard and a magnifying glass?"

I follow her gaze and see a professional-looking setup a few tables away.

"I reckon I can take them," I say, feeling a stray tendril of competitiveness coming out to play.

"That's the spirit!" she answers, leaning back and laughing.

Karim returns with the drinks, and the quiz master comes over to take our pound a person entrance and hand over sheets with little pictures around the edge. The next few minutes are taken up with us debating the shape of Victoria Beckham's nose, me spotting anyone related to films or politics, Karim taking over on the footballers, and Asha displaying a surprisingly in-depth knowledge of reality TV stars.

We chat about nothing at all, and by the time the general knowledge round begins, I am feeling more relaxed than I have all day. Yoga for the mind, I suspect. Being in pleasant company, surrounded by the hustle and bustle of others, my brain distracted just enough by the questions to give the poor thing a break.

Over the next hour, we drink, we talk, and we have one heated discussion about which country has the longest coast-line in the world. I discover that Karim knows a lot about cricket and next to nothing about geography, that Asha is a wiz on cuisine, and that I fill in the gaps with pretty much anything else.

The night ends with a music round that leans heavily toward disco, and we hand our sheets in to be marked.

"I reckon we've won," announces Karim, grinning confidently. He is looking especially good tonight, in a crisp white shirt and black jeans, and my gaze does linger on him in a way that I can only describe as speculative.

He catches it and winks at me. I am usually immune to embarrassment but feel a slight blush creep across my cheeks.

The quizmaster is reading out the scores in reverse order, and I realize I have no idea what our team is called. That is resolved when he announces that tonight's winners are Gemma's Lovely Jumper. I roll my eyes at Karim, and he raises his eyebrows, feigning innocence as he says: "What? It *is* a lovely jumper!"

I can feel Asha soaking all of this in, and notice that she seems pleased. The quizmaster comes over to congratulate us amid a round of applause and presents us with our prize— handmade beer tokens to be used at the bar.

"Right," declares Asha, standing up to her full five foot nothing, "I'm done for the night! I'm pretty tired, Karim; I think I'll head back to the hotel. Can I leave you to walk Gemma home safely?"

It is such a blatant setup that I actually laugh out loud. They both stare at me as though I've breached some essential point of etiquette, and I say: "Oh, come on! I only live around the corner! Karim lives farther away than I do, and who's getting you home safely, Asha?"

She tries to remain stern, but in the end her face cracks into a smile, and she confesses: "I'm just an old lady with a head full of dreams—indulge me, please! I've been talking about baby teeth all day! And my hotel is also around a very nearby corner, and my bed genuinely is calling me. I'm quite exhausted by all that chair dancing to Hot Chocolate."

I shake my head in amusement and stand up to say good-bye. Her head only comes up to my chin, but she still manages to give me a hug that completely envelops me.

Karim walks her to the door, giving her instructions to text him when she lands at the hotel. I know the place where she is staying, and it is indeed only about a two-minute walk away. By the time he gets back, I've gathered up my bits and bobs and I'm ready to leave—alone.

"I don't need walking home," I say firmly. "I'm not fifteen, and I can look after myself."

"I have no doubt about that," he replies, joining me as we leave the pub. "You're a very competent woman."

Competent. Huh. I suppose I am, but it's not exactly the kind of description that sets a heart on fire, is it?

"Competent, and wearing a lovely jumper," he adds. We are standing together on the street, which is still busy with people looking for a late-night drink or a take-home snack. It is noisy with shrieks of laughter and the sound of a karaoke singer torturing "Sweet Caroline" booming from inside a bar. It's a gorgeous evening, surprisingly warm, in that way it can be in September when Mother Nature seems to want a last hurrah.

"Come on," he says, heading down the road in the direction of the beach. "I'm going to walk to your place anyway. You can join me or walk ten steps behind, whatever works best for you."

I give some serious thought to heading in the opposite direction just to spite him, but realize that I am being stupid. I have enjoyed my night out in a way that would not have seemed possible a few short hours ago, but I know with certainty that as soon as I am home and alone, I will dive headlong back into the emotional quagmire of me, Katie, and our possible relationship. It is inevitable, but I don't have to rush into it—not when I have a perfectly good alternative.

We stroll down through the little side streets with their candy-colored houses and toward the beach. It's not the quickest way, but the night seems to demand some meandering.

A path leads us over the sand dunes and onto the bay. The moon is casting silver glamour on the waves, and I slip off my heels so I can walk barefoot in the sand.

"Asha is lovely," I say when we stop to admire the way the world seems to slide off into an indigo eternity. The iron men face out to the water, arms at their sides, standing witness. I wonder if they get bored, seeing this every night, or if it still amazes them.

"She is," he replies. "She's kind of my mum, really. Our actual mum died when I was three and she was sixteen. Dad was pretty hopeless after that, and Asha—well, she was magnificent. I don't ever remember a time she lost her temper, or seemed fed up with us all, or when I didn't have a clean school uniform or get nagged to brush my teeth. Even when she was training to be a dentist, she always had time for us. I love her to bits."

I am silent as I digest this new and sad information. I have my own backstory, my own teenage trauma, and sometimes I suppose I forget that other people have them too. The surface happiness of the big family I envy can hide so much.

"You never told me that," I reply quietly.

"Well, it's a bit of a mood killer, isn't it? It was breast cancer, and she left it too late to get help because she thought it was because of all the babies she'd fed. I don't really even remember her, to be honest—just flickers here and there, certain hazy images, as though the memories are just in the corner of my eye and if I look too hard they disappear. I never felt her loss in the same way Asha and my sisters did, and sometimes I feel guilty about that."

I pause before I reply, then say: "I was about to tell you that's crazy, but emotions don't work in a logical way, do they? Real life isn't as easy as a pub quiz."

"No, it's not. But what about you?" he asks, turning to look at me. "What about your family?"

I blink a few times and am momentarily at a loss for words. I don't want to lie to him, but I don't want to pour out the whole sad saga either.

"It's complicated," I settle for. "Complicated and a bit messed up—and also a bit of a mood killer. Basically, I don't really have any family."

Even as I say it, I wonder if it's true. I have never attempted to find my father—it seems pointless, given the scattered half-truths I know about him. I have never really attempted to heal the fractured thing that is my relationship with my mother, and that knowledge is like a thorn embedded in the sole of my foot—always there, always nagging, never quite painful enough for me to confront.

Mainly, though, I wonder about Katie. I wonder about the baby I held in my arms all those years ago, that genetic thread of red hair and anger, that wild and wonderful creature I brought into the world. I wonder if she is back in it again in the form of Katie, and if so, how that will feel. Wonderful, but disruptive, perhaps—because being alone is addictive.

"A story for another night, then?" he says gently. I like this side of Karim. The quiet and thoughtful version of a man who plays a part like we all do. He is usually so cocky, so sure of himself. Tonight, right now, he is kind and vulnerable.

I lean forward, kiss him on the cheek. Enjoy the look of surprise and pleasure that it provokes.

"Another night," I promise as I turn to leave.

# CHAPTER 8

# TWELVE HISTORY PROJECTS, NINETEEN HUNDRED BABIES, AND ONE CHEAT CODE

**We are holding a meeting** of the history club, which is always an entertaining experience. This time, Katie is not in fancy dress but is wearing a T-shirt that bears the slogan "History Repeats Itself," with the word *History* written five times beneath it. Funny.

She has already settled into the group and chats to the other pupils with a sense of ease that is infectious. One of them is giving her Scouse lessons in Liverpool slang so she doesn't get confused as a big southern softie. Among the usual "go 'eds" and "made ups" are more specific additions, such as "ket wig," "jarg," and "trabs." I don't even know what some of it means and I live here.

"So," she says, frowning as she tries to take in all the information, "if I got some boss clobber and found out it was jarg, I'd be proper devoed, lad?" I think this means "if I got some nice designer clothing and found out it was fake, I'd be devastated." She receives a round of applause and takes a small bow. I have worked in many different places, and they all have their own slang and dialect—but Liverpool really does take it to the next level. There's a whole different language out there.

I smile and let them carry on chatting while I arrange my pens. I count them, several times, as though somehow they might have either bred or escaped in the last five minutes. Without any of the students noticing, I take some deep and calming breaths and prepare to begin.

It is Monday, and I have survived the day only through rigid compartmentalization. I have neatly cordoned my brain off into different sectors, putting everything to do with Katie into one room and locking it tightly. I needed to do that so I could focus on work, and also so I don't actually pick at it all so much that I have some kind of meltdown.

My mum, I remember, used to have meltdowns that started over something trivial—like losing a coin, or running out of cigarette papers for her roll-ups—and escalated with bewildering speed. I think as an adult I'd be able to spot the signs, maybe help her, calm things down. Or maybe not—who knows? My heart breaks for her now, knowing what she must have gone through, knowing how scared she must have been. That she was all alone, dealing with illness and addiction, raising a child.

As that child, though, I was helpless and afraid. I would see those signs—a sideways look, a sudden change in tone of voice, a clenching of fists, a certain way she had of clearing her throat that was quiet but somehow still sounded angry—and know what was coming. Straightaway, I'd feel a tiny seed of tension growing inside me. That seed would grow and expand and blossom into a full-blown poison ivy, until I could barely move or speak.

I'd watch and listen and try to make myself as small as possible, and hope it would be over quickly. I'd know that I would be left alone or, even worse, taken with her when she went off on random visits to friends, to the shops, to the park. I'd look on as she harassed everyone around her for whatever she thought she needed, as she shouted and yelled and became a whirlwind of pointless fury. Of course nobody did help her. She was terrifying. I'd be her shadow, silent and still, having learned from experience that anything I did to intervene would result in some of that fury being turned on me.

Instead, I would gaze around and count how many trees I could see, or how many red cars I could find, or time how long it took for the traffic lights to change. I would use what I later learned were breathing techniques, without even knowing what they were called—I just knew they helped.

I still do all of those things now. I count, I breathe, I close down the parts of me that are soft and vulnerable. I give myself the space to function.

Sometimes I wonder if that ability is a curse—if it has held me back in ways I can't even let myself imagine, including my failed relationships. But at times like this, it is a blessing. I have had a busy day, and I have promised myself that once history club is over, and I am alone and the world around me is quiet, I will get the information I need. I will check Katie's date of birth.

I could have done it at the start of the day, but I forced myself not to. There may be a tiny part of me that simply wants to carry on enjoying the fantasy that she is mine. There may be a part of me that is scared to find out she is—but either way, I knew it was going to shake my world and render me useless for the rest of the day. If I'm going to have a melt-down, it would be better done on my own time. History club, then knowledge, then home to deal with whatever it is I discover.

"So," I say, standing up to gain their attention, feeling twelve pairs of eager eyes turn toward me. "How are we all getting on with our research projects?"

I'd set them the topic at the end of the last term, before the summer holidays, though I am under no illusions that they will have been feverishly working away on it during their break—it was more so that they could think about it, explore some ideas.

I hope it's going to be both fun and useful, develop their research skills, help them become better historians. I've asked them to present a short talk on the history of their own families, and the way it illustrates historical events and the society of the day, in a format where we can all share their findings and learn about different aspects of life and the past.

We are going to make an event of it, combining it with a tour around the Royal Albert Dock and inviting friends and family to the actual presentations, which we'll hold in a small function room that I've booked in one of the museums.

"Miss," says Hannah Maguire, hand in the air, "I found out that my great-granddad was at Dunkirk! He's dead now, obvs, but nobody in the family had ever talked about it much, said he hated even mentioning it."

"So it's like a story that's been passed down?"

"Yeah, but kind of in whispers? Because my grandma knew not to talk about it, because it upset him, so she didn't exactly hide it but also didn't say much. Apparently, he was never the same after."

"That's really interesting, Hannah. Maybe you could do some work around Dunkirk and how terrible it was—a lot of men were left traumatized by it; they lost friends and comrades, probably even felt guilty for surviving."

"I watched the film the other night," she says in tried-and-tested teenage form. "The one with Harry Styles in it."

"Well, that's a good start, but maybe do some reading as well?"

She pulls a face but nods, and I hope she does. There's been a distinct reduction in attention span over the last few years, and I do sometimes worry that if the entire history of the world can't be compressed into a TikTok video, then it is too difficult for them.

One of the other students puts his hand up and says: "Miss, I want to do something about immigration. My grandparents moved here from Hong Kong in the sixties."

"Great idea," I confirm, knowing that his family started off working in restaurants, eventually opened their own, and are now hoping that the current generation will be even more successful. "If they're willing, perhaps you could interview them? Make it an oral history project? Storytelling is one of the most important parts of this subject—today's stories are tomorrow's history."

A few more ideas are discussed, and I try to steer them in the right direction, offering suggestions and ways to find out more. Katie simply tells me she's "still working on it," and I do wonder if this is hard for her—the assignment was set before she was at this school, and before I knew about her being adopted. It might also be painful because of her dad, and I feel a rush of protective sympathy.

"Katie," I say, quickly making up an excuse for her, "you've only just started here, and the others have had months to think—or not—about this. I know it takes a while to settle in and find your feet—so really, if you don't want to do this project, it's absolutely fine."

She looks surprised and shakes her head, red plaits swaying.
"No, miss, it's okay—I'm enjoying it, honestly. Besides, I
wouldn't want you to think I was a slacker."

I smile at that, because we both know she is a million miles
away from being a slacker. Her grades are right up there in the
top percentages, in history and her other subjects. She is a
brain pie with a cherry on top.

We wrap up the meeting, arrange the next one, and I
wave goodbye as they trail out of the classroom, backpacks
hoisted onto shoulders. I hear them chatting and singing as
they wander down the corridor, a minor scuffle of feet on
linoleum, one of them suggesting a trip to the local milkshake
place. They are young, and the world lies ahead of them, and
they will soon be drinking milkshakes while they sit at a table
together looking at their phones in a communal trance.

I sit, and I wait. Eventually, their cloud of activity is gone.
The school is far from empty; there are other clubs being
held, after-school lessons, meetings, music rehearsals, sports
practices. I know Karim will be out there on the field, in his
tracksuit uniform, refereeing football or coaching rugby. I've
only seen him briefly today, on purpose, coming in later than
usual and avoiding the staff room. I don't have space in the
sectored brain for anything extra today, and promise myself I
will talk to him properly tomorrow.

But here, now, in my quiet room, there is only me. Me
and a suitcase full of wishes—I wish that I didn't have to
find out. I wish that I didn't know that Katie was adopted.
I wish that I knew more, and that I knew less. I wish that
she could be mine, even while telling myself that she never
can be—she will always be Erin's daughter, no matter what
biology might say.

I pick up the phone and dial the extension for the school office staff. I make small talk with Cheryl, who looks after our information management system—an almighty affair that records details of the students' achievements, targets, personal circumstances, and shoe size. That last one isn't true, by the way.

I explain that I need to know Katie Bell's date of birth for a project I'm planning. Another lie, and completely unnecessary as well—I'm hardly asking for state secrets here. I could have just asked Katie, but I couldn't bear the thought of putting her in that position, because I don't know how I am going to react, whichever way this goes.

"Ooh," exclaims Cheryl after a few moments of tapping away on her keyboard, "she's got a birthday soon! The third of October."

I already know that the year is right. Now I know that the day is right: October 3.

The day that everything changed.

I somehow manage to finish the conversation in a reasonable way, or at least I think I do, and I put the phone down. It has only taken around ninety seconds to turn my world upside down.

I lean back in my chair, and I bite my lip so hard it bleeds. I don't even feel the pain, just taste the metallic tang of blood. I realize my whole body is numb, like I'm in shock.

She was born on the same day as my baby. She could *be* my baby. It is too huge to process properly, and I am frozen in place.

I shake my head, as though that will help, and start to rearrange my pens. I start to rearrange a lot—internally and externally.

I tell myself that this isn't proof. That this doesn't mean that Katie is my daughter. I remind myself yet again that around one thousand nine hundred babies were born that day, and decide it would be useful to know the statistical probability of them being redheads. My fingers are too fat and slow to work my phone, and maybe that's a good thing. There is a rabbit hole out there with my name on it.

I wipe the blood from the lip that I am still chewing and wonder what to do next. I have to pack up, drive home, see Margie. I have to walk Bill, and cook dinner, and prepare for tomorrow's department meeting. I have to vacuum the bedroom carpets and I have to watch *The Bridge* and I have to reply to Karim's messages.

I have to do all these things, but right now I am incapable even of moving. I am rooted to my chair, my mind well and truly blown, a river of emotions bursting through carefully erected dams.

For the first time in many years, I simply don't know what to do. Should I talk to Erin? Should I try to find out more about where my adopted child went? There is a register you can sign up to, I know, where you can leave your details, and if they come looking for you, they can find you once they are over eighteen.

I have never signed up to that, for many reasons. Eighteen has always seemed a long way off, and I have never been sure that I am strong enough to confront my own past. I am strong enough to suppress it, to ignore it, to function despite it—or at least I used to be.

Now I feel small and weak and scared and elated. I need a plan, but right now I cannot formulate one.

I am vaguely aware of the real world around me, the familiar sights and smells and sounds of this room, of this building—but I feel apart from it as well. I am inhabiting my own strange space and am taken aback when I hear a voice. At first it seems to come from a distance, a whisper or an echo, irrelevant and temporary.

Then it becomes more insistent, and I look up to see her. Katie Bell. Born on October 3. Standing before me, looking worried.

"Miss, are you all right?" she says in a tone that implies it is not the first time of asking. I gaze up at her, drinking in the deep red plaits and the multiple ear studs and the history nerd T-shirt. I drink it all in like I have just emerged from a desert and into an oasis.

"Yes!" I say eventually, a delayed reaction that does nothing to erase her frown. "Yes, I'm fine, Katie—sorry, I was just in a world of my own."

My hands go automatically to the pen parade, pushing them fractionally to make them all touch.

"Okay. I know that feeling," she replies, noticing my movements, noticing the bitten lip, noticing my emotionally disheveled state. This isn't fair, I tell myself—she is innocent in all of this, regardless of who she is or who she isn't. She is still a seventeen-year-old girl watching an authority figure dwindle into a pile of scattered sticks. I pull myself together, sit up straighter, reconnect to reality, and force a smile.

"Did you forget something, Katie? Can I help you with anything?"

A look flickers across her face that I read as "It doesn't look like you can help anyone with much at all right now," but she replies: "Yeah, sorry. My mum asked me to tell you to text her. She accidentally deleted your number, which isn't a surprise to anyone who knows her because her technological expertise seems to have ended at vinyl. She wondered if you wanted to come round to ours for dinner or something. By 'something' she probably means margaritas, and by 'dinner' she probably means a takeaway, I warn you."

I blink and feed the words through the processor that is my mind.

"Right, I will. But would that be okay with you?" I ask. "I mean, would it be a bit weird having one of your teachers in the house? It might be, and I wouldn't be offended if you said so. I could just meet your mum for a drink instead."

"Nah, it's cool. It's not like you're my math teacher from year eleven or anything. I hated him. Anyway, it's nice for my mum to make friends her own age."

The way she says that last part makes me laugh inside— she sounds more like the parent than the child. I have an image of the teeny-tiny dynamo that is Erin, hanging around with teenagers drinking cider on the beach.

"What, you mean complete geriatrics?"

She scrunches up her eyes and looks at me intently, as though she's really looking at me for the first time.

"Actually, you're not even that old, are you?"

"I'm thirty-four," I respond. "Is that old enough to be your mum's friend?"

"Well, she's forty-nine, so I'll let you be the judge of that."

"Wow. She looks a lot younger."

"I know, right?" Katie says, grinning. "And acts it. I kind of wish we were genetically related so I could inherit that fountain-of-youth thing she's got going on. Anyway. Mission accomplished. Off for milkshakes!"

She walks away and pauses in the doorway, gazing back at me. I wonder what I look like to her now, whether she would want to be genetically related to me as well, or if she'd run screaming from the room.

"Have you heard of the Konami Code, miss?"

"No, what is it?"

"Look it up. The way you're jiggling everything around on your desk reminds me of it. Maybe you'll unlock the secrets of the universe if you get it right."

Finally, she leaves, and I manage to function well enough to google Konami Code. I don't know why I do it immediately, but I feel like I have to because she has suggested it. Because it is something she is interested in, because it is a link between us. Because I am desperate to feel closer to her while also keeping my distance. *Huh*, I think as I scroll through the results. It's a cheat code for eighties gamers that seems to have become something of a legend, a pop-culture reference in films and movies and on memes. Up, Up, Down, Down, Left, Right, Left, Right, B, A.

I was never a gamer, but the code appeals to me. I like the idea of a secret set of buttons to press that gives you a power-up or extra lives. I wish you could do that in real life, and it occurs to me that in my own way, I do. All my counting and lists and memorizing of dates—it's like my very own Konami Code, keeping me insulated, keeping me secure.

I move my pens around, down, down, left, right, left, right, but nothing happens. There is no electronic ping, no animated confetti cannon, no superstrength neon light or celestial choir. I do not unlock the secrets of the universe. I suppose it must be because I didn't have a way to do the A and the B. I pack up my pens, my notepads, my phone. I stand up and decide to go home, get changed, and go for a run. Sometimes the only way to cheat-code your mind is to exhaust your body.

# CHAPTER 9

# 999 PARTS OF THE TOWER OF LONDON AND NO NEW ANSWERS

**I am sitting out on** Margie's terrace, her little terra-cotta chiminea keeping us warm, the outdoor lights illuminating the table between us.

It is feeling like autumn all of a sudden, with the sound of geese honking as they fly in formation, the signs of the seasonal change all around us. I have run for miles, in and out of the sand dunes, my feet pounding paths and sinking into hollows and my lungs bursting. The plants have started to fade, the sea holly drying to a bronzed crisp, the rosebay willow herb turning to seed. I have run, and I have showered, and now I am here, my body exhausted, my mind still on fire.

The two of us have been working on a thousand-piece jigsaw showing a garish version of the Tower of London, complete with Beefeaters in their red and gold uniforms. We have mugs of cocoa and have shared a Cadbury's Dairy Milk chocolate bar. Rock and roll.

We have just discovered that we are missing one tiny piece of the puzzle—the body of a cartoonish raven. His feet are securely perched on the crenulations of the tower, keeping it all safe, but his torso and head are nowhere to be found.

We have searched the floor around us and double-checked the box, but most of the raven, it seems, has fled, never to be whole again.

"Maybe it wasn't in the box," says Margie, perplexed.

"It was. I counted the pieces," I reply.

"Of course you did," she responds with a snort of laughter.

We gaze around again, mystified, until Bill raises one eyebrow at us and thumps his tail once on the ground. We both stare at him intently.

"Am I imagining it," Margie says quietly, "or does that dog look guilty?"

"You're not imagining it. That is the face of a dog who has eaten a cardboard raven, if ever I saw one."

Bill chooses that moment to lie flat on his side, turning his face away from us as if to say, *No comment.* I reach down and ruffle his fur with my fingers.

"Well," says Margie, "it is pretty small, so I don't suppose it'll do him much harm. It might mean that the Tower of London falls down though."

I don't reply. I am too busy thinking about a school trip I went on when I was ten, a tour of the Tower and an actor in medieval uniform giving us all the grisly stories in dramatic prose spoiled by the fact that he had really bad acne and a diamond ear stud. I was swept away with the place, and already knew all the stories, and wanted him to shut up so I could just lose myself in my own imagination instead.

That was before I was pregnant, of course, before Katie. Before I gave birth, I remind myself—not necessarily to Katie.

I am making leaps that should not be made, and I need to calm myself down and take baby steps instead.

"Are you all right, love?" Margie asks, reaching out to touch my hand. She knows I'm not the most tactile of people, so I understand that she must be quite concerned. I squeeze her fingers very gently, not knowing how much pain she might be in today, and nod.

I wonder how it would feel to talk to somebody about all of this. How it would feel to hear those secrets spilled, those yearnings unleashed, to let all of this uncertainty fly away from me. How it would feel to share my past and my present instead of hoarding it, keeping it to myself like a twisted treat.

"You're not all right," she says more firmly. "I can tell, you know. My spider senses are tingling. What's up? Is it work? Karim? Have you accidentally misfiled a book that starts with *B* in the D section?"

"Never!" I say, pressing my hands to my heart in fake horror. "And work is fine. Karim is—well, interesting, I suppose."

"I'll say!"

"Hush your mouth, you old pervert—I mean he's an interesting person. And he's asked me out again, and maybe I'd have said yes under normal circumstances, but right now I'm just not sure I can handle any more complications."

I realize, as she twists her mouth into an *O* shape, that I have accidentally said too much. Margie does not need a lot of encouragement to prod and probe, and I have just given her the perfect opening.

Maybe, I concede to myself as I stroke Bill with my bed-socked toes, it wasn't even an accident. Maybe some part of me needs to talk to someone, and I suppose Margie is the best I've got. She's a friend, and I trust her. She knows very little about me, really, and certainly none of the big stuff—but somehow I still feel close to her. She has an accepting approach to life that I find refreshing and comforting.

Perhaps, after all, I need some comfort right now. Perhaps I am not as self-sufficient as I once was, and I'm not sure how I feel about that. I count everything, but I count on no one apart from myself—and even then I always second-guess my motives. Perhaps this latest turn my life has taken is too much for me to deal with alone. I stare at her for a few moments, an internal debate raging in my mind. Some instinct must tell her to be silent, to refrain from launching into an interrogation, and it strikes me that she actually knows me a lot better than I had assumed. That we are all made up of much more than facts. That in some ways, she has slipped stealthily into being pretty much the strongest maternal figure I have ever had.

I don't even see her as old enough to be my mother, but of course she is, easily—and the way she is always interested in me, always supportive, always appreciative . . . Well, I suppose, in a less twisted world than mine, that is exactly what mothers are like.

I know I am safe with Margie, and even as I think it, I feel a knot untangle inside me. Of course, I am made entirely of knots, and it will take time to unravel them all—but this is a start. For now, for this one moment, I feel safe. I make my decision and act on it before I can talk myself out of it.

"I'll be back in a minute," I say, getting to my feet and slipping them into my trainers. "Put the kettle on and bring out a bottle of something with a high alcohol content."

"Aye, aye, Captain!" she replies, giving me a jaunty salute as I leave.

I go round to the front of the building and let myself into our communal door before running up the stairs to my flat. I find what I am looking for immediately, because it is never out of my mind, lying encased in a protective hard-backed envelope in a drawer in my bedroom.

I return to the terrace quickly, aware that if I linger too long I will probably change my mind, that I will chicken out and retreat back into my fortress of solitude. Or, more accurately, my one-bedroomed flat of solitude.

By the time I return, Margie has brought out a bottle of Baileys and two fleece blankets. It is nearing 9:00 p.m., and dark now. It is usually quiet down on the beach on these kinds of evenings, the gentle roll of the waves and the occasional lights of a ferry heading into port the only distractions.

"Didn't bother with more cocoa," she says, wrapping her knees up while I throw the blanket around my shoulders. "This seemed like a strictly alcohol kind of talk."

I smile and nod, and hold the envelope close to my tummy. I have never shown anybody this in my entire adult life, and it feels strange—like I am giving a piece of myself away. My fingers claw against it, reluctant to part with its contents.

I feel Bill shimmy up by my side, the warmth of his large body against my legs. A moth flutters around the chiminea, and somewhere out there a small animal scurries in the dunes.

I open the envelope, and I pull out the flimsy black-and-white square of paper, and I hand it to Margie. She peers at it through her specs, then looks up at me, frowning in confusion.

"Gemma," she says seriously, "are you pregnant? Is that why you're so distracted?"

"No!" I reply, fighting down hysterical laughter. I can totally see why she has jumped to that conclusion, but it's the wrong one. Unless you believe in immaculate conception, it would be impossible, as I've been firmly single for over a year.

"But this is a scan photo, isn't it?"

"It is," I reply. "A scan photo of a baby. But if you look at the date on it, in teeny-tiny writing, you'll see it's very old. About eighteen years old."

"Right . . . and whose baby is this, love?"

I can tell from the gentle way she speaks that she already has her suspicions. She is a sharp cookie, and there probably isn't much she hasn't seen in life.

"It's my baby. I had her when I was sixteen, and I gave her up for adoption. I couldn't cope with a child. I could barely cope with myself. I was in and out of the care system, my mum had her own issues, and—well, I was sixteen!"

"Of course you were," she says, stroking the picture in the familiar way that I have done so many times over the years. It is the only photo I have of my baby. Geoff had offered to take one for me to keep when she was born, but I said no—I was ruthless about it, in a way I barely recognize now, but understand. I couldn't survive the pain of that, of having a reminder of her tiny body and her staring eyes and the sense that she somehow knew that I was betraying her.

What I didn't realize then, of course, was that I didn't need a photograph to remind me of any of that.

"How did it happen?" Margie asks, looking up at me. "How did you get pregnant that young?"

"The usual way," I reply, realizing that she is wondering if the baby was the product of anything more sinister than a teenage girl making a mistake. "A party and vodka."

"Ah. A tried-and-tested method. What about the dad?"

I have, of course, thought about him over the years. Wondered if he is out there, living a parallel life, going about his business unaware of everything that happened after he left.

"I didn't really know him, Margie. I don't think it could be more of a cliché—just one of those stupid things that teenagers do. I didn't even know his name. Nobody else in our gang really knew him either; he was just visiting. After, when I found out—when everyone else found out as well—I did ask around, in case. I mean, I don't know what I'd have done about it, but nobody else knew how to find him either. We weren't quite as connected on social media back then. He was known as D—quite the man of mystery."

"Maybe his name was Derek and he was too embarrassed to say?"

"Maybe, who knows? All I remember is he said he was staying with some relatives, and we met him in the park riding his bike, and he hung around with us for a bit. He wasn't at our school, and he was from the North somewhere, which seemed like a million miles away back then. He was cute, and I was drunk, and—well, these things happen, right? I felt so stupid when I found out I was pregnant. Like such a cliché. But he was . . . he was one of those boys, you know? The ones with the cool clothes and the swagger and the Zippo lighter and the confidence. The ones that make you feel so special when they pay you attention, like the sun's come out?"

"I do know, exactly. We've all had boys like that in our lives, and they're usually the ones that make us do stupid things."

"Yeah. Well. I did. I never thought he'd be into me, and when he was, at that house party, I just—God, I suppose I was just pretty needy back then. I was in a decent enough foster placement at the time, but I never felt like anyone actually wanted me around, really. That little bit of attention from someone was all it took for me to stop being the sensible kid and start being the one who rushed headlong into sex—for the first time. And we used a condom. Even now, it sounds silly—but I've always had this sense of injustice about it, for being so unlucky!"

She laughs, and I have to join in. I sound petulant, after all these years. All the way through my pregnancy I felt like wearing a badge that said, "We Used a Condom, Honest!"

"So he never knew about it?" she asks. "He never knew that you were pregnant?"

"No. Strange, isn't it? That he's a dad and doesn't know it? He's probably better off. I don't think it would have changed anything—he was a kid too."

She nods and says, "So you were all on your own with it. That must have been so hard, Gemma—and obviously there is a lot of stuff I don't know about you. But that's just stuff. I know the really important things—I know you're kind and thoughtful and you don't do anything without thinking it through. Apart from maybe the vodka incident. So I also know that if you did this, you did it for all the right reasons—you did it for the sake of the baby."

I feel tears sting at the back of my eyes, and it is a sensation I am not overly familiar with. I am not usually one of life's criers, but something about her small speech turns me liquid. I'm not sure she's right. I'm not sure that I'm kind, or thoughtful, and over the years I have questioned my motives over and over again.

"I don't know, Margie. Sometimes I think I did—that I wanted her to have a better life than I could give her. A better life than I'd had up until that point. But then sometimes I wonder if I was just being selfish, if I couldn't actually face the fact that it would mess things up for me even more, and take away any chance I had at changing things."

"Is there any reason it can't be both? They're both perfectly good reasons, aren't they? You were a child yourself—you deserved better as well."

I sip some Baileys and wipe away some tears, and think about what she's said. She is, I think, right—it can be both. Yet for some reason I always yo-yo between the two, unwilling to accept the complexity of it all.

"If you were my daughter, Gemma, I wouldn't want your whole future to be derailed by that one mistake. If you'd wanted to keep the baby, I'd have helped you do that in a way that meant you could still chase your own dreams. But from what you say, you didn't have that option—so you did the best you could at the time. For both you and the baby."

"I wish you had been my mum," I say miserably, feeling guilty even as the words leave my mouth. "It wasn't her fault," I add quickly, as though I'm trying to make up for it. "She was ill. She'd had me young, on her own, with no family to help her either. Maybe that was the only thing we had in common. But she couldn't cope, she couldn't look after me, and it was bad sometimes. Sometimes it wasn't, and I do have happy memories of her, but—well, not many. And then I wonder if I'm any better—we both gave up our children."

"I'm sure she did her best, babe, and I'm sure she loved you. But maybe you also put your baby up for adoption to break that cycle, eh? Because you wanted her to grow up in a different environment, with people who made her feel safe and cherished, like all kiddies should be?"

"Yes. And I think she did."

Margie stares at me and takes off her specs, perching them on top of her hair. She'll be looking for them later and forget where they are.

"How do you know? Have you tracked her down?"

"No. Yes. I'm not sure."

"Right," she says. "Well, that clears everything up. Have a drink, take some deep breaths, and get it all off your chest."

She fills up my glass, and I pick it up with trembling hands. This confiding in people lark is a lot harder than I thought; I'm not at all sure why it's so popular.

"Well, I haven't looked for her, no, although I've wanted to every day since. And now something weird has happened. You know that girl Katie from my class, the one I told you about?"

"I do. Suffragette Katie. You seemed very taken with her."

"I was. I am. What I mean is, even before anything else happened, I liked her a lot—you just feel more of a connection with some students than others, and I thought she was going to be one of those. But then I met her mum, totally accidentally, at the yoga class."

"You met her mum at the leisure center?"

I feel a brief flash of impatience as Margie struggles to keep everything straight, and remind myself that even though I have thought about little else for days now, this is all new to her.

"Yes. I didn't know it was Katie's mum; we just started chatting over a coffee, and then Katie turned up, and Erin looks nothing like her, and then they told me—that Katie was adopted. And before you say anything, yes, I know—lots of kids are adopted. But Katie—well, she kind of looks like me. She's tall and has the same hair and she likes history."

"Okay. I trust you to know the statistics on this one, Gem, but what are the odds that she's yours?"

"Long. And actually, I wasn't convinced when it was just that. But Katie had mentioned it was her birthday soon, and so I checked up on the school record, and she was born on the *exact* same day as my baby!"

I lean back in my chair, feeling triumphant, like I should add: "I rest my case, Your Honor!"

I don't know what I expect, but it isn't silence. Margie is so rarely silent that it takes me by surprise.

"So, what do you think?" I ask, prompting her. Now I've managed to tell her everything, I'm oddly desperate to hear what she says. I think I want somebody to tell me what to do next, to take the pressure off.

"I'm not sure," she replies, biting her lip. "I can see why you're thinking what you're thinking. But coincidences happen, love. Did I ever tell you that my hubby, God rest his soul—"

"What? He's not dead, is he? I thought he'd moved to Wales?"

"No, he's not dead—I just sometimes say that. Anyway, the point is this—me and him, we had the same birthday. We met in town when we were both out celebrating our twenty-first. It happens. You can look up your birthday and see how many famous people were born on it, and sometimes you bump into people with the same one, and—well, it's not that unusual, is it? It could just be one of those weird coincidences. Haven't you ever met anyone with the same birthday as you?"

I nod. I have, of course. In fact, there was a girl in my class at school with the same birthday, and she always had big parties and I kind of hated her for it.

"But she looks like me," I say. "And she's adopted. And she's from Middlesex."

"And that matters because . . ."

"Because it's—well, it's not far from London, is it? I never knew where she went, but that could make sense."

She looks at me sternly, and that mothering vibe suddenly feels a lot stronger—and a bit less welcome.

She is bursting my bubble, and even though I know she is right to do so, I am not enjoying it.

"I think, Gem, that anything can make sense if you want it to."

I am silent, trying to drag together enough coherence to explain myself.

"I just . . . I *feel* it as well, Margie. You know I'm all about the facts, but this one is different. She just feels familiar somehow. I can't even explain it properly to myself."

"Well, I'm not going to argue with you on that, Gem—I'm a big believer in instinct, even though I never thought I'd hear you say you were swayed by it . . . So. I suppose, then, the million-dollar question is: What next? Have you thought about that?"

"I've thought about nothing else, Margie. It's so bloody complicated. I want to know for sure, but I don't want to do anything that could put her, or her mum, in a difficult position. And even if she is mine, what do I do about it? I have no right to barge in. I have no right to claim a place in their lives. I don't deserve that."

"Deserve? I'm not sure that's the proper word, babe. It is complicated, yes, no doubt. But it's also not the kind of thing you're just going to be able to forget about, is it? Nobody could, especially not you—not knowing stuff drives you mad."

I nod, and drink, and realize that I am disappointed. I was hoping she'd have a magical solution, some wise-woman advice, a way to untangle this complex web.

"I'd normally just move away," I admit. "That's what I usually do if stuff gets too difficult. But you're right; I couldn't just put this one behind me. Even if I moved to Timbuktu, I'd still be wondering. I don't even know what I want the truth to be."

"Oh, I think you do, hon," she replies, smiling. "You want it to be her, I think. Even though it's complicated and messy and you don't like messy, you want it to be her. And I can completely understand that. So what's the plan? Do you have a plan?"

"Not really, and I hate that I don't! I always have a plan, but with this, it feels like the more I think about it, the less clear it feels. Erin—her mum—has asked me round to theirs for dinner. I don't know how I can do it—how I can sit in their home and talk about their lives and keep quiet about this."

"You'll figure it out—either you'll figure it out, or you don't go. You can't go blundering in there with this. You can't drop this kind of drama over spaghetti and a glass of red, can you? It wouldn't be fair."

She speaks firmly, and I know it's true. Just because I'm messed up doesn't mean I have any right to mess them up as well. They've been through enough in the last year.

"Maybe you can swipe a glass she's drunk from, or her hairbrush," says Margie, raising her eyebrows. "Get a DNA test done secretly?"

I laugh at this because I have already thought through the exact same thing. Apart from the moral implications, it's also not as easy to do in the real world outside a police crime lab.

"Been there, decided that would make me a nutter," I respond. "And if it was her, I'd have a lot of explaining to do about how I found out . . ."

"Yeah, I suppose. Well. Look, I don't really know what to suggest. But for starters, you need to relax and not let yourself get so wrapped up in this that your brain explodes. If you're going round to theirs for dinner, try to switch off for a bit first—go out with Karim or something. Stay in with him, even. I'll put me earplugs in!"

I roll my eyes and reply, "Seriously, you have a filthy mind! And maybe I will go out with him again—but if I do, I want it to be because I like him, not because I'm . . . I don't know, using him as a distraction?"

"In my experience most men don't mind being used like that, but fair enough. Maybe tell him you need distracting and see what happens. But about Katie and her mum, I probably only have one thing to offer."

I nod and say, "Okay. What's that? All suggestions gratefully received."

"I'd say be careful. I'd say this is a situation nobody is prepared for, even you. I'd say remember that poem, the one about treading softly?"

I know the one she means—"Aedh Wishes for the Cloths of Heaven." It's by W. B. Yeats, born 1865, Dublin, died France 1939. The dates are irrelevant, but the idea is not. I run over the last two lines in my mind:

*I have spread my dreams under your feet;*
*Tread softly because you tread on my dreams.*

I look back at Margie and reply, "Yes, I know it. I need to tread softly because I can't crush their dreams, mess up their lives?"

"Yes, that," she says, "but also your own, sweetheart. These are your dreams, whether you've realized it or not, and you are also laying them beneath their feet. I don't want to see you crushed either."

She is right. She is looking out for me. She knows my biggest secret; she has seen me at my weakest. I have talked about Baby to someone for the first time in almost eighteen years, and I am not sure how I feel now. Relieved? Scared? Like I have shared a burden? Possibly all of them.

I am also worried about what will happen next. I have untangled some of my knots, with Margie's help, and do feel freer for it—but I know that even more are yet to come.

## CHAPTER 10

# TWO MISSING BABY TEETH AND ONE MAGIC CUSHION

**I am about to leave** work a few days later when Karim pops his head round the classroom door. We have chatted and exchanged messages, and I have danced around setting a time to go out with him again. I am, I think, being a bit of a prick.

"You're avoiding me," he says, sauntering over to my desk and perching his rather fine backside upon it.

"No, I'm not; I'm in the same room as you right now."

"Only because I tracked you down, and because you didn't have time to climb out the window."

I glance over at the glass and its slightly rusted aluminum frame. We're on the third floor, but I might have been tempted.

"Okay," I concede, leaning back in my chair and trying to appear relaxed. I am far from relaxed, and not just because Karim is here. This is the evening I am due to go round to Erin and Katie's house for dinner. "I'm sorry if I've been avoiding you. If it's any consolation, it's not because of you or anything you've done, or not done, or might do . . ."

"Right. Well, that makes perfect sense," he says, grinning. He runs his hand through his hair, looks me right in the eyes, and adds: "Look, I don't want to be that guy—that guy who hassles someone when the someone isn't interested, but is too polite to say so? In fact, I'd hate to be that guy. It'd mess with my otherwise robust self-image."

"Honestly, you're not that guy, and I'm really not that polite. It's—well, it's like a list of clichés: it's not you, it's me; it's complicated; this isn't the right time; my head's not in the right place. Take your pick—they're all true. I do like you, Karim, and I know your robust self-image tells you that anyway—but I have a lot of stuff going on."

"Any stuff I can, you know, help with?" he asks, sounding genuine. "I'm a good listener. Trained by the best."

Having met Asha, and knowing about his childhood now, I am sure that he is a good listener. I'm sure that he is a kind man, that he has a fine heart as well as a fine backside. That he is someone who could matter in my life—which, of course, terrifies me.

I gaze at him for a moment and realize I am performing some kind of emotional risk assessment. I am wondering how much I can tell him, how much I can trust him. How much space I can allow him in my usually controlled world.

I decide within a few moments that this isn't the right time. That I don't even know what's going on myself, that I still have no real answers. That he is a teacher and Katie is a student and it's all a bit too tangled up and messy. I don't want to drag him into all of this, but at the same time I don't want to lie to him or dismiss him.

"I don't know yet," I reply simply. "I don't know how the stuff in question is going to turn out. My friend Margie, who lives in the flat below me, suggested that I need dis-tracting."

"From the stuff?"

"From the stuff. She also suggested that you might be good at distracting me."

"Ah, a wise woman. It is indeed one of my very best skills. I could probably get business cards made up that say Distractor for Hire. Also, I'm glad to hear you've been talking about me behind my back."

I laugh, and feel a hint of red touch my cheeks, and say: "Don't get too excited. I also talk to her about the postman and the senior hottie who does the quiz at the Hornet."

He smiles at me, and it is an excellent smile. One that comes with a depth of warmth and promise that makes me blink, slowly, and sends a little shiver down my spine.

"Anytime you need distracting, let me know," he says. "Anytime you want to talk, or go for a run, or have a drink, I'm your man. And if you're too busy or too wrapped up in your mysterious stuff, just say so—you really don't need to climb out of windows."

"Okay," I reply, nodding. "I get it. And thank you."

"No worries," he answers, getting up and walking slowly toward the door. I look on with way too much interest, until he says, "I know you're watching!" and disappears into the corridor.

I find that I am mildly embarrassed, unreasonably warm, and grinning. I realize that Karim is, as Margie suggested, the perfect distraction—I haven't thought about my impending visit to the Bell household for the last five minutes.

Now, though, those five minutes of respite are up. I do a quick breath-counting exercise and stay still and silent until I can hear the slowing thud of my heartbeat within my chest. I move my pens in the Konami Code formation before packing them up, and find myself wondering how many pens I have used in my lifetime. I would usually allow this to be almost as good a distraction as Karim, calculating the number of times I need a new one, multiplying that by workdays, adding in my time at school, going back over the years and spending a huge amount of time doing weird mental arithmetic until I come to some random number like seven thousand, which I will find oddly comforting. I am, I freely admit, a very strange person sometimes.

This evening, I don't have that mental energy to spare. I stayed later to finish some grading and plan to go straight to Erin's house on the way home. Katie has had free periods for part of the day and will "probably be lurking around," I've been told.

I make my way to the car park, gulls screeching overhead, the sky a vivid blue, my mind a confused bruise. I manage the drive to their house on autopilot, parking near to the terraced house with the purple door and the green gate and the lavender pots outside. The lavender is fading now, a few late-season bees humming around it hopefully.

For some reason, I stand on the doorstep and smooth down my hair and straighten my skirt before I knock—as though I'm going to a job interview, or facing some kind of judging panel on a reality TV show.

Erin throws open the door, a cloud of white around her. There is a random moment of visual uncertainty: it looks as though she is standing in a cloud of snow, a tiny pixie inside a glass globe. I realize that it is, in fact, flour, whooshing up from coated hands that she's wiped on her top before letting me in.

Bits of it settle in her hair and on her face, and white fingerprints appear on her hips as she holds her hands against her leggings.

She is already laughing as she ushers me inside, and starts to apologize when a small flurry of flour lands on my jacket shoulders.

"Oh lordy!" she says, giggling, "I'm a disaster zone! Come on through, don't mind the mess. I had this idea that I'd bake a pie. It was a pretty stupid idea because I'm crap at baking, and no amount of watching strangers do it on telly ever helps."

I follow her into the narrow corridor, through a door that leads to a long living-and-dining area, the kitchen at the end.

I stand for a while looking around me, taking it all in and letting the assault on my senses have its way with me.

It smells of cinnamon and ginger, which might be from the attempt at baking, or from one of the several scented candles that are burning around the place. The room is cluttered in a way I could never tolerate but which feels wonderful to step into as a guest—piles of books randomly stacked on and around shelves, houseplants curling their leaves over the mantelpiece next to a huge vase of lilies, framed art deco prints of moonscapes against pale-green-painted walls, a huge black sofa covered in mismatched cushions in a kaleidoscope of colors and textures.

A big pine dining table is covered in papers, textbooks, yellow notepads, pens, all scattered chaotically. Erin's work, I think, wondering how she functions like that and also a little bit envious of her ability to do so.

Music is playing in the background, something deep and soulful, and I spot an old-fashioned turntable in one corner, a huge stack of vinyl next to it. I spy albums by Billie Holiday and Otis Redding and Aretha Franklin, alongside Nirvana and the Kings of Leon and Blur. It's quite a mix, and I don't know if some are Erin's and some are Katie's, or if Katie is like most kids of her generation and digital only.

There are framed photos all over the room, and I walk slowly around, inspecting them. Erin is chatting to me from the kitchen, and I am somehow managing to reply even while my focus disappears into the world of their past, of a life lived by Katie and her mum and a sandy-haired man with glasses, who I presume is her dad. I see Katie as a toddler, bundled up in a snowsuit, sitting on Erin's lap on a sled. I see her at a similar age in a high chair holding a bright yellow spoon covered in yogurt. I see Katie as a gap-toothed schoolgirl, beaming smile and ginger bunches. I see Katie waving from a turquoise sea on an obviously foreign holiday, a snorkel mask on her face. I see her in school plays, in a variety of costumes. I see her at parties, in fancy dress, in uniforms, playing a violin, at her high school prom, on sports days. I see her as a tiny tot and as she is now, and every stage in between. I see her grow up before my eyes, and I am not quite prepared for how that affects me.

I am staring at these images and wondering if the face of the baby I held in my arms eighteen years ago could have grown into this face—into this person. I am wondering how I can have lived without her, how I can have missed so much, how I ever could have given this up. But I am also wondering what kind of life she would have had with me, what our photo wall would have looked like—how many magical and carefree moments she would have experienced if I'd kept her in my world. I don't suppose that is a question I can ever answer, but it is also one that I will never be able to stop asking myself.

"Are you all right?" I hear Erin say, her voice miles away. "You look as white as a sheet. Do you want to sit down? I've given up on cooking. It's like that scene in *Bridget Jones* where she makes blue string soup, only worse. Come on, sit down, I'll make you a cuppa, if you fancy? Or get you a pint of Baileys or whatever?"

I let myself be guided to the sofa and half sit, half fall onto it—or into it, more accurately—immediately enveloped in a soft fabric cuddle. It's one of those sofas you can never get out of. Erin passes me a cushion, bright lime-green velvet, super-soft to the touch, and says: "Here. Hug this. It's my Wonky Cushion, for when I'm feeling a bit below par. Pure magic."

I squeeze the cushion as instructed and manage to mutter a few words of apology and fictional explanation. I tell her I forgot my lunch, that I've been extra busy today, that I'm prone to getting a bit light-headed occasionally. And, of course, the biggest fiction of all—that I'll be absolutely fine in a minute or so.

"Don't worry about it," she replies firmly. "At least you've not farted yet, so we're off to a good start. It was probably looking at our ugly mugs made you feel a bit queasy."

She is gazing up at the photos, and I shake my head.

"No, they're gorgeous," I say. "Really lovely. You can see how much you all love each other. No wonder Katie's such a great kid."

"Yeah, she is, isn't she?" answers Erin, grinning proudly. "Even after this last year and a half, she's stayed on top of her schoolwork, handled the move, made new friends. She misses her dad—we both do—and that will never change, but at least now it feels like we're not trapped in the grief—well, she's not anyway. I think I'm just really good at faking it. I'm hoping that if I keep faking it, it'll eventually be true."

Either the Wonky Cushion is working its alleged magic, or Erin's obvious pain somehow nudges mine away. I cannot be so selfish as to sit in this woman's house, surrounded by pictures of her now-dead husband, and make it all about me.

"What was his name?" I say gently, following her gaze to a photo of him and Katie standing by mountain bikes against the backdrop of a rugged green landscape.

"Ian," she says, smiling slightly. "He was only fifty-two. Fit as a fiddle, he was, even though I've never quite understood why fiddles are considered so fit. Pancreatic cancer. Bit of a bastard, that. It was hard for all of us, but I think we were most concerned about Katie. She was only just sixteen when he was first diagnosed, and it was so tough seeing him fight and fight and go through everything he went through, and the way he ended up . . ."

"She told me you both needed a fresh start."

"Yes. We did. We never want to forget him, but we want to remember him the way he was for most of his life, not that last part—and moving away was part of it all, really. I think—I hope—it was the right thing for her. She said she wanted to, was ready for a change, but I always worry whether she agreed for my benefit. Whether I thought I was doing it for her sake and she thought she was doing it for mine, you know?"

"I know," I reply quietly. "But would that be so awful? I think it sounds really sweet, actually."

She laughs and swipes away a tear.

"Maybe you're right—that's a good way of looking at it! Anyway, enough of the doom and gloom. I've totally wrecked the food, which is par for the course. I'll get us a takeaway instead. It's for the best, believe me. I'll just get Katie downstairs. She's in her room playing games with her headphones on, I'm sure, but luckily it's that time of the month, so it'll be easy to attract her attention."

"That time of the month?" I echo, uncertain.

Erin winks at me and walks over to a plug in the corner of the room. "That time of the month when she's run out of data and needs the Wi-Fi to survive."

She flicks the switch off and stands frozen, one ear cocked toward the door.

"Any minute now . . ."

Sure enough, right on cue, I hear the sound of feet thundering down the stairs so fast it seems inevitable that it will end with a thud. It does, as Katie presumably jumps down the last couple of steps.

She bursts into the room, wailing, "Muuuuuuuum! The Wi-Fi's down again!"

Erin has, by this stage, moved away from the wall and is the picture of innocence.

"Oh no!" she says, sounding genuinely upset. "I'd better phone them, see if there's a problem in the area—but while you're here, do you fancy nipping out to collect a takeaway for us?"

"Have you performed your usual culinary miracles in the kitchen, then?" she says, hands on hips, her gaze finally finding me on the sofa.

"Oh! Hello, miss. Are you all right?"

"Yes, I'm fine, Katie. Why?"

"Well, you're holding the Wonky Cushion. Weird, you've got exactly the same shade of hair as me. People always want us to wear green, don't they? But looking at you and looking at that cushion, I'd have to say it hurts my eyes."

I give the cushion a last squeeze and set it aside. I am feeling less wonky. I am feeling the same flush of energy and light that I always get when I am in the same room as this young woman. This young woman who does, indeed, have exactly the same shade of hair as I have.

"Not to worry. I was just a bit tired after a hard day shaping young minds."

She makes a *humph* sound and turns to Erin. "Right then, Mother dearest. Chinese, Indian, kebab, chippy?"

There is some debate between the two of them, some lack of opinion offered by me, and then Katie is finally dispatched with a cash card, a reminder of her mum's PIN (which I will, of course, now always remember), and instructions not to "get abducted by aliens on the way."

As she leaves, the door slamming behind her, the house feels suddenly so much quieter. So much less alive. I glance out the window and see her jogging down the street, hair streaming behind her, wearing some kind of purple cape with her skinny jeans and Converse and looking a bit like a superhero.

"There she goes," murmurs Erin, "Kebab Girl, off on another mission. I don't know what I'll do when she goes off to uni."

I know that Katie has applied to Liverpool, but also to Edinburgh, as well as Leeds, Nottingham, and Brighton.

I'm guessing she'll have the grades to go anywhere she wants.

"She might not go off; she might go to Liverpool—it's a great uni."

"Oh, I know, I went there too—but part of me wants her to go, you know? It's all about spreading your wings, isn't it? Taking those first steps into the big wide world? Leaving home for the first time, but doing it in a safe way? You must remember how exciting it was, that great escape!"

I nod and smile but remain silent. My university experience was different from most people's, and I had never felt safe. I am aware enough to understand that that is why I am usually so careful about my environment now, in an attempt to make up for the underlying sense of threat and fear that defined so much of my younger life. None of which Erin needs to hear.

"He'd have been so proud of her," she says, looking up at that picture of Ian and Katie again. "So amazed to see how well she's doing. What a brilliant creature she is. What brilliant things she might do with her life."

She looks at the picture, and I look at her. Tiny, pixielike, eyes shining. A great mum, a grieving widow. Someone strong enough not to be afraid of showing her emotions, of being vulnerable. Of sharing these moments with me, a woman she has only recently met. Trusting me to honor them.

I am suddenly overcome with uncertainty. I have no idea what I am doing here. I have no idea how I expected this to go. Did I really think it would be the kind of thing I could drop in over dinner conversation? How did I think I could ever approach this particular subject with anything less than a hammer blow? There is too much pain in this house already, too much loss.

I have no right to disrupt their lives. I have no right to blunder in and scatter their certainties, at a time when they are both suffering anyway.

I have no right to tread here, softly or otherwise.

With or without dreams.

I cannot risk hurting Erin, or Katie. I cannot risk causing them further pain. I must keep my questions to myself. I must keep my wildest assumptions private. I must control my need to reach out, and recognize it for the selfish beast that it is.

I must be a friend, a teacher, a good neighbor. For now, that is all I should be. If only I could persuade myself that that is all I want to be as well. If only I could persuade myself that that is all I am. But every minute I spend with Katie convinces me more and more: She is my daughter. I am her mother.

And yet, somehow, we are neither.

# CHAPTER 11

# TWENTY-THREE MILLION BRICKS AND ONE ALMIGHTY PUNCH TO THE GUT

**The Royal Albert Dock is** glittering in the early evening dusk. Lights from the busy bars and restaurants are dancing shadows across the grand colonnades and the covered walkways, and the wind is whipping up the dark water, eddies bumping the moored boats up against the dock walls, flags snapping, bells tinkling.

It's been a moody day with dark gray skies and wind that made the sand howl along the beach this morning. It is almost October, and it is showing.

We are a small and battered group, fighting the breeze as we walk. The students are chattering and excited, still on a high from our tour of the Old Dock. Discovered and excavated during the construction of the new shopping center, it was built in 1715, a precursor to the grand venue we are now exploring.

The docks have always been a favorite place of mine. The sense of immense history, of the coming and going of humanity over hundreds of years. Of the trade, the hope, the dreams, the sometimes dark past, the constant change and evolution.

Of course, I also enjoy the numbers—the statistics of space and time. Twenty-three million bricks, three football pitches, cast-iron columns that are twenty-five feet high.

To the current generation, this is a place that has always been synonymous with good times—with glamorous bars, gift shops, spruced-up visitors and tourists; with the Tate Liverpool, with the city's own museums; with boat trips, nights out, and fun.

"It's hard to believe," says our guide, Natalie, as we pause in a partly sheltered corner by an artisan bakery, "that this was almost lost. There was the Blitz during the Second World War, and it was considered for demolition in the 1960s. It was almost lost simply due to planned neglect—it was closed down, allowed to fill with silt, abandoned for years. Now it's one of the most popular attractions in the city!"

She is doing her best to recreate the scenes for them, and perhaps a cold and gloomy night is in some ways the best time to imagine this place unloved and derelict. They are good kids, and nodding in all the right places, but they are also chilly, wet, and tired. There was a train trip to the city center, the tour of the Old Dock, and now this—their attention spans are wavering, and their phones are being used less and less to take photos and maybe more and more to post tired-face emojis on their timelines.

I meet Natalie's eyes, and we both smile. Time, we agree without even speaking, to call it a day on the educational talks.

"Anyway," she announces, "I hope you'll remember this the next time you're down here having your dinner, or doing your Christmas shopping. But for now, let's head inside and get you all set up."

We follow her to the museum, housed in one of the grand brick former warehouses, and are shown to our room. There is a table with coffee and tea and biscuits, and some of the parents are already there—I guess the ones who work in town have come straight here from the office.

The kids disperse, descending locustlike on the refreshments, and I spot Erin waving at me from a seat in the front row. She is wearing a business suit and makeup and has a briefcase at her feet. She looks totally different than usual but is still grinning in her normal way. I can't imagine her in meetings, being all serious.

I wave back, and then my eyes immediately track Katie, locating her with her friends in a corner of the room, paper cup of a hot drink in her hands. Erin, I see, does exactly the same, locating her daughter among the small crowd. I feel a flash of discomfort, of guilt, of awkwardness—I have no right to be doing the same thing as Erin, not at all. She is her mother, in every way that counts.

We have seen each other at our yoga class, and we have met for coffee, and I have never felt that it would be even marginally reasonable to discuss Katie's birth and adoption with her. I have been alert to opportunity, looking for ways to find out more, to confirm what has moved from a vague suspicion to a near certainty.

It leaves me feeling hollow and dipped in self-loathing, as though I am befriending Erin purely for her daughter.

I know that's not true—that I met and liked Erin before I even knew about her connection to Katie—but, well, now I do know, and I'm not sure how to proceed.

Margie has encouraged me to look at ways to find out more about where my birth daughter went, and I have made halfhearted stabs at research. There are agencies, there are registers, there are ways and means to move forward—but

I have not followed any of them. I don't know why—sheer cowardice, I am beginning to suspect. I don't know when the perfect time will be—when Katie is eighteen, when she is twenty-one, when Erin is truly happy again. Any or none of the above.

For now, I am telling myself that I am content in this limbo, in this netherworld, this twilight zone of factual ignorance and instinctive certainty.

I am telling myself that, and I am staying busy, and I am making sure I am distracted.

Karim, my number one distraction, walks toward me, smiling. He has come straight from work and is still in his PE gear. Black tracksuit, white T-shirt beneath it, a waterproof hiking jacket over his arm. His hair is damp and shining, and his hands linger on my shoulders as he helps me out of my coat.

We have been out a couple of times, and been for a run together, and he has met Bill and chatted to Margie over her fence. He has slipped into my life, and I have allowed it.

We have not kissed, never mind anything more, nor have we spoken of what our relationship is or might be. Neither of us has pushed, and so far, it is working. I feel tiny tremors of fear when I look ahead, when I imagine taking next steps, being part of a couple. If I look too far ahead, I see dates becoming nights spent together, and I see commitment, and I see a level of sharing that I don't dare to ponder. I have not been good at commitment thus far in my life, and I am trying not to ruin the present by worrying too much about the future.

"You look like a wild woman from the hills," he says, and I reach up to try to tame my hair.

It is, indeed, wild, and I realize that Katie had the right idea by putting hers in plaits.

"Which hills?" I say, raising an eyebrow.

"I don't know," he replies, "*the* hills. You know, the mythical ones where wild women live? It suits you. You look like you could hunt a woolly mammoth and cook it for dinner."

I laugh out loud and say, "Wow. That's quite a leap. I'll invite you over for a woolly mammoth roast dinner, if I ever catch one."

"It's a date!" he says quickly, chasing my gaze and capturing it. He has a way, Karim, of flirting without saying very much at all—it's in his tone, his gestures, his body language. It's in the way he looks at me, as though I am a precious mystery to be unraveled. If only he knew—I am not precious. I am made of steel and lead, not silver and gold, and I have spent my whole life ensuring that I am safe from unraveling. At least by other people.

"I'd better get us started," I say, breaking the moment. "I'll be back in a minute."

I nip to the ladies' room, sort my hair out, try to make myself look more like a teacher than a wild woman from the hills. By the time I emerge, most people have settled into their seats, and there is a low-level sense of anticipation in the room.

I drove over yesterday to store what we'd need for the event—props and a few costumes and some handmade artwork and the memory stick with their power points all loaded up and ready to go. I've stuck by my promise to the kids not to watch them first—I trust them not to do anything inappropriate, and they all wanted me to be as surprised as their families.

I walk to the small podium at the front of the room, to the side of a large wall-mounted screen. There is a microphone set up, but I decide I don't need it. This isn't going to be a rowdy crowd.

I take a deep breath and look around as I prepare to talk. I see my students, scattered around the room, all of them with guests—parents, grandparents, maybe aunts or uncles or siblings or family friends. They are all cocooned in their little clusters of support, and it warms me to see that. They are lucky, even if they don't realize it. They have people in their lives who care enough to brave a rainy night on the waterfront to see their school projects, to hear them speak, to applaud them. It makes all the difference, having a cheerleader.

I lost touch with the ones I did have—with Geoff, with Audrey—after my graduation. I moved away, I kept moving, I edged into a different life; one that didn't contain foster parents or social workers or even, eventually, my own mother. Looking back, it sounds so harsh and clinical and ungrateful— but it wasn't. It was never any of those things. It was simply what I felt I needed to do to survive, to build my own world afresh, to give myself a chance. I hope that none of the young people I see before me is ever faced with similar choices.

"Hi, everyone!" I say, my voice sounding calm and confident, comfortable to stand here and talk in front of a room full of people. I have no problem with that—it's a room with only one or two people I struggle with.

"Thanks for coming," I continue. "I know that I and the wonderful members of the history club appreciate you being here. They've worked so hard on these projects, and they're both deeply personal and historically revealing. For those of you who always thought history was boring, or irrelevant, I hope this goes some way toward changing your minds. We'll start with Hannah . . ."

Hannah clambers out of her row of chairs and makes her way to the front. She looks embarrassed in that way that some teenagers can, for no specific reason—just the unbearable fact of existing is enough to make her feel awkward. The round of applause seems to make her even more stressed, and her voice is a bit of a squeak as she announces her name and the title of her project.

I click on the opening slide and have to smile as Harry Styles fills the screen, all disheveled in his Dunkirk uniform. That seems to break the ice, and Hannah takes heart from Harry and begins her talk. It's not the most in-depth version of Dunkirk I've ever come across, but it has a powerful personal element that has everyone spellbound and her mother in tears. She ends by passing around her great-grandfather's medals.

David follows, with a superb presentation on the contribution of immigrant workforces to the economy and culture of Liverpool and the UK. We play videos of his interviews with his family, interspersed with facts and figures and the history of the city's Chinatown. He even comes up with a few things I never knew.

Next up is a student named Sally Duncan, who brings the Merseybeat era of Liverpool alive with a presentation about her granddad, who was in a skiffle band that once supported the Beatles at the Cavern. She has clips of their music and photos from the night, and does the whole thing dressed in a sixties wig and clothes.

On and on it goes, filling the room with light and color and emotion, with *oohs* and *aahs* and clapping and cheers. Some of it is funny, some of it is moving, all of it is interesting. I am very proud of them, of how hard they've worked, of how much they've learned, of the way they're sharing it with the room. I might not be a mother in the traditional sense, but I also allow myself a flicker of satisfaction at my own part in encouraging and guiding them.

Katie is up last, and she takes a couple of minutes to get ready behind the privacy screen we've set up in a corner. I am tingling slightly as I wait for her to emerge—I don't even know what topic she chose in the end, as she was insistent that she would just get on with it on her own. I have enjoyed all of the presentations, and I am proud of all my students, but—well, this is different.

This is Katie.

I glance into the crowd in the darkened room, see Erin's blond head, the smile on her face. I find myself wishing that her dad was here too, which is a strange thought to intrude on my mind.

I introduce Katie, explaining that she is a new student, and she emerges from behind the screen to polite applause.

At first, I'm not quite sure what she's dressed as. She's wearing a school uniform that is either an old one of hers or one she has picked up from a charity shop—there's no uniform at our school. She looks like a parody of Britney in the "Baby One More Time" video with her red hair now in bunches and her tie dangling loose, skirt short. I had wondered why the lime-green Wonky Cushion had been among her prop items, but now I know—she has shoved it under her shirt, to make herself look pregnant.

"Hi," she says as she reaches the front of the room, "my name is Katie Bell, and today I'll be talking about adoption in the United Kingdom. Years ago, the teenage mum was a figure of dread for parents—and before the common availability of contraception, unwanted pregnancies were more common. They were also, in earlier times, a source of much shame.

"Being fifteen and pregnant in the past would have meant the end of respectability. Even in the sixties, seventies, or eighties, for many it would have meant the end of education, of a girl's hopes and dreams. In different eras, it resulted in different behaviors."

I press the buttons on the power point as she indicates, and she talks about the Catholic forced adoption scandal, and about young women who were mysteriously "sent away" to school, only to return months later much thinner. She talks about changing attitudes toward sex, about the patriarchal approach to unwed mothers, and about the way that celebrities like Madonna and Angelina Jolie adopted babies from other countries.

She weaves in humor, political commentary, and even a reference to witchcraft before drawing to a close with a picture of herself and her mum and dad as a toddler. It's the one I saw in her house, where she has a yogurt spoon in her pudgy hand.

"This is me," she says, grinning. "And it's a precious photo in our house, because it was taken on the very first day I spent with my parents. I chose this topic today because I was adopted myself, when I was two years old. My mum and dad were always honest with me, and when I was old enough to understand, they explained—and they made me feel special. They made me feel special because they chose me, because I was so very loved, and so very wanted. They made sure I never felt rejected—only chosen.

"Like I say, I was only two when I was taken into care. I don't remember my birth parents, and I choose not to see that as a loss—I choose to celebrate all that I am now. All that my mum and dad made me. Thank you."

It is a powerful and emotional statement, a wonderful close to an enlightening presentation. The room erupts into applause, and I am aware of Erin standing up, cheering the loudest of all. I am aware of someone switching the lights back on. I am aware of a ringing sensation in my ears, and a flash of white zigzags clouding out my vision, and a sudden weakness in my knees.

I hit the floor, and am aware of nothing more.

# CHAPTER 12

# BRANDY NUMBER FOUR, CHAIRS FOR TWO, AND ONE WORLD-CLASS KISS

**"God, that was embarrassing," I** say, holding my face in my hands.

"Could've been worse," says Karim, shrugging. "At least you did it at the end when everyone was due to go home anyway."

I nod in agreement. He's right there. At least I didn't ruin the whole night for everyone. I still feel trembly and weak, the physical remnants of an emotional wound. It was, of course, more than embarrassing—it was like a blow to the stomach. One minute I was watching Katie, feeling that now-familiar sense of connection to her, and the next, everything changed.

Every silly dream, every ridiculous hope, every stupid thought I'd ever entertained about her was shredded by that one sentence: *"I was only two when I was taken into care."*

She was two when she was adopted. She was two when she left her old life and joined her new one. She was two—not a newborn baby.

Katie is not, never has been, never will be, my daughter.

I feel woozy, shaken, like I have just had my carpet of could-it-be pulled from beneath my feet.

I don't think I'd realized how much it had become part of me—how quickly it had crept into my being, become almost fact, how well I had shaped it into what I wanted it to be. How many tiny ways I had allowed myself to start thinking of her as mine.

I have missed my baby girl every single day since she was taken from my arms in hospital. I have thought about her, and wondered about her, and grieved for the loss of her. I under-stand now that I am more injured by it than I ever let myself believe—why else would I have so readily embraced the idea that Katie was her?

I am a woman of facts, of dates and numbers and data, but on this one issue I hid away from them. I avoided finding out, I swerved around logic, I deliberately turned a blind eye to reality. I did all of that because I wanted so very much to be in her life again.

I'd been worrying about how to tell them that I was Katie's biological mother. Planning scenarios, rehearsing speeches, even considering drafting letters. That's how solid my convic-tion was, even if I never truly admitted it to myself.

I don't just feel embarrassed—I feel devastated. Like part of me has been chopped off, and now all I have left is the phantom pain where my fantasy once lived.

Karim, of course, does not know this. He, like everyone else there tonight, simply believed me when I said I was fine. That I'd just been diagnosed as anemic, and that I was on iron supplements that obviously hadn't kicked in yet. The lies just flowed out of me, easily, perfect little lies that left everyone reassured.

There had been some fuss about calling a first aider, some talk of getting me to a hospital, but I insisted that everything was okay. Another lie.

Karim had helped clear the room, students and families full of concern but also chattering in that hushed and excited way people do when they've been on the periphery of a drama. He'd loaded everything into his car and driven back around to the side of the dock to collect me, finding me huddled in my coat in the rain.

Erin had wanted to stay with me, to make sure I was all right, but I convinced her and Katie to leave. It wasn't their fault, of course, but I couldn't bear to be around them, not just then, when I was feeling so raw. So injured.

Katie had whipped the Wonky Cushion out from under her shirt and handed it to me to hold. I'd hugged it tightly, told them it was working its magic, persuaded them to head home. I needed to be alone, if only for a few minutes.

I'd sat on a low wall in the drizzle, watching them walk away, Katie so tall, her hair glinting under the streetlamps, Erin by her side. They walked closely, arms linked together, their bond so strong you could almost see it.

I watched them walk away, and I held back tears and told myself it was for the best. That it had all worked out the way it should. I wasn't mother material, after all. I didn't have the right skill set.

By the time Karim pulled up in his Nissan, I was able to fake it. Able to put on a brave face, to talk, to mock myself for being a delicate damsel in distress, to make jokes about needing to eat more steak dinners.

He was going to take me home, but I'd asked if we could stop off somewhere on the way. I just couldn't face it, going back to my flat. To its emptiness, its tidy rooms, its bare walls. For years I've taken comfort in solitude, in living my life with minimal clutter, in keeping my various homes so uncomplicated that I could move out within a day without any bother like a character in a spy film who keeps a go bag under the floorboards.

Now I see that for what it is—fear.

I have a lot of thinking to do, about my life and the way I live it, about choices I have made and about how to move forward. I promise myself I will do that hard thinking—but I know I am not capable of it tonight.

Now I find myself at a small corner table in a quiet pub in the city's Georgian Quarter. As we drove through the damp streets, along glistening cobbles and past graceful gardens, the hulk of the cathedral and the elegant townhouses that surround it, I mentally recited the facts: planned by John Foster Senior in 1800; Gambier Terrace, former home of John Lennon; Canning, named after former Prime Minister George; St. Bride's Church, neoclassical. It is beautiful, and it is timeless, and it is the home of many very fine pubs.

Karim is sipping a Coke and has placed a brandy in front of me. Several packets of crisps and nuts are on the table, bags torn open so we can help ourselves—"Scouse tapas," he calls it.

I sip my drink, feel the initial burn turn into liquid heat, and say: "I've only ever had brandy three times in my life. Four now."

"Seriously—you even keep track of how many times you've had a drink of anything?"

"Don't be silly. That would be impossible—I don't keep track of water!"

He shakes his head, but he does it with a sense of amusement, as though he finds my personality traits endearing. That, I think, is how it starts in my experience—at first it's an amusing quirk. That's before the irritation sets in, and the petty quibbles, and the small frictions that build into a fire that burns down the whole relationship. Admittedly, I might have a one-sided view, as all my relationships have gone up in smoke.

"Are you seriously all right?" he asks. "And no jokes allowed."

I pause, let the warming effects of the brandy take hold, and wonder how to reply. Again, I find that I do not want to lie to him, even though it would be so much easier. I like him, and I respect him, and at the very least he is a friend—possibly much more.

"I'm not completely all right, no," I say eventually. "There is a thing going on in my life that is causing me some—I don't know, let's just call it anxiety, shall we? It's a complicated thing that I don't want to talk about just yet."

"The stuff you mentioned a bit ago?"

"Yeah, the same stuff—or an evolution of the same stuff anyway, which now sounds like something from a horror film. Anyway, it's all linked to what happened tonight."

"So you're not actually anemic or anything?"

"Nope. I'm just a frighteningly good liar."

He raises his eyebrows and smiles. "Good to know," he replies. "And thanks for being honest about the fact that you were lying."

We both laugh at that one, and I feel a slight easing of the tension that has been clamped around my skull for the last hour. Maybe it's the brandy. Maybe it's Karim. Who knows?

I enjoy his company but still feel slightly uncomfortable about it all—I am not sure if I am capable of making a relationship work, but I am also not sure what it is he's looking for. I am not arrogant enough to assume he is planning on asking for my hand in marriage, but there is a vast array of possibilities between our current gentle flirting and that. I don't even know what I want, never mind what he wants.

"Why do you like me, Karim?" I ask. "Really, why do you bother?"

He stares at me, takes a sip of his Coke, and answers: "You do realize that's a completely fucked-up question, don't you?"

"Well, maybe I'm a completely fucked-up person—which makes the question even more relevant. I avoided you for ages. Then I said I wanted to use you as a distraction, and now I'm still not telling you things you clearly want to know. I can be frustrating to be around, in a million different ways. You're a great bloke, funny and decent and, yes, before you butt in, you are also extremely good-looking—so why bother? You could find any number of women who'd be thrilled to be with you."

"Well," he says, "there's the flippant answer—that I fancy you rotten—and there's the obvious answer—that I'm a competitive kind of guy and I like a challenge. Then there are a few other things. I like the way you're so committed to your job, how you always see the positives about it even after a long day that ends with more work. I like the fact that you offer those extra catch-up sessions to the students who're struggling, on your own time. I like the fact that you look after your neighbor Margie, but at the same time make out that you do nothing at all for her. The way you pretend to be all tough but your actions say different.

"I like the way you listen to everyone respectfully, even if you don't agree with them. I enjoy your lists and your dates and your other coping mechanisms, and the way you're weird but open about it so it doesn't even feel weird. I like the way you bundle your hair on your head in that odd bun that looks great, even though you don't care. I like that you go for runs with me. I like that you know about my childhood and reacted sympathetically but didn't treat me as a pitiable motherless baby-man. I like the way that sometimes you're quiet but you're never shy. I appreciate your advanced knowledge in a pub quiz. I am intrigued by you, I find you funny, you're gorgeous, and I've never met anyone quite like you. Does that answer your question at all?"

I am, as he has just said, sometimes quiet—but I am rarely at a loss for words. My silence seems to amuse him, and he adds: "See? I'm deep, me. I bet you thought it was just because you have good legs."

I shake my head and reply, "You are a very interesting person, Karim—and I like you too. I'm not going to compile a list, but I do. I just feel the need to tell you a few things first."

"Oh no—are you on the run from the Russian Mafia? About to move to Japan? Actually gay and not at all attracted to men?"

"No to the mafia, no to Japan, and although I've had my wild moments, I'm definitely attracted to men. But—well, I think maybe sometimes I should come with a health warning, you know? Some kind of label that tells people I have issues. I'm not good with commitment. I love sex but I'm not great at intimacy. I tend to move around a lot, and I tend to live in my own little bubble as much as possible, and I'm . . . basically not a good bet."

"You're a woman, not a racehorse," he answers, frowning. "I'm not interested in what the odds are. Nobody is perfect, and no relationship is either—or I wouldn't be single at thirty-four. I undoubtedly have issues of my own, though perhaps I haven't spent quite as much time cataloging them as you. I just think we're good together. I just think we should both take it slowly, see what happens, keep an open mind, I don't know, but how about this for a crazy plan: maybe not decide right now, before anything's even happened between us, that it's going to fail? Maybe just have some fun?"

I bite my lip and know that he has battered the nail right on the head. That is exactly what I'd been doing, and exactly what I've done in the past—it's like I've gone through the motions of having partners but never really, truly tried to make a go of it. I've been so convinced that the relationships were going to fail—so convinced that that's all I deserved—that I've always contributed to their demise. I've been rejecting myself on behalf of others for a very long time now, getting in there first before they have the chance.

It is a sad and defeatist way of living, I know. The way I have felt recently, despite the confusion and the worry and the what-should-I-do-next, has shown me that I am capable of feeling bigger things. Better things. Imagining Katie in my life in a permanent way opened me up, made me peel back some layers, forced me to become vulnerable.

All it got me, I suppose, was ending up collapsed on the floor in front of a roomful of people—but perhaps, eventually, when I am feeling less hurt and less bereft, it will have been something positive. And perhaps, as well, I need some fun—and it doesn't come in much better packaging than Karim.

I nod firmly, as much to myself as to him. I glance at my watch, see that it is only just after 8:00 p.m., even though it feels as though I have lived a whole lifetime today.

Still, it's after 8:00 p.m. And in my mind, 9:00 p.m. is a reasonable bedtime. I'm wild and crazy like that.

"Did you know," I say slowly, as though I'm building up to something truly mysterious, "that on this day in 1066, William the Conqueror invaded England at Pevensey Bay in Sussex?"

"Of course I did."

"You didn't, did you?"

"Of course I didn't. I'm just a PE teacher, you know."

"You're much more than that, Karim," I reply. "And thank you. For looking after me. For listening. For being so kind and patient with me. Now I think I'd better get home."

We make the half-hour drive back to the north of the city in a comfortable silence, windscreen wipers swooshing against the rain, roads streaked with neon. I cradle the Wonky Cushion on my lap for the whole journey, telling myself that its magic power is indeed seeping through me. That I will heal, that I will be whole.

Karim is content to leave me to my thoughts, and as he pulls up outside my flat, I hear Bill let out one welcome woof. He seems to know it's me, even in a strange car—dogs are surprisingly clever for creatures that spend so much time with their noses near bottoms. I realize, as I sit unmoving in the passenger seat, that I am still not ready to be alone. I am still not ready to face the fallout of tonight's revelations. Not ready to put myself and my failings under the microscope that I so bluntly wield.

That "fun" comes in many shapes and sizes, and just might involve being in the company of another human being. I realize that I have opened up to Margie in ways I never thought possible, and that I can change—that I am capable of living more fully than I currently do. I have to believe that.

"Would you . . . like to come in?" I say, trying not to sound as eager as I feel. "Though I have to admit, I am using you as a distraction again."

"I've been used for worse," he says simply, switching off the engine and helping me carry the boxes of history project props up the stairs. I consider letting Margie know I am home, but she will already know—Bill has woofed, and she will hear my feet on the stairs. She will, knowing Margie, also hear Karim's feet on the stairs and be full of questions in the morning. I smile at the thought of how excited she will be to interrogate me as I open the door.

He follows me in, puts the boxes down, and looks around with interest.

I follow his gaze and see my flat through his eyes: neat, clean, orderly. No pictures on the walls, no knickknacks, no clutter. Everything perfectly set up for one person to live a simple life. I know, because I am that kind of person, that I have four forks and four knives and four plates and four everything else—but most of them have never come out of their respective cupboards and drawers.

I feel the thread of some kind of cutlery-based analogy coming on, about how I have everything it takes within my grasp but have simply never chosen to use it.

"Nice place," he says. "Better than mine purely on the basis that it doesn't smell like unwashed socks." I smile and potter around. I light the scented candle, put on some music, get out an extra glass. I pour myself a glug of white wine that's been open in the fridge for a bit too long, ask him what he would like, and laugh when he requests a glass of milk.

The rain has died down a little, and I open the French windows to the balcony. I grab us both a blanket and lead him outside. There is, as usual, only one chair—because I have never invited anyone here before.

That has never felt strange to me until tonight, but now I decide it is. I have lived here for a long time, and the only other person who has been inside was a plumber fixing a leak in the shower. Margie struggles with the stairs, so I always visit her, and none of my other so-called friends have ever felt significant enough to bring home. I know the other teachers at the school hold book clubs, dinner parties, sleepovers for their kids—all of that has seemed superfluous to me before.

Now, as I drag an extra chair outside for Karim, I wonder if it isn't superfluous at all—or if the casual connections that other people make so easily simply scare me.

We settle together, blankets wrapped around our shoulders, chairs close enough together that our thighs touch. We look out at the water, at the bright red lights of the cranes and gantries, at the distant harbor, at the dark and windswept beach.

The foghorn is blaring, a single solitary note that always sounds like mourning. A sound so specific to this place that I will never hear it again without thinking of this view, this small corner of the world.

"It's beautiful, isn't it?" he says, sounding slightly awestruck. "I grew up in the Midlands, and I never get tired of this—this feeling that we're looking out at the whole of the universe laid out before us."

"It is beautiful," I reply, smiling, "and that was very poetic for a PE teacher."

"I have my moments," he says, smiling back.

We sit, and we look, and we drink our drinks. Eventually, I feel his hand reach for mine, and our fingers entwine. It is a simple thing, a simple human thing, but it is what I need. I hold on tight, and wonder how I have convinced myself for so long that I need nobody.

I still feel a deep sense of loss about Katie—about my actual daughter, I suppose. About Baby—beautiful Baby, wherever she may be.

But I also feel a sense of discovery, of taking tentative steps into the possibility of a different kind of life.

The music gently floats out from the living room, swirling around us. It shuffles on to Florence and the Machine. "Never Let Me Go."

"Ah," he says, nodding his head wisely, "Florence. I think I once told you this was going-to-bed music."

I stroke the skin of his palm. I look out at the whole of the universe, laid out before us.

"Well," I reply. "Who am I to argue?"

I stand up, and he joins me. He reaches out, strokes my hair back from my face. His touch is gentle, warm, fingers tracing a soft path along my cheekbones, down to my neck. I lean into him and feel the solidity of his body pressed against mine. He is here. He is real. He is gazing at me in the darkness, his eyes intense, a small smile on his lips as his hands settle on my shoulders.

I smile back and, for once, neither of us has anything to say. He kisses me, and it is a sublime kiss. A kiss that blanks out the rest of the world. A kiss that will not allow me to worry, or be sad, or even to count.

A kiss that promises the whole of the universe—at least for tonight.

## CHAPTER 13

# 112 STEPS TO A DIFFICULT CONVERSATION AND ONE ANGRY GARDEN GNOME

**When I wake up, I** can still smell him on the pillows; a vague echo of his aftershave. My senses luxuriate in it, and in the vivid memories of the night before. I allow myself a few brief moments of respite before I force my eyes awake, force my brain to become alert, force myself into a new day.

He is gone, I can tell immediately. I have a second where I am both disappointed and relieved, and then I see the note that he has left on the pillow next to me.

I pick it up and read:

*Doing the Drive of Shame home to get a shower before work. See you later, gorgeous. PS: On this day in history, I discovered that Gemma Jones snores!*

I hold the paper, roll onto my back, smiling at the ceiling.

"No I don't!" I protest to the empty room. Though I am forced to concede the point that I usually sleep alone, and therefore can't really make a solid case for my defense.

It is still, for a little while, a distraction, this thing with Karim. This undefined, ever-changing, pretty damn spectacular thing with Karim—but I know that it will not distract forever. That I must reenter the real world at some point. I glance at my phone on the bedside table, see that it is almost 9:00 a.m. I should be at work by now.

I bite my lip, screw up my eyes against the weak fingers of sunlight that are curling around the edges of the curtains.

I pick up the phone and do something I have never done before in my entire working life: call in sick. In all my years, through coughs and colds and all the other sniffles that students like to share, I have managed to fight my way in to teach.

Perhaps it is because I am so committed to my job. Perhaps it is because I don't have anything much else to do that is more important. It is easy for me to be committed, I know— easy for me to be organized, to cope with the long hours, the meetings, the politics, the planning, and the grading. Easy for me not to get ground down by it all—because it is the biggest single thing in my life.

I know my colleagues have to fit a lot more life into the hours they have available. They need to make marriages work, look after babies, their own teenagers, in some cases care for elderly parents. In the case of a few of the women, they have menopause thrown in as an extra treat. It is hard to find the time and energy and have anything left over for themselves.

I have none of those commitments or challenges, and it frees me up in a way that is a strength in my career—but, I suspect, a weakness in my life.

Today, I decide, rolling around on the sheets and building up to a dismount, I will be kind to myself. I will be gentle in the way I think, delicate in the demands I place on my time and my mind, as polite to myself as I would be to anyone else.

I will "throw a sickie," as they say here, to buy myself the day I need to rediscover my equilibrium.

I get up, shower, eat a slice of toast. I tidy up the glasses from last night and smile at the thought of how it ended.

I lounge around the flat, imagining it filled with laughter and love and light. It is a strange idea, a foreign concept, the thought of deliberately opening myself up to what will probably end badly.

That, of course, is what I am up against: the mental road-blocks that tell me nothing good can come of all of this.

By the time I am dressed in my running clothes and ready to pop down to see Margie, it is almost 11:00 a.m. I have wasted so much of the morning, and it feels decadent.

I jog down my fourteen stairs, planning to take Bill out and then to take Margie out. We will go to one of the nice coffee shops in town, possibly in disguise in case I bump into anyone from work. I tell myself it will be good, that we will eat over-priced pastries and watch the world go by while I tell her all about Katie. I will tell her how sad I feel, how empty, how I had pinned so many unspoken hopes and dreams on it all—but I will also tell her that I will cope. That I will grieve for my losses, that I will look to the future, and I will be better and stronger for it.

I might even, I decide, tell her all about Karim—the edited version at least. She's getting on, after all; I don't want to give her a heart attack.

As I make my way around the side of the building to Margie's terrace, though, I hear voices. This is not unusual—Margie is well known in the area, and dog walkers often stop to chat to her as they stroll past.

But this time, the voice sounds familiar. The southern accent, the lighthearted tone, the infectious laughter.

I come to a standstill and peek round the corner, seeing that I am right. Erin is standing at the gate, scratching Bill behind the ears as he stands on his back legs to get closer to her, licking her fingers and making her giggle.

I pause, consider turning back—neither of them has seen me, and Bill has been distracted by affection. I could still make a run for it. Immediately I give myself a telling-off—so much for my brave new world if I run and hide at the first sign of an awkward situation.

I arrange my face into something approaching okay and push myself onward. *I can do this*, I think. These people are friends, and I need all the friends I can get. Normal people have friends, and even if I don't always feel normal, I should at the very least bloody well try.

"Hi!" I say breezily as I walk round the corner, feigning surprise. "I see you two have met!"

They both look at me with odd expressions, and I wonder if I have overdone the breezy and edged into manic.

"Gemma! You look . . . okay," says Erin, frowning slightly. "After last night, I was a bit concerned, and then Katie messaged me to say you were off sick today. I didn't have your address, but you'd described this place and Bill and Margie to me so well that I thought I'd amble along and hope for the best."

Margie is brandishing a jar, a bemused look on her face.

"Erin brought this for you," she says.

"Thank you. What is it?"

"It's beetroot juice," Margie replies, "you know, to help with your *anemia*?"

Margie's tone adds an unspoken "that you don't have" to the end of the sentence, and I feel a flush of embarrassment creep onto my cheeks.

"Oh. Right. That's really thoughtful. Except, well, I was lying last night, Erin—I'm not anemic, as far as I know."

"I see. Are you pregnant, then?" she asks, eyebrows raised in curiosity. Clearly, that is the only other reason she can come up with for my incredible fainting-woman routine, and possibly my odd behavior. It makes a lot more sense than the real reason, that's for sure.

I shake my head, and all three of us are silent for a moment. I have no idea what to do or say next.

"Tell you what," says Margie, breaking in and saving me, "why don't you two take Bill for a trot while I get the kettle on? I'm sure you've got plenty to catch up on."

She meets my eyes and purses her lips, and I know that she is trying to telepathically communicate with me. To tell me that I should come clean, open up, confess all.

Or maybe she's just cold and wants to get rid of us so she can go inside and watch *Homes Under the Hammer*.

"Good idea," I reply, "if you're up for it, Erin?"

She nods, and I unlock the little gate that marks out Margie's territory. Bill knows what's afoot and slinks out, wrapping himself around Erin's legs before bounding off toward the sand hills.

We follow and make small talk about the history project as we explore, heading along one of the paths that crisscrosses the dunes until we reach the shoreline. One hundred and twelve steps for me, maybe more for Erin.

We come to a halt by the steps that lead down to the sea, and I perch on them, as I usually do, but this time with Erin by my side. It is cool but sunny, the sky vivid blue, zigzagged with streaks of white cloud. The storm from last night has left the waterfront battered and wild, debris strewn across the sand, the plants that edge the dunes flattened and damp and tangled.

Bill is frolicking in and out of the frothy waves, living his very best life, playing with a little brown spaniel called Twig. He runs out of the water, starts to inspect a pile of driftwood, and pees on it.

Erin laughs, and I say: "Yeah. He's like a one-dog comedy routine, isn't he? At least he isn't bringing us any gifts. One day over summer he found the decapitated head of a gull and brought it over to me, spinal cord still attached."

"Nice. Sounds like something from a horror film."

"It was a bit. You get quite a lot of jellyfish washing up, but he's learned to leave those alone . . . Anyway, I'm sorry I lied."

"About being anemic?"

"Yeah, and—well, I haven't lied about anything else, but there have been what you might call some omissions."

She nods and looks serious, and I see the side of her that is capable of working in law and seeing through nonsense for a living.

"And these omissions, they're my business, are they?" she says gently.

I nod, and suck in some air, and decide I might as well jump right in. I like Erin and would enjoy continuing to see her. I want to be honest, to clear the air, but I'm also concerned that it is going to freak her out. That my clearing of the air is her horror story, with or without a decapitated seagull head.

Katie is my student, and her daughter, and even though we have formed our tentative friendship outside of the school environment, there are still probably a million and one safeguarding protocols being broken.

Damn it, I decide—it's either trust that she'll understand, or never see her again outside parents' evenings. To which I will wear a disguise.

"It's a bit of a long story," I say eventually. "In fact, it starts over eighteen years ago."

"Crikey. That *is* long. Come on, then, let's be having it!"

She smiles encouragingly and pats my hand, and it is enough—enough to give me the final push over the edge of reticence and into honesty.

"Right. Yes. Well, when I was sixteen, I had a baby. I had a baby on the third of October almost eighteen years ago. She had red hair, just like mine, and she was perfect, not like me, and—well, she was adopted, for lots of good reasons, and I've never seen her since." I speak briskly, in a matter-of-fact fashion, as though I am discussing the best way to assemble an IKEA wardrobe, not the darkest day of my life. It is, I think, the only way I will be able to do it.

I speak, and I wait. She is no fool, of course, this woman, even if she is wearing a pink bobble hat and has a passing resemblance to a garden gnome today. I see Erin process the information, see it register, see a flicker of emotion cross her face. I can't quite tell what the emotion is, though—maybe it's a lawyer thing.

"Same day that Katie was born," she says quietly. "Same hair. Not the same child, though. Katie came to us from a—well, from a difficult background. She was in care on and off from when she was born, and finally removed by the courts when it became clear that nothing at home was going to change, that she wouldn't be safe. That's when she came to us."

"I know that," I reply. "Now. After last night." She nods and is still and silent for a moment as she pieces it together.

"But before that," she says, "you didn't. You thought, what, that Katie might be your daughter?" I feel wretched and miserable and oh so out of my depth here. I am not good at this stuff. I am not good at honesty, or people, or friendships, and it feels unnatural to be laying myself so bare and exposed.

I count the Iron Men for a few moments while I gather myself, then reply, "I did. And I'm really sorry."

"About what?"

"About everything. I mean, I had no idea you were Katie's mum when we met at the yoga class—I just liked you. And I had no idea Katie was adopted until then either—I just liked her too. Of course I did—she's very likable. But when I did find out, and also discovered when her birthday was, it just—I don't know, it grew and grew in my mind. I think I might have gone a little bit crazy."

"So that evening, when you came around for dinner, you were already wondering about it?" I nod and bite my lip. I want to say more. To apologize more. To humble myself somehow—but I don't have the right words to express it all.

"That's why you went a bit funny looking at the pictures, right? And that's why you passed out last night."

"It is, yes. It was a shock, and I just suddenly—suddenly knew how wrong I'd been, and how stupid I'd been as well. And now I feel like you must think I'm some kind of lunatic stalker, and I'm not, I promise.

"I didn't say anything because it didn't feel right. Even back then, when I thought I might actually be her birth mother, I knew you were her *real* mother. I never, ever wanted to intrude on that. Especially because of what you've both been through recently—I didn't want to just make everything even more messed up for you."

"So, what, you just thought you'd hang around with me, teach Katie, and hope that one day you'd magically find a way to know for sure? How did you think that was going to happen, Gemma?"

Her voice is level and calm, but I can see a red sheen to her cheeks and know that she is angry. I shake my head and clench my eyes against tears. I am not the wronged party here. I have no right to tears.

"I don't know. I just don't know. I completely get why you're pissed off. This whole thing is a mess, and it's all my fault. I probably shouldn't have even told you."

Bill runs back over to us, nuzzles Erin's hands. He has abandoned me in my hour of need, and I can't say that I blame him.

She strokes his long head and says, "Why did you even tell me? You could have gone with anemia, and we'd have been none the wiser."

It's a good question, and right at this second I'm wishing that's exactly what I had done. Blame the emotional rollercoaster, blame the sex, blame loneliness—whatever the reason, I'd felt the need to come clean.

"I know," I reply, laughing bitterly. "I probably should have! It's—well, I don't really know what it is, Erin. Except that I like you and hope we can be friends, and I like Katie so much too and want her to do all the brilliant things I know she can with her life, and—well, I guess I wanted to be honest. Believe me, it feels weird at my end too."

She does not speak for a while, simply gazes out at the horizon, jaw clenched.

"I totally understand," I say when I can't take the silence anymore, "if you want me to get Katie moved into a different class. Heck, I totally understand if you want me to leave completely."

"Leave the school?"

"Yes. I will, if you want me to. I've made an almighty mess, and—I don't know, maybe it's for the best anyway. I've already been here too long."

She stands up suddenly, catching both me and Bill unawares. He responds quicker, trotting alongside her as she walks briskly back toward the dune path.

When we near the houses, she stops. Somehow, even though she is almost a foot shorter than me, she makes me feel intimidated with the look on her face.

"Look," she says seriously, "this is all a bit weird. I suppose you might have hit a nerve with me—no matter how confident you are as the mum of an adopted child, there always seems to be a bit of you that knows they must wonder, they must at least consider their 'other' mum. We've never hidden anything from Katie and have always said we'd support her if she wanted to look for her birth parents, but so far she's said she doesn't want to—and if I'm honest, even though I know it's selfish, that's been a bit of a relief. So this . . . this is a bit of a . . ."

"Head fuck?"

"Precisely that. I know, when I think it through and get my balance back, that I will understand it all better. I know I like you too, and that Katie thinks you're the bee's knees, and that it's probably best that you've been honest. Right now, I'm just a bit caught off guard, and freaked out, and in the same spirit of honesty, a bit angry as well. So I'm going to go home and have a glass of wine, even though it's not even lunchtime, and have a soak in the bath, and later on talk to Katie about all this."

I cringe slightly as she says it, and she notices.

"I have to. We don't keep secrets from each other, but I'll make sure she's discreet—she won't be sharing your secrets with the rest of the students, I promise," she says.

"I know. That's fine. I'm also happy to talk to her directly, if that helps. Whatever I can do. And I'm sorry. Sorry I was such an idiot."

"I'm sorry too," she says, reaching out and holding what I see is my trembling hand. "I'm sorry you were ever in this position. I can only imagine how much it hurts."

She strides away, and Bill lets out a resigned whimper as she disappears into the distance.

I know exactly how he feels.

# CHAPTER 14

# ONE BOX TICKED, ONE ESCAPE PLAN HATCHED

**"Do you want your beetroot** juice?" Margie asks as I trudge toward her gate.

"Only if it's actually whisky," I reply.

"Oh. That bad?"

I let myself in, and Bill heads inside to lap noisily at his water bowl. Margie gestures toward one of her chairs, but I am not in the mood for comfort.

"I don't know," I say simply, shrugging. "Obviously it's a bit of a strange thing to explain to someone, isn't it? She was a bit . . . unsettled?"

"'Course she was—you've been mulling it over for ages, but it was all a shock to her, wasn't it? She's lovely, though, isn't she? Erin, I mean."

"Yeah, she's really nice. We clicked as soon as we met. I liked her before I knew about Katie, and I still do. But maybe I've screwed that up now—I could totally get it if she never wanted to see me again. I'll have to stop going to yoga. And the takeaways near hers. And—"

"Did she say that, love, that she didn't ever want to see you again?"

"Well, no. She said she was going to talk to Katie in confidence and let it all brew."

"That seems reasonable, don't you think?"

I nod, because it is impossible to disagree. Of course it is reasonable.

"Then you're just getting ahead of yourself now, aren't you? Worrying about scenarios that haven't even happened?"

I narrow my eyes at her and reply, "That's what I do, Margie! It's kind of my specialist subject!"

"I thought that was knowing something weird that happened on every single day of the year, and being able to quantify exactly how many tea bags you'll need for a month."

"Well, they're also specialist subjects. God, I really am crap, aren't I?"

"Sit down," she says firmly, pushing me physically into one of her chairs. "You're in a proper tizz, and I've never seen you like this before. Normally you're Little Miss Calm, Cool, and Collected. Now take a chill pill, will you?"

"Take a chill pill?" I echo, the phrase so incongruous coming from her lips that it almost makes me smile.

"Yeah. You need to do some of your fancy breathing, or count some spoons or something. I can practically see steam coming out of your ears. Everything will be all right, hon. Have a bit of faith."

"Ha! Faith . . . that's definitely not one of my specialist subjects, but okay. I will indeed try to chill. I think this is my blind spot, Margie—anything to do with my baby, real or imagined, just seems to override all my usual factory settings."

She leans forward, pats my hand briefly, then winces. She is in pain, and she is ignoring it to comfort me. That small fact, that small sacrifice on her part, works better than any technique

I could have devised deliberately. It immediately diverts my attention away from the obstacle course that is my brain.

"Are you all right?" I ask. "Shall I get us a coffee?"

"I'm okay, Gem. Just need to go back to the doc, I think. Might ask him about acupuncture or something. I already take so many tablets that I rattle when I walk. Anyhow, that's for another time. So, I think you need to give Erin a bit of space, and you need to give yourself a bit of a break. And I think you need to give me all the filthy details of what you got up to last night, madam! We heard you, Bill and me, getting home past nine o'clock, a man's footsteps on your stairs, a mysterious Nissan still outside this morning . . ."

She is grinning like a demon on drugs, cackling and pointing at me as she sees my embarrassed expression.

"You're a dirty old woman, Margie, did you know that?" I ask, finding it impossible not to grin back.

"I do. That's one of *my* specialist subjects . . . so. Spill the beans!"

"Well, I'd not been well at the history club event, as you heard from Erin."

"Poor anemic child that you are . . ."

"Yes, well. So Karim and I went for a drink, and then he drove me home, and he helped me bring all the stuff back upstairs, and then we stayed up all night binge-watching *Bridgerton* on Netflix."

I announce this very seriously, and I can see from the disappointed look on her face that she completely believes me. Good to see my fibbing skills haven't completely deserted me.

"Really?" she murmurs. "I mean, I do love *Bridgerton*, but . . . I was hoping for more!"

I wink at her, and she widens her eyes and laughs again.

"Oh, you! You got me there! So . . . there was more?"

"There was more."

"And was it good more, bad more, or mediocre more?"

"It was excellent more. And that is all you're getting—a lady should never kiss and tell."

I can tell that she is delighted, both with my new romantic developments and at my apparent change of mood. While that lasts, while I can maintain the subterfuge, I get to my feet.

"Right, I've got stuff to do. Is there anything you need, Margie? I was thinking of a trip to town later, or to the shops, if you want to keep me company?"

I always have to phrase it like this, so she doesn't think I am being too kind, that she is being a burden to me. She has her pride, and I have my need for solitude, and somehow we manage to dance around both.

"Well, I'd have to check my diary," she replies, "but that sounds lovely! I'm surprised you've got the energy after all that more-ing."

We make a loose arrangement to check in with each other later, and I make my farewells. I manage to keep the smile in place until I am back round at the front of the building and making my way up to my flat.

Once I'm inside I shut the door firmly behind me and lean back against it, closing my eyes and letting out what feels like a long-held breath.

Being with other people has been hard this morning, for all kinds of reasons. Being honest with Erin was draining; pretending with Margie was tense. Now I am alone again, and I feel the bubble burst—the bubble of having to care what other people think, what other people feel, how other people react.

I like them, these other people—Margie, Erin, Katie, Karim. I like them, but I know it will always be a struggle for me to *be* like them. To form easy relationships, to not overthink everything, to simply sit back and go along for the ride. To be myself around them, when part of me still doesn't think I should take the risk. To have faith, as Margie puts it.

It is all so complicated, this simple stuff, and I am feeling the pressure build inside me.

I tell myself it is just that too much has happened in a short space of time. I can even calculate how many hours, if I really need to. Minutes, if I get extra fancy.

In that short space of time, over those minutes and hours and days, I have met someone who I became convinced was my biological daughter. I have discovered that I was wrong, and felt the pain of that discovery. By telling Erin about it, I have knowingly put myself in a vulnerable position, and I now have to deal with the consequences of it.

There are the personal consequences—that I may lose my budding friendship with Erin before it has even had a chance to grow. That it has roused all kinds of yearnings and secret hurts that I have been suppressing for years. But there are also professional issues, like facing a difficult situation with my star student at school, and making her life more complicated too. If Erin really wants to, she could make life difficult for me by making some kind of official complaint.

I have behaved recklessly with their feelings, with my own, and with my career. With hindsight I can see the mistakes I made, but I cannot change them. It is like watching a car crash happen in slow motion.

I also seem to have started something up with Karim, which was hard to resist last night, but in the cold light of day doesn't seem quite so wise. The poor man has no idea what he's letting himself in for.

I have, basically, become tangled up in a very messy web of life and emotions and potential disasters. Now I feel trapped, and like a giant spider is heading in my direction.

I splash some water on my face in the bathroom, make a mug of coffee, and walk over to my desk. It is, unsurprisingly, neat and tidy and well stocked. I usually spend at least a couple of hours a day here, so it's got to be.

I open up my laptop and log in to my account at a recruitment agency I have used several times in the past. At the moment, I am marked as unavailable, so new job opportunities don't get sent to me. I tick the box, indicate that I am once again looking for gainful employment, and log off.

I close the laptop lid, lean back in my chair, and feel an immediate sense of relief.

It is just a box on a form. It is just a net being cast. It does not mean that I am moving on. It does not mean that I am giving up. It does not mean that I will run.

It just means that I could.

## CHAPTER 15

# SIX BILLION DANCE STEPS AND THREE TIRED WOMEN

**I have just dropped Margie** back home when the message from Erin lands on my phone.

I am tired and feeling gray and washed out despite my best efforts. I think Margie enjoyed our trip to an elegant café near the cathedral, where we ate cake and admired the waiters and watched the beautiful people go by.

It was hard, though, to stay chatty and cheerful when all I really wanted to do was retreat beneath my duvet and cry.

Walking back into my flat, that is exactly what I hope to do when I hear the ping. I have already had a message from Karim, checked in and told him I am fine, that I will see him tomorrow. I want the whole world to leave me alone now, but it seems insistent on snapping at my heels.

Come to ours at 7 p.m., the message says, and wear comfortable shoes. I sit down and hold my face in my hands. It is not far from seven now, and the very last thing I want to do is see more people. I have reached the upper limits of my ability to interact socially, and I give at least a few moments' thought to ignoring it, or replying saying I can't come.

I take a deep breath, remind myself that this morning I was determined to make changes. To evolve, to move on. I can't give up at the first hurdle—and I owe it to Erin and Katie to try harder, be better, to at least attempt to make things right, for all kinds of reasons.

I take off my going-to-town shoes and slip on my socks and sneakers. I have no idea what they have planned for me and am too exhausted to even try to guess. I suppose I will simply have to take my medicine and hope it doesn't kill me.

I drive to their little terraced house, even though it only would have taken fifteen minutes if I'd walked. I need to feel safe, cocooned, and a few minutes in my car gives me that. I park nearby, glancing over at the lavender pots, and force myself up and out.

I knock on the door at exactly seven, and Katie answers. I don't know what I expect to feel when I see her again, but embarrassed and humiliated pretty much covers it. I feel very much like the child, and she seems very much like the grown-up, standing in the doorway smiling at me.

She is wearing black leggings, a black top, and a hot-pink tutu. I have no idea why, but it works.

"Come in, miss," she says, ushering me into the hallway, "and don't look so scared. It'll all be okay."

She is comforting me, and I am grateful. She might not be my biological daughter, but she is still a fine and admirable young woman.

Inside the living room, the clutter has been cleared, the sofas pushed back to the walls, and a large space created in the middle of the room. Erin is dressed in black with a pink boa, and on top of her head there is a wig made of glittery strands of gold. Her blond hair peeks out, and she looks like she could be in an Abba tribute band.

She walks over to me and passes me a beret. It is tartan, red and green, and will look awful with my hair. I wordlessly accept it and put it on. I have no idea what is happening, but none of it feels hostile, which is more than I have a right to expect.

"We're going to dance it all out," she says seriously, gesturing at the TV screen. "It's what we do, Katie and me, when things are tough or sad or complicated. We dance it out. This seems like a situation that could be improved by a bit of sweat."

"I'm not the world's best at dancing," I murmur, feeling apprehensive beneath my beret.

"That's even better," she replies, nodding. "It's like karaoke— it's not fun if you're actually good. Now, all we ask is that you give it everything—no half measures, no pauses, no worrying about how you look. The key to successfully dancing it out is commitment. Can you do that?"

I look at her kind eyes peering up at me from beneath her glittery fringe, and at Katie, standing next to her in her tutu. They are completely mad, these two.

"Yes," I reply definitely. "I can do that."

"Then we shall begin. Katie, can you do the honors?"

Katie draws the curtains and turns off the lights. The room is dim and quiet, and that all changes the minute she presses a button on the remote control. The TV screen bursts into life, and I see that it is a YouTube video of a band called Blackpink, singing something catchily entitled "DDU-DU DDU-DU."

She pauses it and explains: "Blackpink is my favorite K-pop band. There are four of them and only three of us, but that's okay. You're the one with the dark red hair. Just do your best, copy as well as you can, and remember—it's all about the oomph!"

I nod nervously, and she starts the video. It is a jaunty tune, and there is all kinds of stuff going on in the video. They are sitting down, then standing up; they are dressed in shorts and boots and then rainbows and sequins and there is a lot of pink powder being thrown around; there is a Chihuahua with super-long ears and there is a pastel-colored cockatoo and a giant chess set, and it's all pretty damn weird and full-on.

Katie and Erin are flailing around in a vague way—as though they are petting dogs, holding birds, brandishing umbrellas and swords, whatever "their" one is doing on-screen. I try to join in but am completely at a loss until all the women come together on a platform for the chorus and the dance sequence. Boy, can they dance.

There are jumps and kicks, and their hips swivel in ways that no human being should be able to swivel. I do my very best, encouraged by the fact that Katie and Erin are almost as bad as I am, despite having done it before, and I am barely breathing by the time we get a break, while the girls ride sequined tanks and swing from chandeliers and other bizarre actions that we have to imitate without the props.

There is another ferocious dance sequence chorus, another break, countless costume changes, a whirlwind of color and sound and movement. It's like being on an acid trip inside Willy Wonka's Chocolate Factory.

We all try to copy a sinuous movement where the band members seem to have turned into snakes, and we end up sitting in prim poses while we sweat and pant.

"Again, again!" Erin shouts, and I feel like karate chopping her. Instead I grimace, and Katie presses play, and we do it all over again. It is easier the second time around, not less exhausting but less surprising. My spine will probably never be the same again, but I am learning to count the steps, and finding that helpful in many ways. By the end of the second time around, though, I am done. I am physically fit, but this is a kind of activity my body is not used to, and it has destroyed me. It is a huge relief when the two of them collapse onto the sofa laughing, wiping the sheen from their faces, sucking in air.

I fall back onto a chair, and my legs feel like jelly. My lungs are sore, and my heart rate feels three times as fast as usual. I am, though, smiling—which is weird.

"See!" announces Katie, pointing at me. "Told you it works! How do you feel?"

"Knackered," I reply. "Out of breath. Like I'm about a hundred years old. But better than I did when I arrived."

I have no idea why I feel better, but I do.

"It's good, isn't it?" says Erin, still in recovery, sounding tired but looking thrilled. "And we needed it, I think—all of us did."

Katie jumps up to her feet with absurd speed, goes into the kitchen, and returns with three bottles of water that they seem to have chilled in advance. Experience pays.

I take some relieved glugs, and we are all silent for a few moments.

"I've never even heard of K-pop . . . ," I say, shaking my head. I tug off the beret and instantly feel better.

"It's a whole new world," Erin replies sagely. "So. I told Katie all about everything."

I nod and feel some of the familiar tension seep back in.

"She was far cooler about it than I was," she continues, looking at Katie in wonder. "In fact, her first reaction was to feel sad for you. To explain to me, her little old mama, that it must have been harder for you than you ever let on. That you were in pain, and that you probably still are, and that as your friends, we should support you, not be pissed off with you. In fact, she is wise beyond all her years, and I adore her."

Katie nods, accepting the compliment, and says: "I am indeed. And while you're in an adoring mood, can I get a new phone?"

I fight the urge to jump in, to say that I'll buy her a new phone, anything she wants—because I am so pathetically grateful for her kindness, her understanding, her generosity of spirit.

"I don't adore you that much," Erin responds quickly. "You can get a new phone when you save enough money to buy one."

Katie sticks her tongue out at her, in a not-very-wise way, and looks over at me.

"Have you tried to find her?" she asks. "Your daughter?"

I shake my head, and drink some more water, and gather my thoughts. It is a complex situation, and I need to tread carefully. Beneath my feet lie dreams, of course.

"No," I reply. "For any number of reasons. I suppose partly I don't want to upset her life. And partly, if I'm honest, I don't want to upset my own; I've imagined all kinds of lives for her over the years, all of them good. All of them better than the one she would have had with me. I suppose I'm also a bit scared of finding out what actually happened. I still feel guilty."

"About what?" Katie asks, leaning forward, elbows on her tutu-clad knees.

"About . . . everything. About being stupid enough to get pregnant in the first place. About letting everyone down, making my own mum's life even more complicated. Mainly, though, about giving her away. Letting go when maybe I should have held on tight."

"Why did you, then?" she says. "If you wanted to keep her, why didn't you? Were you under pressure not to? Wouldn't it have been possible?"

"It would have been possible, yes, which is maybe why I feel guilty still. Possible, but not good, for either of us. My mother wasn't capable of looking after herself or me—she had her own issues, and I was in care at the time it happened. I wasn't ready. Financially, emotionally, in any way—I just wasn't ready. But that wasn't her fault, was it?"

I leave that out there, and feel a sudden chill go through me as my dancing-it-out sweat dries against my skin.

"If that was me," Katie says after a few moments' thought, "I would understand. I would understand that a sixteen-year-old girl who was in care herself might not feel ready to be a mum."

"Yes, but as has just been pointed out, you are wise beyond your years. What if she doesn't understand? What if she feels rejected?"

"What if it's both?" Katie counters firmly. "She's probably not stupid. She's probably capable of understanding it on one level and still feeling hurt on another. And if the people who adopted her were anywhere near as good as the people who adopted me, she'll be able to cope with that."

"Katie, it's my wildest dream that she was raised by people like your parents—people who loved her and cherished her and gave her everything she needed. Who certainly gave her more than I could have done at the time. When I met you, when I started to put two and two together and come up with seventy-eight, I felt elated—and relieved. Relieved because of how well you'd turned out. Relieved that I'd made the right decision all those years ago."

I look over at Erin, who has stayed unusually silent during this exchange, wondering what she thinks of it all. Whether Katie's accepting the situation is enough for her, or whether she still has her doubts about me.

"And how do you feel about it all now?" she asks, making eye contact with me. "After this thing with Katie, after this . . . disappointment, I suppose you'd call it?"

It's a very good question, and the answer is that I'm not sure. I have never allowed myself to fantasize about a reunion, about seeing her again, about actually finding out what her life after me has looked like. I have told myself that it has been enough to know that she was better off without me. Until now.

"I don't know," I say simply. "I think . . . I think it's opened up all kinds of feelings in me that I've hidden away for years. I think it's taken away any certainty I had. I think it's made me . . . want to know more. But I'm still not sure it's right to try to insert myself into her life. I didn't even feel it was right with you two, when I was convinced that Katie was her. I don't want to cause any damage. I feel like I've caused enough already. Truth be told, no matter how sorted I look on the surface, I'm still a bit of a disaster zone myself."

"All parents are, Gemma," Erin replies gently. "It's a little secret we all have. Nobody is sorted."

"Even someone who arranges her pens and counts dance steps out loud!" adds Katie. Damn. I didn't know I'd been doing it out loud.

"How's this for a plan," says Erin. "We order in a pizza, crack open a bottle of wine, and look at how it all works?"

"How what all works?"

"How the Adoption Contact Register works. You can sign up. You can choose to not sign up. But I think it would be good to know your options."

I nod and think she may be right. I can look, at least. I could fill out a form, maybe. It doesn't mean that I will find my daughter.

It just means that I could.

# CHAPTER 16

# TWO SECRETS SHARED

**"So, did you register, then?** Did you sign up?"

Karim is gazing at me intently, his glass of Coke halfway to his lips. We have driven out to a countryside pub for dinner, and we are sitting in the garden together, beneath a gazebo. The evening is mild—and warm, as long as you are sheltered from the wind. Fairy lights are strewn across the roof, and it is cozy and Christmassy, even at this time of year.

"I did, yes," I reply, keeping my hands clasped between my knees because I know they are trembling.

It is a few days after I danced it out with Erin and Katie, and I have finally told him all about it. I have given him the abridged History of Me, sticking to the facts, not letting my emotions spill over into what is already a difficult accounting. He is now up to date, and I am exhausted. I have talked about myself more in the last week than I have for the rest of my life, and I am not that interesting.

Now I feel laid bare, like a wire stripped of its insulation. My nerves are raw and jagged, and I look around at all the other tables nearby. I have already calculated that the outdoor capacity of the pub is forty-eight, and there are only twelve of us here. I look back at Karim and remain silent.

He has listened carefully to my sad tale and now seems to want to know more. Which is understandable but also disturbing—I was steeled to say my piece, but hadn't quite prepared myself for any further probing. I tell myself that it is fine, that he is friend not foe, that it will all be okay.

Of course, part of me doesn't believe that. Part of me thinks that Karim will hear all of this and disapprove. Think badly of me. Judge me and find me wanting. At the very least, that he will decide I am way too messy and complicated and screwed up to waste any more time on.

That thought process in itself is bad enough—but the fact that I might actually be relieved if he walks away is even worse.

If he walks away, I will be hurt. But I have been hurt before, and I know I will recover. If he stays, if we carry on with this thing we have together, then I will get in deeper and deeper and the hurt will grow bigger and bigger. It has already become so much more than I expected it to. More than I planned. How will I cope when it all goes wrong?

"And what happens next, then?" he asks quietly, rudely interrupting my internal catastrophizing.

"Well, I've registered my details and what I know about her—the dates and places and names and stuff. Obviously, I don't know what her name is now. When she was born I didn't want to choose a name for her; I just thought that was the job of the people who were adopting her, and—well, I suppose I didn't want to make her even more real.

"So, I signed up and said that I would be open to being contacted, and now I wait. She can go on there when she is eighteen, and then—well. I don't know what happens then."

It had been simple to fill in, that form. A straightforward act of bureaucracy, submitted to the General Register Office, which bizarrely turned out to be just down the road from us in Southport.

Simple, but not—those dates, those times, those names, all so heavily laden with history, with emotion. And the final kicker— the question that asks you if you wish to be contacted or if you do not; a delete-as-appropriate option that hides a world of potential pain and rejection. The same option is given on the form for adopted people as well—once they are eighteen, they can register and specifically say that they don't want to be contacted.

Such clear-cut options for something that is so very complex.

Katie won't register when she turns eighteen because she says she isn't interested in her birth parents yet. She knows their names and knows the details that would allow her to contact them, but doesn't feel the need. That might change, but for now she is content to keep her distance.

It might be the same with my daughter—or it might be that she registers but says she doesn't want to be contacted. In which case, it's game over unless I wanted to work with some kind of tracing agency or whatever—which I don't. I would have to respect that wish.

I explain a little of this to Karim, and he nods, processing it all, before replying: "And she's eighteen in a few days' time— that's tough, Gemma, isn't it? That waiting. And tough if she does register but says she doesn't want to hear from you?"

"I suppose it is. But I've been through tougher."

I am trying to sound calm, but even I hear the waver in my voice, feel a tremor in my lower lip.

I have been through tougher, and I have no real desire to go through it again.

Karim is sitting next to me, and his hand slides beneath the table, takes one of mine in his. I hadn't realized how cold my fingers were until I feel the warmth of his skin. I hold on tight, more relieved than I could have expected beneath his touch.

"Thank you," he says, squeezing my hand, "for telling me. It explains a lot about the last few weeks. And I see why it wasn't something you wanted to share straightaway."

"I'm not sure it's something I want to share even now, truthfully," I reply. "I wasn't sure how you'd react."

"I knew you had a past, Gemma. I didn't think you were a virgin. What happened to you—it's sad. It's a small tragedy, in its own way. You were only sixteen—younger than a lot of the kids we teach. Can you imagine any of them being responsible enough to raise a child?"

I think of a few prime suspects, and I shake my head.

No. I can't. Most of them still seem so young. Too young to even remember to bring a pen to class, or to study for a test, or to wear matching socks.

"I can tell it still affects you," he continues, "and it's probably affected the whole of your life. Maybe you should allow yourself a little bit of pride for what you've achieved, rather than a great big dollop of guilt for what you didn't. Not many people from your background do as well as you have done."

"I don't think you can tell how well someone has done just from looking, can you? I mean, it depends on how you judge it. Health, wealth, happiness, whatever."

"You're right. You can't tell from looking. But you got your degree. You've built a career. You're building a life that is good and full."

I look into his dark eyes and see nothing but understanding and support. It is almost as unsettling as seeing contempt and horror.

"I'm trying," I say quietly. "But none of this comes naturally to me. I wasn't raised to expect much of myself, or the people around me, and it's hard to . . . unpick it, I suppose."

He nods and replies, "Yeah. I can imagine. Have you ever thought about getting some help? You know, some counseling?"

I snort out a bitter laugh, and wonder why. It's not exactly the world's worst idea—but it's also not an idea that I can ever see myself following up on. I am too self-contained, too boxed in, scared of revealing too much of myself.

"I think I'd end up lying to the therapist," I say. "Making up easier stuff to confess to so I wouldn't have to deal with the bigger issues."

He smiles and rolls his eyes, like he can totally imagine that scenario.

"I had counseling, for a while, a few years ago," he answers simply. He leaves it at that, opening the door but not shoving me through it.

"Why?" I ask. "And did it help?"

"It did help, and as for why—well, on the surface, it was because I lost a baby."

I look up at him sharply, frowning. This is not what I expected him to say.

"Tell me about it," I urge gently. "If you want to. But if you don't, I understand—I'm hardly in a position to criticize anyone for keeping secrets, am I?"

STATISTICALLY SPEAKING 179

He shrugs and gulps down some of his Coke. We both have plates of food in front of us, untouched, fries wilting, salad curling. The unloved burgers of the beer garden.

"You had your reasons for being secretive," he responds. "And this isn't something I talk about often either. When I was younger—twenty-two—I was engaged to a girl called Zara. We'd been together since we were sixteen, stuck it out through uni, and—well, we were going to get married. Looking back, we were way too young, and probably not even right for each other. But my sisters liked her, and our families were pleased, and I think we were both happy enough to go along with it."

He pauses, and I give him the silence and the space to gather his thoughts.

"Sex before marriage, of course, was technically discouraged—but we were only human. When Zara found out she was pregnant, we didn't tell anyone. We were shocked, and maybe, to be honest, a bit worried, and we had no idea what to do. So we kept quiet, and we—well, we adapted to the idea. Sometimes accidents can be happy, we decided. Once we'd got over the initial panic, we were both pleased. And then— long story short—she miscarried at eleven weeks."

We are still holding hands, but now I am the one doing the comforting as I wait for him to continue.

"Nobody else knew, so we only had each other. And—well, that wasn't enough. She was devastated, and I was too, but I had no real idea what to say or how to help her, and I was so sad myself, and we were both a mess for a long time. Eventually, we split up. We just couldn't get over it, and maybe it made us realize that we shouldn't be together at all. Now she's married with four kids and I see her every now and then when I go home. Her older kids go to the same school as my niece and nephews. I'm happy for her, I really am, but I carried that pain for a long time. I still do."

"It's hard for the dad, I'm sure," I say, "when that happens. You've both suffered the loss, but she's the one going through it physically."

"Exactly that. I had to focus on her; it was the right thing to do. I was useless, but I tried. The problem is that to do that, I bottled up all of my own grief, and eventually I was angry.

"Not just about the baby but about everything. It felt like the universe was against me, and I was pissed off. When we ended things between us, I felt lost. I reacted by behaving badly. I moved away from home, I was drinking, even though I never really had before, and I was—well, let's just say I was doing a lot of stuff that was out of character for me. It wasn't making me happy, and it was scaring the heck out of my sisters, and it was threatening my career just as it was really starting. It was Asha who made me get help. You've met her. She's a tough lady—and when she tells you to do something, you do it."

I laugh a little at that. He's so right.

"Well, sometimes it's good to have people in your life who care enough about you to boss you around. Is that when you saw a counselor?"

"Yeah, and it was so good for me. She helped me understand my problems—that the loss of my mum had affected me so much more than I ever thought it had. That everything was tangled up together, that I was grieving for her, for my baby, for my relationship. It was the making of me, really."

I reach up to stroke his cheek, see the sheen of tears in his eyes. Lean in to kiss him briefly.

"See," he says, smiling sadly, "we all have secrets. Now you know something about me that nobody else here does."

"That makes me feel special," I reply, finding that I like the feeling.

"Good. I think you are. The big question, though, remains—do you still fancy me, now you know I'm not the one hundred percent pure alpha male beefcake you signed up for?"

We look at each other, and there is a sense of openness, of sharing, that I don't think I've ever felt before. I push aside my own concerns, my worries, my insecurities, my cowardly fear of where this might all be leading, and reply, "I don't think I've ever found you more attractive."

"What? What about that time when I took my top off on the cricket field last summer term, and you were almost salivating?"

I whack him on the arm but remember it vividly. I blushed whenever I thought about it for days afterward.

"Even more than then. Thank you. For listening, and for talking, and for just . . . being you, I suppose."

"Being me is one of the things I'm best at. Have you finished with your food? Do you want to get out of here?"

"I do," I reply, grinning. "Let's go home. Let's go to bed. Let's make each other happy. Let's enjoy the simple stuff for a while after all this complicated stuff."

"You know me," he says, winking, "I'm always up for the simple stuff."

# CHAPTER 17

# EIGHTEEN YEARS OF MISSING HER

**The day of October 3** falls on a Saturday. I wake up with Karim by my side, his hair in dark tufts and his bare chest slowly rising and falling. He is one of those people who kicks all the covers off himself at night and wakes up cold. I look at him for a moment, syncing my breathing with his, trying to calm my own heart rate.

I have been trapped in anxiety dreams all night long. Dreams where my fingers have turned into actual sausages that are too big to operate a keyboard. Dreams where I have forgotten my phone passcode and get locked out so many times my phone actually explodes in my hands like a grenade, leaving me with bloody stumps. Dreams where I am in hospital and nobody will let me out of bed to check my emails, tying me to the headboard with surgical stockings.

Over and over I have woken up, slicked in sweat, exhausted and drained. It has been about as much fun as it sounds.

I slide out of bed as quietly and softly as I can, trying not to disturb him as I pull the duvet up over his sleeping form. I put on a robe, creep out of the room, and stand alone in the lounge. I need coffee, I tell myself, and go through the motions of putting a pod in the machine, pressing the button, and realizing too late that I haven't put a cup on the stand.

I clean up the mess, do it all again, sip brown liquid that I do not taste, so hot it scalds my lips.

It is 5:54 a.m., and I know there is zero chance of me getting back to sleep. I give in and go out onto the balcony. It is raining heavily, the sky is dark, the sea a black, roiling smudge that stretches on forever.

I open my phone, relieved to find that the passcode is the same as it always has been, relieved that my fingers are not made of minced meat, that nothing explodes.

I check my emails, hands shaking, forgetting to breathe until I wheeze. I have imagined this moment so many times. Pictured getting a notification, opening it, seeing that she has found me on the register. That she has agreed to contact. That my details have now been passed on to her so she can get in touch.

In my wilder moments of fantasy, everything has happened at once—there is already an email there from her, inviting me into her life. It is chatty, and friendly, and curious—just the way I hoped it would be. Understanding and non-judgmental and full of colorful details about how good her life has been.

We will arrange to meet, and that meeting will be the beginning of something wondrous that will make me whole again.

That, of course, was fantasy—and this is reality. This is a cold, wet pre-dawn morning, and there is nothing. Nothing at all.

I sit down and I go slack. I hadn't realized how scrunched up I was until I'm not, and then suddenly I feel like all my muscles have stopped working.

She is eighteen today. Only eighteen. She probably has other things on her mind. She probably isn't even out of bed yet. I have been in too much of a rush, and I need to be more rational about this.

I sit, that hope-killing phone on my lap, and I remember that day eighteen years ago. The aching agony. The fatigue. Geoff with a G, and the Irish midwife, and the blood and the gore and the sheer perfection of my baby. I remember her ten tiny fingers, her ten tiny toes. I feel tears on my face, and I let them be. I am sad. I am allowed to cry. I wish that I had a mother to console me, to tell me that everything will be fine. But now, as it was then, I do not.

I have more than I had this time last year, I remind myself. I have Margie and Bill. I have Katie and Erin. I have the man who is lying in my bed. I have more than I had—but right now, at this exact moment, it feels like nothing at all. It feels empty and hollow and sour.

I hear the door open behind me, feel a warm hand on my shoulder. I do not look round. I don't want him to see that I am crying. I don't want him to see me like this at all.

Karim doesn't go along with that plan and crouches down in front of me. He is only wearing boxers, and must be freezing out here in the damp, not-quite-awake air.

He puts his hands on my knees and looks up at me. I bite my lip, and swipe away those stupid tears, and meet his eyes.

"Anything?" he asks. There is no need to explain. He knows exactly what I am doing out here. We have not discussed it, but of course he knows. He insisted on staying over last night, even though he has to take the school's football team on an away match to Manchester later.

I shake my head and close my eyes. I don't want to see his sympathy. It might break me.

"Well, it's still early," he says gently. "Not everyone gets up before six, especially teenagers. Come back to bed."

I let him lead me back inside, and I clamber under the sheets with him, and he wraps me in his arms and kisses the top of my head as I cry.

"You're right. It's too early, isn't it?" I say eventually. I don't know if I mean it's too early in the morning, or too early for her to come anywhere close to forgiving me.

"It is too early," he agrees. "Everything could change. For now, just stay here, nice and warm with me. Lie here and see if you can get some more sleep."

"I don't think I can," I reply, letting my head rest on his chest, feeling his hands stroke my hair.

"Just try," he murmurs softly. "Just breathe, and keep your eyes closed, and try."

Some kind of small miracle occurs, and I actually do fall back to sleep. This time, it is deep and solid and devoid of dreams. I don't know whether it is because of Karim's comforting presence, or because my own mind understands that it really must rest.

I sleep, and I sleep, and I sleep. When I finally come to, it is a gradual and gloriously gentle thing—a slow stretch of arms and legs, a fluttering open of eyelids, a luxurious emergence into consciousness.

I know, of course, that this is where the problems usually start, so before I even pull the covers back I tell myself that I have had my indulgence for the day. That I will not spend every waking moment checking my phone. That I will not cry, or mope, or sacrifice myself on the altar of self-pity.

I will be my own mother and set my own boundaries. I will allow myself to check my phone once more today. No, I decide—that's not realistic. I have to be realistic. Five times, I think, sounds more like it. Five more times before midnight, I will let myself hope, in the full knowledge that hope can be crushed as completely by nothing as by something.

Karim is gone, a note left again on my pillow. It is a scrawled doodle of a love heart. Nothing more, nothing less, but enough to make me smile.

I take my time getting up and potter around the flat, tidying and cleaning things that are already clean. I have slept through the whole morning and some of the afternoon, and by the time I emerge into the world it is almost 2:00 p.m.

I do some grading and prep for a meeting on Monday, and I read about a job that the recruitment agency has sent me. Head of History for sixteen-to-eighteen education at a school sixth form in Norwich. It is a good job, the logical next step for me—but it is in Norwich, and my life is here.

Even thinking that scares me. I reply to register my interest, agreeing that they can pass on my details. There is no harm in finding out more, I think, in keeping my options open. If nothing else, it will be something tangible to think about—I will not move. I will not run. But it might give me a little boost if they want me, a small win in what might be a short term that is not littered with wins.

I check in with Margie, agree to her invitation to have dinner with her later, and take Bill with me to walk round to Erin and Katie's house. The rain has settled into a gray drizzle that coats my hair and seeps through my jacket, and the people I see are hunched and hurried, keen to get back inside their cars and their homes.

I smile as I reach their house. The whole of the outside has been decorated with balloons, birthday-girl banners, and a giant cardboard cutout of Katie herself, with "18 Today!" emblazoned across it.

I can hear music blasting inside, and all the lights are on to fight off the seeping dimness of the day.

I take the now slightly soggy envelope from my pocket and quietly slip it through the door. I know I could knock. I know they would welcome us inside, feed me cake, allow me to share in their celebrations.

But I also know that it would be wrong. I don't want to intrude on their happiness, or to suck them into my own turmoil on a day that should be all about Katie.

They both know what this day means to me as well, and they are both too damn lovely not to try to make me feel better.

I hear the card gently thud onto the mat in the hallway, and I turn away quickly before I can change my mind. Before I am lured in by the soft light and the laughter and the promise of the kind of familial warmth I have always longed for.

I walk with Bill for another hour, in and around the dunes, along the beach, to the coast guard station and back. I would have been content to carry on, but Bill is a dog with his own strong opinions, and when he simply started walking back toward home I had no choice but to follow. Margie opens her terrace doors and he slinks off inside, shaking rain from his shaggy fur and making her yelp as she gets splattered.

I give her a wave and go back upstairs, where I fill in more time with a long bath, with a book I'm too distracted to concentrate on, with a random episode of Ru Paul's *Drag Race*, with cooking. I make a huge pan of spaghetti Bolognese to go with the garlic bread and tiramisu that Margie has promised. I suspect there will be alcohol as well, and I also suspect that she has been very deliberate in this dinner plan.

She, like Karim, knows that today will be difficult for me, and she is providing me with respite care for my worn mind.

There is still a small corner of me that resents this. Fears it, even. If I start to depend on them, does that mean I can depend on myself less? Does it even matter?

I've depended on myself for my whole adult life, and I can't say that it's brought me a lot of joy. Contentment, yes; a quiet life and security. But joy? No. Definitely not, as my previous boyfriends can testify.

My past default settings have been to back away when any-one gets too close, like some strangely choreographed dance of shifting emotions. They take a step toward me, I take two steps back. Eventually, I am always dancing alone.

Changing that will take time, I know, but I am at least will-ing to try.

Just after 6:00 p.m., I make my way downstairs, carefully carrying the pan of pasta in front of me. Margie has left the door unlocked, and Bill is waiting for me right inside the hall-way. I have food, so he is on high alert. If I were to trip over now, or lose my grip, he would turn into a slavering wolf and gulp down the lot, then belch in our hungry faces. The love of a dog only goes so far. I walk round him and put the pan on the stove to warm up. The garlic bread is out and laid on a tray, so I pop that in the oven as well.

I walk through the flat, which is pretty much the oppo-site of mine, despite having the same layout. Margie's place is fifty shades of stuff—books, DVDs, family photos, magazines, plants, candles in wine bottles, cuddly toys, crossword-puzzle compendiums, a collection of wooden elephants. No surface is left uncovered, no corner left empty.

I find her outside, where she has set up the table beneath the pullout awning she uses for shelter. She is struggling to move chairs so I take over, and she sighs a breath of relief.

"Thanks, love," she says, rubbing her fingers. "It's raining sideways, isn't it? Can you move everything back a bit?"

I do as I am asked, and notice that she is wearing makeup— that bright red lipstick she said she used to love—and has swept her hair up and tied it with a gold scarf.

"You look nice," I say, examining her. She gives me a very slow twirl, making her skirt puff out, and replies, "Well, this is Italian night—thought I'd make a bit of an effort."

She goes inside, puts a disc into her CD player, and I hear the sounds of opera waft out toward us. She's usually more of a Fleetwood Mac kind of girl, so she really is making an effort. I feel shabby in my leggings and trainers, and run my hands over my hair in an attempt at looking a bit better.

When the food is ready, we settle down to eat, to drink, to chat. It is pleasant, and it is good for me. She doesn't ask if I've heard anything, and I don't raise it. The whole point is to switch off, I think, to let myself go along with this distraction.

We are tucking into our tiramisu when Bill starts barking. It's not his full-alert bark, not his terrifying deep growl that tells us a stranger is lurking. It is a woof of anticipation that means someone he knows is here. He gallops through the flat and I follow.

I open the door and find Erin outside. She has clearly been ringing my doorbell, which I didn't hear due to not being at home. She looks glum and is holding a carrier bag.

"Hi!" I say brightly. "Come in—you're just in time for cake."

Her eyes widen slightly in pleasure, the universal response to the mention of dessert. She follows me through, Bill dancing around her legs in excitement. I lead her out to the terrace, grabbing an extra glass on the way.

She takes off her raincoat and slouches down on the chair I give her, brandishing the plastic bag at Margie.

"I came to get my Wonky Cushion back," she says simply. "And I accidentally fell into the liquor store on the way round."

"That used to happen to me all the time," answers Margie, taking the wine and placing it on the table. She pours us all a fresh glass from the bottle we have open, and Erin glugs hers down like it's lemonade before pulling a face.

"This is nice," she says, glancing around at the fairy lights and the heater and the pots of now-fading flowers. "And the music too. It'd feel quite exotic, if it wasn't for the rain. Sorry to turn up unannounced. I didn't really plan it. I wasn't thinking quite right. I just didn't want to be in on my own. Katie's gone to *town*."

She says the last word as though she really means that Katie has gone on a swingers' holiday to Sodom and Gomorrah.

"Thanks for the card and the cash you dropped off, Gemma," she adds. "She'll probably use it to buy drugs on a shady street corner, and then she'll get bundled into a kidnap van and I'll never see her again."

Margie and I share a look, and I say, "Probably not. Do you want me to go and get your Wonky Cushion from upstairs?"

"No, any old cushion will do," she replies sadly. Immediately I grab one of Margie's many cushions from the living room, and Erin hugs it to her tummy.

"What's wrong?" I ask, pouring her some more wine. It feels like a night that calls for more wine. "When I called past earlier, everything seemed great."

"It was! It is . . . everything's great. Katie's had a brilliant day, and she's so excited about going out with her friends, having her first legal drink, going clubbing . . . Honestly, it was a joy to see. She looked so beautiful and so happy, and so carefree. It was perfect. Then she left, and I felt . . . God, just so sad, you know? He should have been here to see this. He should have been with us, singing 'Happy Birthday.' He's missing so much—and I'm missing him so much too."

Margie reaches out and pats her hand. "It's bloody horrible, love, what you're going through. It's not the same, but when I got divorced, the nights were the hardest—getting used to being on my own after all those years together. Have you thought about getting a dog?"

Erin gazes at Bill, who is curled in a snakelike ball at her feet, and says: "Maybe, one day. I had a border terrier when I was little, but he hated me and used to bite my toes—but maybe. And thank you, both of you. For listening, and for putting up with a misery-moo when you're trying to have a nice night. Oh, I love this one!"

The music has changed, and "Nessun Dorma" begins in all its showy glory.

"This could be us, if we sing along," she adds. "The Three Tenors, live in Liverpool!"

"More like the Three Terrors Tena-Ladies!" Margie cracks, then descends into a throaty cackle. It lightens the mood, and Erin seems to perk up. Or maybe she's just drunk.

"What about you, Gemma? How are you doing? Any . . . news?" she asks.

I shake my head, and realize that I am possibly a little drunk as well.

"No. I'm trying to be reasonable about it all. I've set myself a phone-checking limit. Five times before midnight."

"Wow," she replies, "that's brilliant. That level of self-discipline is amazing."

"Thank you. So far I've checked it sixty-eight times."

We all laugh at that one, and I start to wonder if Three Witches might actually be more appropriate than Three Tenors. None of this is amusing—loneliness, grief, regret—and yet somehow, together, we seem to be managing to see the funny side of life. Maybe this is what I should have been picturing all these years when I told myself there was safety in numbers.

"You know, it might not be that simple at her end," says Erin, leaning forward and sniffing the tiramisu. "Apart from the emotional stuff and whether she wants to meet you or not, it might not be easy logistically—she's only allowed to register when she's eighteen, which I know, technically, was midnight, but probably she wasn't up late filling out forms. Plus, it depends on how much information she has, whether she has her original birth certificate or has to apply for one, all that kind of stuff . . ."

I do, of course, know all of this. I have just allowed myself to ignore it—to build this day into something it was never going to be. It was a mistake, but I seem to have no control over myself when it comes to this particular subject. It's like all of the order and perfection I see in the rest of my life counts for nothing, and all of the chaos and mess and craziness gets channeled into this one thing.

"Yeah. You speak sense, Erin, I know . . . I'm just not feeling very sensible."

"That's not like you!"

"I know, right? What's a girl to do? I'll feel calmer tomorrow, I'm sure."

We all sit with this last sentence, and I suspect we all recognize it for the benign lie it is.

"I was thinking," says Margie eventually, in a slow, hear-me-out tone, "about all of this today. About your baby, Gemma. And yours, Erin. About families, I suppose. None of us know what's around the corner, do we? She might get in touch, Gem, she might not—either way, she'll have her reasons. But I was also thinking about your mother."

That catches me unawares, and I reply, "My mother?"

"Yeah. Your mum. I know you said she had lots of issues, and I know you were in and out of care, but I know you also said she did her best with a bad lot, and I was thinking . . . in the same way you miss your daughter being in your life, maybe she does too? Maybe you're not the only one who wishes things had been different with their child? Just saying. Don't be offended."

I'm not sure how I feel, but offended isn't it. Confused, maybe. Mentally jarred. A little dizzy from Margie phrasing her question in a way that forces me to see things from a different perspective.

My mother moved on, it always felt like. Nothing says "thanks but no thanks" like changing your phone number without telling someone. She moved on, and so did I. But I never really made the effort to find her, to stay in her life, to build a proper adult relationship with her. I never thought of her missing me, feeling sad at not being able to give me what I needed.

*Why is that?* I wonder now. Was I too selfish? Too angry? Was I too damaged by my childhood and incapable of separating her from that trauma? Was I scared that if I stayed in her orbit, she'd pull me into her own whirlwind of instability? I can't pinpoint one exact reason—and perhaps I don't have to. Perhaps it is allowed to be a mess.

"It's complicated," I say to Margie and Erin, which I think sums it up.

"It's complicated!" says Margie with a snort. "I've heard that from you so often, girl, I think you should have it on your gravestone!"

She is joking. It is funny. We laugh. But somewhere deep inside, she has planted an image: a cemetery full of headstones, dedicated to loved ones. Engraved words to much-missed mothers and the best dads in the world and wives who were soulmates and children whose smiles lit up a room. And mine, all alone, and none of those things—not important enough for anyone to miss. Here Lies Gemma Jones: She Was Complicated.

Being complicated is overrated, I think. All the happiest people I know are also the most straightforward. Hidden depths just give you farther to fall; still waters can drown you, and too many layers can be suffocating. I don't want to be complicated. I want to be simple.

I want to love and laugh and live. I want to find my little girl, my baby who is now a young woman—but perhaps I also need to find the little girl that I once was as well.

Perhaps, right now, I can't be in my daughter's life—but maybe I can be in my mum's.

# CHAPTER 18

# 221 MILES INTO THE PAST

**The bus is full and** awash with noise.

There are forty-nine seats, and all of them are filled with either students or staff. Two other buses are with us, and we have driven in convoy to London.

It is the annual field trip to end them all—science students will be going to the Science Museum and to Imperial College; English students will be touring Dickens's London and seeing a play at the Globe; PE kids will be taken to Wembley and Lord's; historians to the Tudor buildings on High Holborn and around St. Paul's. There is something for everyone.

It is educational, but it is also fun—the atmosphere on board has been infectious, despite the fact that we left Liverpool at 6:00 a.m.

We are nearing the end of the long journey, and the air is filled with the sounds of excited chatter and laughter and tinny music leaking from headphones.

I still remember the intensity of being a teenager, of being at that crossroads in your life where everything is still possible.

Where disaster and success are both beckoning, and the most important things in life revolve around looking good, feeling cool, chumming with your friends, and muddling through great big crushes of the kind you can only truly endure when you are that young and inexperienced.

My own dalliance with D changed my life and created another—but nobody imagines that happening, do they? When the hormones are coursing and the flirting is high and the possible liaisons are tantalizing.

A trip like this, away from home, together for a night, is a melting pot of feverish hopes and dreams. Literally anything could happen—and it's down to boring old fuddy-duddies like me and my colleagues to make sure it doesn't.

I've been on trips before, so I know the score. I know I will need to shout, a lot. That I will need to keep my face straight even when I want to laugh. That I will need to find new levels of energy just to keep up with them. That I will need to be hyperalert to creeping footsteps in the corridors of the hostel we are staying at, and always be on the lookout for illicit booze and other contraband.

I might be called upon to use the first-aid kit, or hunt down a missing student, or clean up sick when the booze sneaks past us. I might be on the receiving end of tears, or tantrums, or abuse.

But I will also have the pleasure of seeing them *ooh* and *aah* at the places we visit, of laughing at their jokes, of living vicariously through their fresh eyes.

We draw up outside the hostel, and I shout uselessly for everyone to stay in their seats until we've come to a complete stop. It has about as much effect as a chocolate kettle, as Margie might say. They're up, grabbing backpacks, stowing phones, pushing and shoving and giggling as the final jolt of the engine shutting down whooshes them all forward.

The door opens, and I am first off the bus, along with Jenny from the English department and James Monroe from Art.

One of the other teachers is already heading into the building, where I am sure the staff are trembling in delight at the thought of having 150 teenagers take over the place. They've probably all had tetanus shots in advance.

We split the students into groups according to subject, and I shepherd the history crew to our rooms. The noise is phenomenal, like an invading army, as everyone troops along. I check off their names, escort them into same-sex dorms, announce the ground rules yet again: no smoking, no drinking, no misbehaving of any kind.

There are cries of "Yes, miss!" and shouts of agreement, followed by raucous laughter and plenty of eye rolls. Some of these kids are eighteen, of legal pub age, but we have emphasized over and over again that they are not allowed to enter licensed premises, even during their free time.

*Huh*, I think, as I look at them all, hear the thundering of feet from the floor above, the vibration of freedom in the ether—*good luck with that*.

Katie gives me a wave as she climbs into a top bunk, and I smile at her. She's a good girl, Katie, but she's still only a girl—and she'll need as much watching as any of them. Erin has made me promise personally that she won't come back to Liverpool wounded, pregnant, or with a tattoo. As I close the door behind me and leave them to settle in, I am starting to wonder if I was rash in making such a promise.

I dump my own bag in the room I am sharing with a new teacher called Lucy, who seems almost as excited as the kids. She's fresh out of training, in her early twenties, and I wonder if perhaps I should be warning her about drinking too much as well.

It tends to be the younger staff who come on the trips, those of us without our own children to supervise—or those wanting to escape their own families for a night.

I freshen up in the en suite we are lucky enough to have and then head down to the foyer, where the staff have agreed to meet before taking the students out into the city in stages to avoid a stampede.

I spot Karim across the room and make my way toward him. He is in jeans and a white T-shirt, chunky boots on his feet, a plaid shirt tied around his waist. He looks extremely dishy, and he grins at me as I approach.

"Bet you're wondering how you're going to keep your hands off me, aren't you, Miss Jones?"

"I think I'll manage," I reply, laughing. "Are your lot off soon?"

He nods and looks around for his deputy, who is sitting in a corner looking slightly scared.

"Yeah. We have one of our activities in about half an hour, then lunch, and then they've got their free time. I'll be on call, but it's also our free time—you want to sneak off somewhere?"

I nod and chew my lip. I have an idea of where I want to go, but it isn't exactly on the tourist track. I was planning to go alone, felt that I could go alone, but now that we are here I am not quite so convinced. Even driving into the city has brought up so many memories, so many strange feelings. I haven't been back to London since I left the first time around, and although I will be fine while I am with the students and doing my job, I am not sure about how I will cope with the unexpectedly powerful trip down memory lane.

"I was thinking," I say, weighing each word carefully in case I change my mind midsentence, "about going to the place where I grew up. To the last place I knew my mother was living."

I look at him to gauge his reaction, and his face is a study in neutral. I am immediately flooded with a combination of embarrassment and regret.

"But you don't have to come," I add hastily. "I can go on my own, it's no big deal. You could just chill out, and I'll tell you how it goes, and we can see each other later. Honestly, it was a stupid idea. I might not even do it myself, now I come to think of it . . ."

We are in public, so we are limited in our allowed behaviors. We can't be lecturing the students on the need for celibacy one minute and groping each other the next. Despite this, he reaches out, very briefly squeezes my shoulder.

"Don't be like that," he says seriously. "Don't go back into your cave. It took me by surprise, that's all. Of course I want to come with you. Of course I want to see where you grew up. I was just wondering what you'll do if she's still there, I mean? Will you visit her? Will you go in, have a cup of tea, catch up on the last decade or so? Are you sure you want to do this? If you are, then I am one thousand percent with you, okay?"

I nod and am about to reply when we are interrupted by the arrival of the first batch of students. The science group, all wearing T-shirts that have a DNA double helix on the front. All the groups have their own—ours is a portrait of Elizabeth I.

These are not mine or Karim's students, not our responsibility, but their being here is enough—it breaks the moment. Suddenly there is noise, chaos, and hyped-up teenagers are milling around. It is not a time or place for subtlety.

"I'll see you later," I say quickly before we are swept up into the vortex. "I'll text you, all right? Have a great day. Good luck!"

I stride away before he can object, needing to go and stand outside for a moment, to make the most of the ten minutes I have before the history group is scheduled to come downstairs.

I head round the corner of the building, where I find a single student having a sneaky cigarette. I recognize him and see from the Van Gogh sunflower on his shirt that he is with Art. He practically eats the cigarette whole, then runs away, apologizing and trying to wave the smoke away. He'll probably spend the next hour worrying that he's going to get into trouble.

He's not the only one. I suck in some deep breaths, the air heavy with lingering smoke and the diesel-heavy smell of London, and count the windows on this side of the building.

I have spent some time trying to track down my mother, with no real success. I suspect I have been halfhearted in my attempts, calling the same number I know has been disconnected, and searching for her on social media—but with a name like Sharon Jones, it's not easy. She's probably not even on social media, I know.

I want to find her, yet also I do not. It isn't a straightforward thing. It has been sixteen days since Katie, and my baby girl, turned eighteen. I have not heard from her, or from the Adoption Contact Register, and I am slowly and sadly lowering my expectations that I ever will.

It is a hard truth to swallow, but one that I must face—I may never know what became of her, and all the wishing and hoping in the world will not change that.

As I have reluctantly taken these first steps toward finding my own mum, I wonder if she feels the same. If she thinks about me, is it with yearning, or guilt, or regret? Is she well enough to even think about me at all? This trip, coming here, being so close to where everything happened and didn't happen, feels like one of those moments in life when you have to make some tough decisions. I am here, and she might be here, and this is an opportunity for me to decide. Do I knock on her door, or do I leave the past behind me, where it has always so firmly been?

"Miss Jones?" says Lucy, popping her blond head round the corner nervously. I have told her repeatedly to call me Gemma, but I must seem too old to be granted first-name status. I see her eyes flicker to the discarded cigarette butts and realize that she assumes I have been out here having a quick smoke.

"Yes?" I reply, dragging myself back to the here and now and the fact that I am needed.

"They're starting to gather for our Tudor tour. Are you . . . are you all right?"

"I'm absolutely fine," I say and walk toward her.

# CHAPTER 19

# SIXTEEN CONCRETE STEPS AND TOO MANY MEMORIES

**The estate, the social housing** project where I grew up, is both the same as I remember it and yet very different.

Karim holds my hand as we walk across what used to be a concrete jungle but now has tubs of greenery, and solar panels, and a small playground full of primary-colored swings and slides. A young mum sits on a bench checking her phone as her toddler plays, swathed in a thick puffer jacket that makes him look entirely round.

The shop is still there, the place where I was sent to buy cigarettes and boxes of off-brand cereal, where I lurked after school. I see the huddled figure of a man behind the security screen, wonder if it is still run by Arif and his sons. They were always nice to me in there, letting me sit in a corner and read magazines for hours on end when I was desperately finding excuses not to go home.

I see the familiar pathways, the steps, the balconies, the doors with wire-meshed windows. I am silent as I look around, taking all this in, feeling the invisible hands of my childhood tighten around my neck.

This is not a place devoid of happy memories, but neither is it a place that makes me smile when I think about it. I had friends I played tag with, neighbors who were kind to me, dogs that would jump up to lick my face when I came home from school.

But it is also the place where I saw my mother cycle in and out of normality, where I spent countless hours and days alone. Where I often went hungry, or felt scared, or simply didn't know what to do when I was thrust into situations beyond my control and beyond my ability to understand as a child.

It is the place where I first learned the valuable art of counting, where I learned to rely on myself and nobody else, where I learned to stop expecting much of the world. None of those lessons should be learned by the time you are seven.

It is beyond strange to be here again, and I think I may have made a mistake . . .

It is a shock to the system, not only this trip into my own past but the contrast with our trip into the past earlier in the day. Our tour of Tudor London was brilliant, and I think I enjoyed it as much as the students. They took endless photos and dressed up in silly hats and Elizabethan ruffs and listened to everything our guide had to say. I have no idea how much of it they actually registered, and how much they were pretending so that they didn't get told off, but I was happy enough to take it as a win.

It was good to switch off for a while, to ignore the turmoil in my brain and in my belly, to focus on something far simpler.

By 2:00 p.m., though, it was over. We'd done our tour, had our lunch, and the students were pretty much trembling with excitement at the thought of being let off the leash. Lucy and I gave them The Talk again, made sure they all had our phone numbers, checked they had the address of the hostel and knew they had to be back by six, and uttered the magical words they were all waiting for: "You're free to go."

I half expected air punches and cheers, but instead they simply disappeared en masse, a human tangle of backpacks and joy. I said a silent prayer for their safe return, and for the people of London, before saying my goodbyes to Lucy. Apparently, she was off to "the biggest Paperchase in the city." Part of me wanted to go to the stationery shop with her—looking at notepads would probably be a lot more fun than what I had planned.

Now I am here, and feel all of my grown-up confidence and sense of safety being stripped away from me, one step at a time. I'd kill for an Elizabethan ruff right now.

"This is . . . nice?" says Karim, obviously alarmed by the depth of my silence. I look at him and smile.

"It's not really, is it?" I reply. "But it is a lot nicer than it was when I was little. We moved around a bit but always stayed on this estate. She lost the flat she was in when she went to prison for a spell, but then got another one here. I always wondered why she didn't move somewhere else—it was like this place had some sort of hold on her."

"Maybe she was just too scared to be somewhere she wasn't used to?" he suggests tentatively.

I think, looking at it now, he is right. She didn't have much family that I knew of. Didn't have friends who lasted beyond the next bottle or the next high. Didn't have much, really—but she did know everybody here. That wasn't always a good thing, and she wasn't always known for good reasons, but I suppose it was enough to anchor her down.

"That's probably true," I reply. "This was her home, for good or for bad, I suppose."

"And what about you? Do you see it as home?"

"I think I'm still looking for the place I see as home, Karim. And maybe I'm getting closer, who knows?" He looks around, and I wonder how it all appears to his eyes. He grew up in Birmingham, which has its own places just like this, but I know his family lived in a middle-class suburb. It must be odd for him, trying to match up the me he knows today and the image of me as a child, here.

"I know you were in care when you were a kid," he says eventually, "but what was she like? What might she be like now, if we find her?"

I frown and find that I can't even begin to answer the second part of that question.

"I have no idea what she'll be like now," I answer. "But as for what she was like then . . . well, she had a mental illness, and she was an addict. I still don't know which came first, or if one caused the other, or if they just went hand in hand. But the addiction and her lifestyle almost certainly meant that she didn't get the full benefit of any health care or treatment she was offered—I do remember going with her to doctors' appointments, sitting outside in the waiting rooms and playing with wooden abacuses and the like.

"She was . . . *unpredictable* is probably the best word to use. I tell myself she did her best, and I know she did—but it still wasn't easy. It was all I knew when I was young, though, and kids accept whatever their normal is. They don't realize it's not normal, do they, until they're old enough to glimpse into other people's lives? I'd go round to friends' houses for tea or whatever, and it was like being in a different world entirely. There was always food for a start, and they had tellies in their bedrooms, and their mums nagged them about homework. That looked like heaven to me."

"I'm sorry," he says, pulling me in for a hug. "I'm sorry you went through all of that."

"It wasn't entirely awful," I reply. "She had some very good days, which I think now probably coincided with when she was feeling well, or maybe when she was on medication that actually worked so she didn't need to self-medicate? I don't know for sure. But she could be so much fun, and so loving, on those days. In some ways the contrast made it worse when she wasn't—and even on those good days, I could never really relax, because I was always waiting for the change. Waiting for the signs that she was feeling bad again."

I pull away from his embrace, feeling better for the hug, and lead him toward the staircase I'm aiming for.

"And how long is it since you've seen her?"

"A long time. At my graduation from uni."

"Right. Did you just . . . lose touch?"

I can tell that this is confusing for him, raised as he was in a close-knit family, a solid community of people who loved each other. I'm sure he can't ever imagine losing touch with his sisters and their extended families. They are part of him, part of who he was, who he is, who he will become. His family are his heart—mine was more of a septic appendix.

"Bit by bit. I moved away, but we spoke on the phone now and then, until she changed her number, or got it cut off or whatever. I sent her a Mother's Day card that year, to this address, with a note inside telling her where I was—but I never heard back. I know this doesn't cover me in glory, but part of me was relieved—it meant I could reinvent myself completely."

And I did, maybe too well. I became so independent that the new version of myself needed no one else—and if the last month has taught me anything, it's that the flip side of that is no one needs you either.

We climb the steps, still the sixteen that I remember, and emerge onto the concrete balcony. I can feel the tension seeping up through my body, my feet reluctant to move on. It is the same feeling I used to have coming home at the end of the school day: a bleak certainty that whatever awaited me was not going to be good. A paralyzing, unformed sense of dread.

Karim feels me tense up and tightens his grip on my hand.

"It's okay," he says gently. "I'm here."

I turn to him and smile.

"Yes. You are. Thank you for that."

We carry on, and then we are outside the place she last lived, the last address I had for her. This is a place I never even visited in person, but which is only one floor beneath the flat where we lived together when I was a child. It is the exact same layout, the exact same style, built from the same materials. It even smells the same.

I take a deep breath and knock on the door. It is a quiet and halfhearted knock, one that betrays my reluctance, my uncertainty that I am doing the right thing.

I suppose I had been hoping that there would be no answer, that we could leave, flee the scene of the crime; that I could tell myself I'd tried but it simply wasn't meant to be.

Too soon, I see a figure moving toward us down the hallway, blurred behind the small glass square in the door. I inhale sharply, a rush of emotion flooding through me, wanting so desperately for it to be her and wanting so desperately for it not to be her.

The door opens, and it is not. It is a man in his fifties, bald, a cigarette in his mouth. He looks us up and down suspiciously, and I realize that even in our casual clothes we are too well-dressed.

"Yeah?" he says, breathing out smoke. "Can I help you?"

I can hear the sounds of daytime television in the background, smell just-cooked toast, see past him to the living room. The same living room as ours, on the floor above our heads. It is like nothing has changed. Like I have never left. I freeze. I am suddenly unable to speak. Unable to explain why I am here. Really, I have no idea why I am.

"Hi," says Karim, after a brief glance at me, "sorry to bother you. We're looking for a woman called Sharon Jones. I believe she used to live here?"

The man relaxes slightly when he understands that we are not looking for him. That whatever trouble or debt or dispute he was worried about isn't what has brought these two strangers to his door. That even if we are the police or social services or working for a collection agency, we're not bothered about harassing him.

"Nah, sorry, mate," he says, shaking his head. "Nobody here called that. We've lived here for about four years now."

"Do you remember her?" I ask in a hurry as he tries to close the door again. "The woman who was here before? She had red hair. Could be a bit . . . strange sometimes?"

If he was new to the area he might not—but just like my mum, a lot of other people never move on. They just move around, in ever-decreasing circles.

I see him turn it over in his mind, and he answers: "You mean that mad one who shouted a lot?"

I nod. It is a terrible description, an awful thing for a human life to be reduced to—but it is also accurate.

"Yeah. I remember her. I didn't know she was called that, though, and she wasn't living here when we moved in—that was a young couple, come from Syria, had a couple of kids so they didn't want to live by the balcony. Why are you looking for her, love?"

"Do you know what happened to her?" I ask, ignoring his question. "To Sharon Jones? Is she still on the estate?"

"No, don't think so. To be honest, I heard she was dead."

"Dead?" I echo, as though I've never heard the word before.

"Are you sure?" asks Karim, frowning. "It's her mother, you see."

The man's eyes dart to me, and his expression softens.

"Right. I'm sorry—look, don't take it for gospel, all right? But . . . well, she was into the drugs, wasn't she, if I remember right? And someone told me she OD'd. She definitely isn't on the estate anymore. Wish I could be more help. Do you want to come in? Have a cuppa, slice of toast?"

He looks tough, this man, and I can see the scars that a hard life has left on him. But still, he is trying to be kind. Trying to help. Somehow, it makes me feel even worse.

Karim glances at me, obviously worried, but I shake my head. Going inside won't help. It will only remind me more of the past, of what I have lost.

"Thank you, but no," I reply.

The man nods and moves to close his door. Before it shuts entirely, he pauses and says, "Good luck to you, darling. Doesn't matter what anyone else says about her—she was still your mum, and you only get one."

He retreats back inside, and Karim and I are left standing there together, on a dull October afternoon, on a concrete walkway lined with doors. Lined with windows. Lined with lives being lived. Lives possibly coming to their ends. Happens all the time.

I am stunned, and silent, and still. I have never imagined that she could be dead. I have never imagined it, despite the logical evidence—she was ill. She made poor choices. She was isolated and had nobody to pull her back from the abyss she stared into on a daily basis. I left her, and there was nobody else, and now the abyss might have taken her. The woman I was relieved to escape from could be gone forever.

"We don't know it's true, Gemma," Karim says reassuringly. "He wasn't sure—it was only something he'd heard, something he'd assumed. It's not necessarily a fact. That wasn't exactly a reliable witness right there, was it? He might even have said it just to spite us. He was that type."

I nod, because he is right.

He is right, but everything still feels so very wrong.

# CHAPTER 20

# THE FIFTH-EVER BRANDY AND ONE CUNNING PLAN

**Karim is determined to remain** positive and refuses to agree with any conviction that we should believe my mother is dead on the say-so of a chain-smoking stranger.

He is undoubtedly right to take this approach, and I am grateful to him for his support—but I am also exhausted by it all. Going back there—to that nonhome—has shaken me so much more than I thought it would. The news about my mum has numbed me, and I am struggling to keep my engagement levels up. The dark side of me is calling, and I would dearly love to be alone.

We are now standing outside the hospital where I gave birth. It is only a ten-minute walk away from where we were, and near to a tube stop, so I'd gone along with his logic.

"If she died, someone would have told you," he insists. "She would have had that card you sent. Maybe an address book?"

I laugh out loud at that one. The thought of my mum being organized enough or bothered enough to keep an address book is the most amusing thing I have heard all day—though admittedly there hasn't exactly been stiff competition.

"Perhaps," I say, when I see his crestfallen expression. He is trying, so very hard, to keep hold of me. It's as though he can see me slipping away from him, sense that I am dissolving from the inside out.

*"Who else would know?"* he'd asked as we'd walked away from the estate and onto busy roads lined with kebab shops and Subways and nail salons.

*"I don't have a clue. I don't know which doctor she was with, if she even was. I could probably search for a death certificate with the records people, but I don't have any dates or know what address she was at or . . . I don't know. Maybe her social worker, if she still had one?"*

He doesn't understand how chaotic she was, of course. He doesn't know that she had a loose relationship with reality, that she missed appointments, that she imagined people were against her and went on huge rants about them before dropping out of the system. She was hard to keep hold of too—maybe I'm more like her than I've ever admitted to myself.

So now we are here. Outside a monolithic building that has crawled along since the 1960s, growing and expanding in ever-uglier incarnations. Ambulances come and go; cars zoom to the new parking garage; staff trail, exhausted, to the bus stop. It is, as all hospitals are, constantly in motion, a busy landscape of life and death and everything in between.

We are near to the automatic doors, running the gauntlet of illicit smokers. Every time Karim moves, he sets off the sensors and the doors whoosh apart.

"He might still work here, you know—it's not that long ago."

"It's eighteen years, Karim," I say, too tired to put up much of a fight. I am screwing up my sore eyes, the memories of the last time I was here whooshing open just like the automatic doors.

It was the day after she was born. I'd had a long labor, but a straightforward one, and I was declared well enough to leave the next morning.

I remember standing outside the maternity unit, just around the corner, the school bag I'd taken with me clutched to my still-flabby belly. A belly that was now empty, lifeless, useless. My boobs were sore, and I was bleeding into a sanitary towel they'd given me, and I still felt in shock.

I stood there for so long, leaning against the wall, watching other women arrive, other women leave. Women with parents, with partners, with people who loved them. Women with husbands who carried car seats containing their precious cargo, heading to their new lives. Women who weren't me.

I was sixteen, and I was alone. Geoff with a G had said he'd arrange a taxi back to Audrey's for me. That he'd meet me there if I could wait for him until the afternoon.

I couldn't. I had to get out. I had to escape the smells and the babies and the other people and the all-consuming sense of loss.

In the end, I got the bus. I sat there, pale and shaking, school bag on my knees, every swerve and every stop jolting my sore body. I spoke to nobody. I heard nothing. I told myself that eventually this would all seem like a bad dream. That one day I'd look back on it from a better place.

And now here I am. In my so-called better place. Looking for a kind man who was part of my world a lifetime ago, in case he can help me find my mother through her social-work records.

I follow Karim into the lobby, past the small shop with its chocolates and newspapers, past the café. He heads for the information desk and starts to chat to the woman behind the counter. She looks about twelve years old—but maybe that's just because I feel about a hundred.

"What was his surname, Gemma?" he asks over his shoulder.

"Wainwright," I reply, "and it was Geoff with a G." The receptionist pulls a face and says she doesn't think there's anybody called that working there, but is helpful enough to check the staff directory for us.

"No, sorry—though it could be he's only here part-time, or he's down as a guest instead? I do know most of the social-work staff, though, and I don't think there's a Geoff. With or without a G."

"That's fine, thanks for looking," I answer, managing a polite smile as I tug Karim away. He looks more disappointed than I do.

We go back outside, and I sit down on a bright yellow metal bench. He sits next to me, puts his arm around my shoulder.

"I'm sorry, Gem," he says, dropping a kiss on my head. "I thought I was helping, but you look wiped out. I wish we were at home so we could just climb under the covers."

"So do I. And I suppose we'll be back there soon enough. But I don't think I'm good for much else now, to be honest. I need to sit still, and maybe have a drink, and then we should get back to the hostel. I'll be all right in a bit. I'm just . . . running on empty, you know?"

"I know. I just wanted to help. And now we've stopped for a minute, I'm sorry. I think maybe I'm a bit more sensitive about dead mothers than most people are, and I didn't want it to be true for you, and that's not your fault. There's a pub near the hostel—maybe I should ply you with your fifth-ever brandy?"

"Aah, you remembered—how sweet!"

"I remember everything about you, Gemma Jones. I've always thought you were pretty amazing, but seeing all of this today—well, you're even more amazing."

"Yup. That's me. Gemma the Amazing. That sounds like my magician name . . ."

I am feeling a bit spaced out, and I'm aware that I'm talking nonsense. Karim wisely realizes this as well, and manages to flag down a black cab after it drops someone off. He helps me inside, and fastens my seat belt for me, and is the very model of loveliness.

This time, at least, I tell myself, I am not leaving the hospital alone. I am leaving with someone who cares about me. I can't quite rejoice in that now—my senses have been ambushed by the past, by the news about my mother. I am shell-shocked by it all. But I lock it away, a small, happy note in a gray day, to look at later.

The pub is Victorian, called something to do with a horse, and is draped with fading flowering baskets outside. We find a small spot in a corner, and Karim gets drinks at the bar. I look around, at the dark wood and the heavy red-velvet curtains, and realize I am automatically scanning the room for any stray students. I don't see any, so I assume those of pub age have at least been savvy enough to sneak into one that isn't right by our home base and where angsty teachers might also be taking a medicinal snifter or two.

Karim returns with the drinks and his usual selection of snack products. For a PE teacher, he puts away a lot of junk food.

"Okay," he says, sitting down next to me, "I have just one more thing to suggest for today."

"Unless it's a shower and sleep, I'm not sure I'm up for it," I reply.

Sleep, I know, might be hard to come by tonight—and not only because of the day I've had. The students are going to need some supervision, and it seems unlikely that I'll get through the whole evening without being disturbed by someone or something. Entirely possible it will be Lucy climbing out of the window so she can have a night on the tiles.

"Well, Geoff with a G, as you always call him, sounds like he was a great bloke."

"He was. One of the few."

"And you lost touch with him as well?"

I pull a face and nod. "I did—but I think that was the right thing to do, really. I mean, he was a great bloke, like you say, but he was just doing his job. Admittedly doing it well, and definitely doing more than he needed to, but it's not like he was my friend or anything. He was ancient—or at least he seemed it at the time. I invited him to my graduation, as a kind of thank-you, really, and after that—well, I had his work phone number, but that was it. I knew he was there if I needed him, but I didn't."

I shrug, wondering if this sounds harsh. It didn't feel it at the time, and I was sure Geoff had lots of other people to help. We just both seemed to know that it was time to let go, to drift out of each other's orbit.

"And what about the woman you lived with? Audrey, was it?"

"Now, she did die, I know for certain. I googled her for some reason a few years back—one of my rare idle moments—and found a local newspaper article about it. She'd fostered over a hundred kids, apparently. I sent a card to her husband, but that's a—"

I pause, wrinkling my nose.

"You want to say 'dead end' but think it's in poor taste, don't you?" he responds, smiling.

"Yes! And Audrey was good to me, in her own way. She wasn't one of those touchy-feely mumsy types—she was quite professional and strict with us all—but I actually appreciated that. She gave me a lot of stability at least. So. What's your cunning plan?"

"It's not exactly cunning. I'm not sure it's even a plan. But his name isn't that common, so I thought maybe we could find him online? I had a quick look while I was at the bar, and there are some on Facebook that look about the right age."

He gets out his phone and leans close as he shows me the screen. I flick through them, cursing the ones with avatars and pictures of motorbikes as their profiles, and finally come across one that could very well be Geoff with a G.

I get my own phone out instead, and find the right page. He has the privacy settings on so I can't see posts, but I can see a photo and a brief "about" section that describes him as "Dad, granddad, fan of fishing, retired social worker."

I enlarge the picture and stare at it as I sip my fifth-ever brandy.

Obviously, he looks older. He has different glasses. Less hair on his head, more on his face—but the same kind smile that I first saw when I was sixteen, sitting across from him in his cubbyhole office at the hospital, determined not to like him or to admit that I needed anyone.

"I think it's him," I say quietly. "But I'm not quite sure how you think it will help?"

"I think, my darling girl, that it will help in a few ways. First of all, he might know more about what happened to your mum—I presume he met her, knew about her situation? Maybe even liaised with her caseworker or whatever?"

I nod. All of that is true.

"So, social workers are like teachers—they talk to each other. They swap stories. They stay in touch. So he could be able to fill in some of the gaps for you. But also—well, maybe it'd just be nice? To say hello to him? I bet he'd be so proud of what you've made of your life."

I look away from the phone and into Karim's eyes. I make a promise to myself that I will never take this for granted—this support, this encouragement, this strange belief he has in me. If only I could always see myself through his eyes—sometimes I think he perceives a totally different Gemma than me.

"You're kind of cool," I say. "Do you know that?"

"I do," he replies, shrugging. "Just comes naturally, what can I say? Now send the man a message!"

I nod, send off a friend request, and type a message.

"He probably won't even remember me," I say as I tap the keyboard, a few bland lines reintroducing myself and saying I hope he's the right Geoff and if not, to ignore me.

I finish off, put the phone down, and drink the brandy. I feel strangely better—maybe it's simply getting away from the place I grew up. Or actually doing something that feels proactive.

Now, of course, I have to wait—in the same way that I am still waiting to hear from my daughter. My whole life seems to consist of waiting.

In this case, the wait is considerably shorter—a notification pings within a minute. Karim and I look at each other, eyes wide, and he gestures for me to check it.

I see that my friend request has been accepted and there is already a message. I read it out loud for him.

Gemma, how lovely to hear from you—and of course
I remember you! I would love to catch up and hear
how you are. I always expected great things from you.
Would you mind doing it by email instead? I always
find these messages a bit fiddly! Hope to hear from
you soon, Geoff.

"Wow," says Karim, grinning. "He doesn't actually call himself Geoff with a G?"

"I don't suppose he needs to when it's in writing, does he, because you can actually see there's a G. Only when he's talking."

"Fair point, Lieutenant Logic—so, will you email him?"

I nod and reply, "I will. I want to, for all the reasons some hot PE teacher guy gave me. But not now—now, we probably need to go back over the road and deal with a bunch of hungry and hormonal teenagers."

He glances out of the window and pulls a face. I guess some of the hungry and hormonal teenagers are lurking outside.

"You're not wrong," he says.

# CHAPTER 21

# TWENTY-ONE DAYS OF SILENCE AND 500 METERS OF SWIMMING

**Erin and Margie are in** the smaller pool, leaning together against one of the edges, arms draped along the side. I have just finished twenty lengths in the bigger pool and feel exhausted, in a good way.

I pull myself up the steps and join them.

"I thought you were supposed to be exercising?" I say, raising an eyebrow.

"We are!" says Margie. "Look down below!"

I gaze lower and see that both of them are kicking their legs, slowly but consistently. There is no movement above, but sure enough, I have to concede that some form of exercise is indeed being taken.

This is an experiment we are trying, at Karim's suggestion. He thought it might help Margie, with both pain relief and flexibility, and as soon as he mentioned it her face lit up in excitement. In fact, it seems remiss that we hadn't thought of it before, but I suppose we were too busy drinking and doing jigsaws most of the time.

I join them, leaning against the wall, lazily scooping my legs around in the water. I have already done my proper exercise for the day and will allow myself to slack.

"How is it?" I ask Margie. "Are you okay?"

"Oh, love, it's marvelous—I can't remember the last time I felt weightless like this, you know? I'd forgotten how much of a joy it is to just float around! I feel like a mermaid!"

It is good to see her so relaxed, and good to at least try to relax myself. I feel edgy these days, vaguely disturbed and in a constant state of flux. Like I'm a can of pop that keeps getting shaken into a fizz every time I come near to settling.

It is now twenty-one days since Katie, and she-who-cannot-be-named-because-I-don't-know-her-name, turned eighteen. Twenty-one days of checking, of telling myself off for checking, of checking again. Also thrown into the mix at the moment is the almost-as-strange knowledge that, any day now, I might hear from Geoff, might find out more about my mum. Or I might not. It could go either way, and I am not sure which way I would prefer.

*No*, I think, *I do want to hear*—I do want to know, one way or another. I need to, even if I don't exactly relish the prospect. It is, though, adding to the blend of anxiety and weirdly creeping fear that I am feeling.

*Fear* is a strange word to use, but I think it's the right one. On the surface, I am the most settled I have ever been in my life. This is the longest period of time I have lived in one place and done one job as an adult. I have friends I am closer to than I have ever been. I have Karim, and the wonders of that particular relationship continue to surprise me. I almost have a dog. I have sneakily laid down the roots I never thought I would manage to lay down.

The thing about roots, though, is that you can get tangled up in them as well—and there is part of me, part that I know is rubbish and wrong and made entirely of badness, that worries about that. About entanglement. If you're tangled up in roots, how can you make a run for it when the boogeyman comes chasing? You only need to watch any horror film ever to know that roots can be the difference between life and death when you're running through the woods at night with a slasher in a mask on your heels.

I dip my head under the water, shake it about a bit, come back up and gasp in air. I need to stop thinking like this. Stop expecting the slasher in a mask to appear around every corner.

In my case, though, the slasher in the mask feels like he's cleverly disguised himself as The Past. The Past is coming for me, and it is undermining The Present. The two could meet, quietly and calmly, and say hello to each other and arrange to go for coffee. Or they could spectacularly collide and blow me to pieces as collateral damage. *Boom.*

It is an uncomfortable way to feel, but no matter how hard I try to shake it off, it persists, like fine drizzle in your hair on a damp day. You barely notice it's raining, but you get soaked through and chilled to the bone anyway.

"What's Katie up to today?" I ask, changing the internal subject.

Erin's face breaks out into a smile, and she replies, "She's at a gaming workshop in town. Making little figures of trolls or whatever and painting them. She's the only girl who goes, and I suspect she is the subject of a lot of crushes."

"I'd imagine she is," I say, knowing exactly the kind of boys who get into those kinds of games. Nice ones, usually. As eighteen-year-old pastimes go, it is extremely benign.

"Could be worse." Erin shrugs. "It certainly was when I was her age."

Margie cackles and adds, "I was a bit of a handful myself back then!"

"You still are!" say Erin and I at exactly the same time. Margie pretends to look offended, but I can tell she is secretly delighted to be considered a source of trouble.

Once she's had enough, Erin and I help Margie out of the pool and into the changing rooms. It takes her a while, but Margie manages alone while I sit in the cubicle next to her, listening to her swear and curse. I am alert for any signs of distress, but hear only mild frustration as she dries off and gets back into her clothes. We head for the café, and Erin gets the coffees in while Margie and I settle at a table by the vending machine.

A half-in, half-out Mars bar tells a tale of bitter sadness and disappointment.

Margie is recounting a story about one of her grandchildren winning Reader of the Week at school, and about her plans to visit them in the new year. She seems happy, animated, her hair damp on her shoulders as she chats.

I am half listening but am also distracted by a group of toddlers being led in a line toward the small pool, like brightly colored ducklings. They're wearing inflatable arm bands, and there are eight of them, so sixteen inflatable arm bands in total. Which is, of course, completely irrelevant to anything in the world but automatically noted by my whacked-out brain.

My phone is out on the table, and as Erin returns with a tray of drinks that she is merrily sloshing all over the place, it does a little jump as it chirrups and vibrates.

"Ooh! Get that!" cries Margie. "It might be a pic of your Karim in the nude! If it is, I want to see . . ."

I grab the phone, knowing that it won't be a picture of "my Karim" in the nude. At least I don't think it will. I see that it is my email app. That I have a new message from Geoff with a G. The subject heading is "your mother."

I feel a sudden rush of nerves, and the sound of the pool— the giggling kids, the slosh of the water, the background chatter of the café—recedes into the distance. I grip the phone so hard I see my knuckles go white, and I have a strong urge to just delete it. Slasher in mask, just ahead.

"You all right, love?" asks Margie, reaching out to touch my arm. I jump, as though I had forgotten she was there. Maybe I had.

"Yep. Just a work thing. I'll be back in a sec."

I get up and stride away, heading outside to the car park. I have no idea why I lied. Why I felt the need to escape. Why I do many of the things I do.

I shelter in the doorway, hiding from the rain, and calm myself down by watching the cars for a few minutes. Audi seems to be the favored brand of the local swimmer, and most of them are black.

I take a deep breath and open my inbox. I have shared a few messages with Geoff, and he is chatty and friendly even in writing. He has told me about his retirement, about his children and his three grandchildren, and about his dog, a springer spaniel called Mabel. He seems genuinely very pleased to hear from me and is delighted at the way my life has gone. I suppose it must be good to hear a success story when much of his career was probably taken up with meeting people at the lowest point of their lives.

When I broached the issue of my mum and told him I was trying to find out what had happened to her, he was supportive but also professional. He said he was still in touch with some people from that place and time, but also that even though he was retired, there were still rules. Protocols. Matters of confidentiality.

I told him that I understood all that and would be grateful for anything he could do. And now, here it is—the moment I've been partially dreading. I could, of course, open the email and find that he has discovered nothing. I could find that he has discovered she is in fact dead. I could find that she has been abducted by space aliens and is currently running a vaping shop on Venus. Or I could, of course, actually read the damned thing.

Dear Gemma, the email says.

I hope you're well, and not too busy with work! Now I'm retired I find myself always a bit concerned about overwork in others! Anyway, I have news about your mother. As we've discussed before, I am limited in what I can say, and what I can share. However, would you be happy for me to pass your details on to my former colleague, who could then pass them on to the relevant parties? Your phone number and email address, perhaps? I think, then, maybe you could get all the information you need from the horse's mouth, so to speak. Let me know either way—best wishes as ever, Geoff.

He is not of the generation that posts kisses after signing off, and I am glad, as I still think of him as an adult talking to the teenage me and that would be weird.

I look over the email again, and again. I am reading between the lines, I know, but I think he is telling me that
my mother is still alive. I think he is asking me if, via some
convoluted process, I would be okay with her being given
my contact details. Or am I completely misinterpreting that
"horse's mouth" comment?

Where did that saying come from, anyway? I've never heard
a horse speak, so I'm unsure about why they're considered to
be such a reliable source. And while I'm at it, what are gift
horses, and why shouldn't we look them in the mouth? Why
are there so many phrases about horses? And why am I so
bothered about it, right now, as I stand in the rain clutching
my phone?

I am bothered, I know, because it is a distraction from what
is really bothering me. Saying yes to Geoff's question will open
doors—possible stable doors, allowing horses to bolt. It will
open doors to my mother getting in touch, or even my mother
choosing not to get in touch, and I wonder if I am ready for
that.

I went looking for her, but I never felt ready. I asked Geoff,
but I wasn't sure if I wanted to know. Remembering my life
with my mother in it makes me feel dizzy. My life with my
mother in it was uncertain, and unpredictable, and those are
not qualities I am renowned for liking. My life without my
mother in it is undoubtedly simpler, easier, safer.

But still . . . she is my mother. She is the only blood relation
I know of, apart from my own daughter. Isn't it hypocritical of
me to expect my own offspring to want me in her life, while
turning my back on my own mum? It is, I decide. I understand
why I feel like this, and I think it is reasonable—but it is also
going to be hard to turn my back on. She is part of me, whether

I like it or not. I owe it to her, and to myself, to at least have the backbone to take these first steps.

I am an adult now, and things are very different. I reassure myself that I am too strong, too grown, too bloody rooted, to be sucked into her chaos again. It is the fear of it that is controlling me, and I refuse to be controlled by fear.

I tap out a reply, tell Geoff I am out and about and will send a longer email later, but that yes, I would be happy for him to pass along my details.

I press Send before I can change my mind. I close the app down, switch off my phone, and go back inside.

I have, I realize, added yet another person to the ever-expanding List of People Who Might Not Actually Want to Know Me. Talk about setting yourself up to fail.

# CHAPTER 22

# ELEVEN UNKNOWN NUMBERS ON A MOBILE PHONE SCREEN

**I am at the end** of an especially tedious staff meeting a few days later when my phone rings. We have been discussing exciting issues like budgetary constraints, renovations in the science block, and student parking passes being shared illicitly. Nothing gets the blood flowing quite like an illicit parking pass.

I have been avoiding Karim's eyes for most of this endurance test because I know he will make me laugh. He will roll his eyes or mouth something at me or mime shooting himself in the head, and I will not be able to help myself. I will giggle. We will behave like the students and disrupt the very important business being very earnestly discussed.

I have forgotten about my phone, which very rarely rings anyway. Margie knows not to contact me during work hours, and either texts or uses my landline. Karim, the only other person likely to actually call, is sitting here in the same over-full room, the breath of the assembled staff steaming up the windows.

So when it rings I jump in surprise, rummaging around in my handbag so I can pull it out and silence it. There is a moment of quiet and I feel all eyes on me, some in sympathy, others in rebuke. Naughty Gemma. Behaving like a student even when I tried not to.

I mutter an apology and the meeting wheezes to an end, everyone running out of steam. The head of maintenance finishes his talk and asks if there are any questions. I look around and see that everyone is steadfastly refusing to put their hand up—if we ask questions, we will have to stay longer. This is already like detention and I'm not the only one keen to leave.

We draw to a close and everyone shuffles out, forming into small groups of friends and colleagues, all keeping their comments to themselves until they are safely away.

I am sitting near the door—I am no fool; I plan this stuff—and am one of the first out. Karim catches up with me in the corridor, the subtle scent of his aftershave warning me he is near. And, weirdly, making me smile.

"Who was on the phone, Miss Jones? Who was so important that they could interrupt the G8 summit?"

"I don't know," I reply, walking briskly, knowing he will easily keep up. "I think it might have been Leonardo DiCaprio. He won't leave me alone."

"Want me to have a word? I think I can take him."

I laugh, and we finally reach the exit and walk together toward the car park. I pull out my phone as I reach my car and check the number that called me.

"Huh," I say quietly, "it's not one of my contacts. And I don't recognize it. So it might actually be Leonardo DiCaprio."

He peers at the screen, shakes his head, and replies, "Could it be the Adoption Register people? I know you're deliberately not mentioning that very much, but I also know you probably think about it a lot."

"You're right, on both counts," I say, unlocking my car. "But no, it won't be them, or . . . her. The way it works is that if she gets in touch, if she asks for my details, they notify me. And they haven't. So she hasn't. If that makes sense. My money's still on Leo. See you later?"

He is standing close to me, a small crooked smile on his face. He is doing that thing where he somehow manages to do sexy flirting without saying a single word. We are not "out" at work, so he does not touch me—but somehow his gaze lets me know that he would like to. I feel a flush of heat and know that I am blushing.

"It's a date, Miss Jones—see you at the pub quiz," he says, the crooked smile ramping up into a full grin. He gives me a wave and saunters off to his own car. As ever, I seem powerless to remove my eyes from his rear view as he leaves.

I sigh and climb into the driver's seat. I slam the door, switch on the engine, and turn up the heater.

I was, of course, joking about Leonardo. We ended it years ago. But something about that call, something about that mysterious number, has rattled me. Put me on high alert. No voicemail was left, and I have no real reason to feel as I do.

Except . . . except I know that Geoff with a G would have passed it on, down the chain, through the top-secret Social Worker Fight Club. Possibly all the way to her—to my mother.

When I was little, I didn't have a mobile phone—not many people did. They were nowhere near as ubiquitous as they are now; nowhere were they seen as essential to modern life. For most of the time, we didn't even have a landline—we'd have spells where the phone was hooked up, but then there would be a bill that went unpaid, and magically it was gone. I used pay phones, which seem to be a thing of the past now.

By the time I was at Audrey's, I had a very simple pay-as-you-go brick that did phone calls and texts and nothing else—it was way before the era we live in now, when everyone carries the Internet around in their pocket. I'm not sure my mother ever called me on that little Nokia, even though she had the number.

I try to recall the last time I heard my mother's voice on the phone, and realize that it was so many years ago I don't even remember what we talked about. Just that it felt like an ordeal for both of us.

The car has heated up, and I turn the engine off again. It is dusk, and all around me yellow headlights swoop and sweep across the car park as staff leave. It is like a carefully choreographed dance, bathed in illumination. Soon, I am the only one there. One small Hyundai in a sea of space.

I decide that I will call that number. That I will do it here because, for some reason, I do not want to take it home with me. Back to my safe place, where it might somehow take hold and invade and infect in a way I cannot control.

I call the number back, telling myself as it rings out that it could be anything—it could be a sales call. It could be phone junk. It could be a Hollywood superstar asking me out to dinner.

It is none of those things. It is, as I suspected, as some buried instinct told me, her. My mother.

"Gems? Is that you?" she says.

Those few simple words plunge me back to a different world. Her voice, the rasp of cigarettes, the surprisingly gentle tone. When she was calm, she spoke so softly, it was almost lyrical. And Gems. She was the only person who ever called me that, before or after. I have not been Gems for so many years, and I feel the sharp sting of tears when I become her once more.

"It's me, Mum," I reply, swallowing down the unexpected lump in my throat. It is fast and it is strange and it is inexplicable—but I am engulfed in a rush of warmth. Of relief. Of a comfort that I rarely felt when I was with her, but which I have never forgotten, which has never been replaced. It is a ghost of our real life, a shadow at the edges of harder times, but it is there—the long-ago memory of my mother making me feel safe and loved.

We are both silent, and I try to imagine her—over a decade older, sitting who knows where. I hear the grind of a cigarette lighter sparking into life, and smile. The sound of childhood.

"How are you, Gems? It's . . . it's been a while, eh, babe?"

"It has, Mum, yeah. I'm good. Really good. It's so nice to hear your voice again."

She laughs, and I laugh too. I can't believe what I've just said, but it's true—all of the ambiguity, all of the borderline dread I was feeling about this conversation has gone up in a puff of smoke. Her lighter has burned it away.

"Where are you, Mum? Are you still in London? I came to the estate. Tried to find you. Someone told me they thought you were dead." She coughs, and I hear her move the phone away while she does it, before she can speak again.

"Almost, love, but not quite! Can't believe you went back to that place, Gems. Can't have been easy for you."

"It wasn't, no."

There is a pause, and I feel the weight of our mutual silence, the words we have not said, the thoughts we have not shared. The years that separate us, the blood that binds us.

"I'm sorry about that, love. I left a few years ago. I ended up—well, it's a long story, not a pretty one. But I left, and I'm living

in Stoke-on-Trent now. Did one of those house-swap things the
councils do, someone who wanted to move to London when I
wanted to get out. Didn't care where I ended up, to be honest,
as long as it wasn't there, you know? I needed to leave it all
behind."

I nod, even though she can't see me. I nod because I do
understand—I understand the power of leaving it all behind.
I, I have to assume, was part of the past she needed to escape
from. It hurts, but I get it. Sometimes we have to make tough
decisions, and the brutal compartmentalization of our lives
seems to be a thread that connects us.

"What's it like?" I ask, not even sure where Stoke-on-Trent
is. Somewhere in the middle, I think, my mind conjuring up
images of Wedgwood and fine china factories.

"It's okay. People are nice. What about you, Gems? Have
you settled anywhere?"

"I'm in Liverpool," I say simply. "Kind of settled. Can I—
can I come and see you, Mum? Would that be okay?"

I am as surprised as she is by those words. I had anticipated
possibly speaking to her—but I have shocked myself with how
strongly I want to sit with her. To be in her company. To feel
her arms around me. I know it is probably a fantasy, but I still
feel it.

I have no idea what her mental state is these days, or if she
is still in love with the various substances that overwhelmed
her love for everything else. But she sounds well—she sounds
in control. Sad but sane. It might be a phase, or she might
have picked a clear day to call me. It might be an illusion, but
it is one that I desperately want to be true.

She does not reply immediately, and I feel a leaden churn
in my stomach, the creeping doubt, the opening tremors of

rejection. It is not an unfamiliar sensation. She has rejected me before, in many different ways. I wonder for a moment if I have been a fool to lay myself so open to being rejected again.

"I'd like that, Gems," she says eventually, her own voice heavy with emotion. It must have been hard for her too, to make this call. To not know what reception she would be given. To anticipate her own rejection, another in a long line from a world that has never understood her.

"Okay, Mum. I will, I promise. I'll see you soon."

CHAPTER 23

# ONE DISAGREEMENT, TWO SORRY PEOPLE

**That night, Karim and I** have our first-ever argument.

I avoided telling him much about my conversation with my long-lost matriarch while we did the pub quiz—I had to concentrate on remembering the answers to every subject that didn't involve a ball or a bat or an athletics field. Though, to be fair, he did get a very tricky Eurovision question (1971—Monaco—Séverine taking the country's only ever win with the forgotten classic "*Un Banc, Un Arbre, Une Rue*").

After the quiz has finished, we walk back to my place, enjoying a night that has taken an unexpectedly warm turn. The drizzle has cleared and the temperature has climbed, and we both end up carrying our jackets instead of wearing them.

As we walk toward the coastal path, he says: "So. Tell me more about it. How did she sound?"

"She sounded . . . good. Better than I remember. Better than I hoped for, I suppose. I think I expected the worst; it was way too believable to accept that she was just another druggie who died young. I suppose maybe one step up from that would be alive but just as messed up as she always was."

"And this was a few steps up from that, was it?"

"It was," I reply, smiling in the darkness. We are holding hands as we walk, finding an easy rhythm, paces matched. "She seemed really clearheaded. Maybe it was the move that did it. Or maybe she moved because she wanted to get more clearheaded . . . or maybe it was a blip, and I'll turn up at the weekend and she'll be running around naked hitting people with a frying pan."

There is a brief hitch in his step, and I know that I have surprised him.

"You're going to see her this weekend?" he asks.

"Yes—is that a problem? Had we arranged to do something that I've forgotten? I thought you were going home for your niece's birthday party?"

He laughs, squeezes my fingers, and says, "I think we both know that it's extremely unlikely that you'd have forgotten something, Gemma. Yeah, I was planning on popping back to deliver presents and be the favorite uncle. The only uncle, actually. So I won't be around after you see her. Will you be all right?"

He is concerned for me, and it is still a strange sensation. Still something that doesn't sit entirely right with me.

"I'll be fine, don't worry," I say, throwing as much confidence into it as I can.

He is quiet for a moment, then continues: "So . . . random idea, but it occurs to me . . . Stoke is kind of on the way to Birmingham—just a little detour off the M6, almost Alton Towers . . ." I know this now, of course. I have looked it up.

Planned my route. Learned way more about the history of the pottery industry than I ever needed to.

"I don't think it's going to be as much fun as Alton Towers," I reply, wondering what he is getting at and feeling tense when I begin to suspect what it is.

"Few things are as much fun as Alton Towers," he answers. "I love theme parks, by the way. That's probably something you should know about me. But no, I wasn't thinking we'd call in for a quick go on the Runaway Mine Train or anything."

"The Runaway Mine Train? Isn't that for kids?"

"No! Well, okay, it's not as big as some, but it's my favorite, all right? Don't hold it against me. Anyhow, forget Alton Towers— what I was thinking is that we could maybe go together? Down the M6?"

"Down the M6" sounds so innocent, I think. Just a drive on a busy motorway. What's a few miles between friends?

But the reality is that what he is suggesting is much more complicated than that. In our case, "down the M6" leads to a world of family, and a world of complexity, and a world of unspoken commitment.

"I'm not sure," I say as we reach my flat and I get my keys out. I hear Bill's welcome woof as we lurk outside. "I mean, I haven't seen my mum for so long. I don't know how it's going to go. There's every chance I might just chicken out and turn into a Runaway Gemma Train myself. I don't think it'd be . . . comfortable for you?"

He takes my keys out of my hands, as I'm making a god-awful job of talking, thinking, and door-opening at the same time.

"I wasn't saying I should come to your mum's with you," he explains as we walk up the stairs and go into the flat. "That would be inappropriate right now. Though obviously, if you wanted me to, if you thought it would help for me to be there, then I would."

I sit on the chair instead of the sofa, not knowing why. We usually get back here and curl up together on the couch while we talk rubbish, holding a casual postmortem of our days. He notices—of course he does—and looks confused when he finds himself on the sofa alone.

"Thanks, Karim," I say, "I appreciate that, but I think I need to see her by myself."

He nods and replies, "I agree, that's probably for the best. What I'm thinking is this—we could drive there together. I could drop you at your mum's and maybe hang out in Stoke for a bit."

"What would you do there?" I ask, although it really is irrelevant. "Do you know the place?"

"I've been there. Well, to be more precise, I've been to the football stadium . . . but you know, it's a city. There'll be cafés and shops and fleshpots of earthly delights."

I frown. From what I read when I googled my mum's new hometown, I'm not 100 percent sure about the fleshpots.

"But why?" I ask eventually. "Are you worried in case I become such an emotional wreck it's not safe for me to drive?"

He puffs out a slightly exasperated breath, and I realize that I am annoying him and that he is trying to remain calm. He thinks I am being deliberately obtuse, and he might, of course, be right. I think what I am actually doing is stalling for time.

"I would never worry about such a thing," he answers. "I know you'd be able to handle it. But as I'm planning to go home as well, maybe it might make sense? Maybe you could see your mum, and then we could . . . go to Birmingham. Together. See my dad and my sisters. Eat birthday cake and stuff."

He is leaning back, trying to appear casual, but I can tell that I have made him feel edgy. This is probably not going how he imagined it would. I am probably not reacting like a normal girlfriend should. He runs his fingers through his thick hair and looks around the room while I consider what he has said.

"You want me to meet your family?" I ask dumbly.

"Yes. I do. Why wouldn't I? Though I'm kind of getting the vibe right now that I've made a mistake. That the timing isn't right. That I've loaded too much into one weekend. I didn't think it through properly. I just thought it'd work for both of us, but now I see that meeting your mum again and meeting my lot for the first time would be . . . excessive."

It would, I think, nodding. *Excessive* is the right word. It would be a lot to deal with, and there are too many variables. I have no idea how I will feel after visiting my own mother. I might be upset, I might be sad, I might be hurt. I might end up creeping into Karim's family home like a wounded animal escaping a trap, and that would not be a good start. It would be too much tension for one day.

All of that makes sense. All of that is logical; all of that could be reasonably explained. But beneath the sense and the logic and the reason there lies something more instinctive, more deeply ingrained: I am terrified at the prospect of meeting his sisters and his father.

Not because I won't like them—I have already met Asha, and I am sure the others are wonderful too. But because it is a big step, isn't it? Meeting the parents. I mean, they've even made films about it.

I am happy with Karim. I enjoy his company, and I have made space for him in my world as well as I can while still being me. I also fancy him rotten, and am relishing our love life. I do not want this to end, this precious thing we have— but I also do not feel ready for this. For this entirely next-level shit.

I realize that I have not answered him. That I have sat here quietly, hands folded on my knees, probably looking calm while my mind raced through all of the various scenarios and failed to find one I feel comfortable with. He is looking increasingly less calm himself, and I know I need to open my mouth. I know I need to say some reassuring words, explain myself, get us over this awkward moment. I need to communicate.

"Do you want a glass of milk?" I say.

The look on his face is priceless. Under other circumstances I might have laughed.

"No, Gemma, I don't want a glass of milk, thank you. Maybe I should just go?"

*Don't go,* I think. *Please don't go. Hold me in your arms and take me to bed and tell me everything will be all right. Shout at me, scream at me, call me names. But please, don't go.*

"Okay, if that's what you want," I reply.

He stares at me and shakes his head sadly. I am frozen, immobile, incapable of speech. I am not good with needing people, and this has made me realize how much I need him. I stay silent as he stands up, grabs his jacket, and leaves.

I hear the door slam shut behind him, and Bill lets out a howl downstairs. I feel like howling myself.

I stay where I am, jacket and bag on my lap, and feel a rising tide of panic. I know I have broken something, and I am not sure how to fix it.

I automatically start to take some deep breaths, counting them in, counting them out. I think of this day in history. Christopher Columbus first sights Cuba and claims it for the Spanish, 1492. *Gulliver's Travels* is published in London, 1726. The Volstead Act is passed in the US, bringing in Prohibition, 1919. *Donnie Darko* comes out, and I go to see it at the cinema with my friend Cally, passing as fifteen with a full face of slap and a pushup bra. None of it is helping. None of it is soothing me. I am sad, and I don't want to be sad. More frustratingly, I think perhaps I don't even need to be sad. It has all been a horrible mistake, and it came out of nowhere. I was ambushed, and so was he. He only meant well, and I reacted badly—my stupid, stupid mind told me I was in danger, when in reality I wasn't. In reality I am lucky to have a man who cares about me, who is proud of me, who wants me to be in his family's life as well as his.

I have never had any family to introduce a boyfriend to, and I never went home with any of my previous partners—though I now see that *partner* isn't even close to the right word. I avoided it, always had things to do, was always too busy. I made excuses until they gave up asking. This stuff—family that matters, family that cares—is all new to me, like something I've seen from the outside but never really experienced.

He didn't know how much it would throw me off course. He miscalculated, which I can forgive—not everybody counts as precisely as I do. He miscalculated, but he did it for the best of reasons.

I pick up my phone, start typing a message. I am going too fast, and I keep making spelling mistakes or triggering weird words on autofill. My fingers are flying, but not fast enough. I need to tell him that I didn't mean to hurt him. That I am just made weird, that I am not built like other humans. That I am an idiot. That he needs to be patient with me. Above all, that I am sorry.

I am interrupted in my frenzied mistexting by a quiet knock at the door. I jump up, run down the hallway, and open it.

He is standing there, looking half angry and half amused. His hair is in tufts where he has been shoving his hands through it. I have driven him to dishevelment with my magic touch.

"I'm not happy with the way we left that," he says simply. "Plus, I want a glass of milk."

I stand back, and he comes inside. Before he can take another step, I throw my arms around him and kiss him as thoroughly as a man can be kissed. When we finally pull apart, we are both less interested in talking, and more interested in doing.

I lead him to the bedroom, and we show each other in the simplest way possible that we are sorry.

## CHAPTER 24

# FOUR WEDGWOOD PLATES AND ONE DEMENTED PARAKEET

**In the end, we drive** in a two-car convoy as far as a service station that lies just before the exit for Stoke-on-Trent.

I park slightly later than him, and he has already bought me a coffee. I accept it gratefully, and we go and sit outside in what could very loosely be described as a garden. There are some planter boxes full of half-dead flowers, and three scrawny pigeons fighting over the remains of a sausage roll. It is very picturesque here, among the car fumes and the sounds of traffic.

"So," he says as we finish up, "I hope it goes well. Give me a bell afterward if you feel up to it. You know I'll be thinking of you."

"No, you won't. You'll be in a sugar coma and all your sisters will be fussing over you." He smiles and replies fondly, "Well, they do get excited when the little prince comes home . . . and I'm told there will be a popcorn machine."

"Lucky swine. I love popcorn."

He nods, acknowledging his luck, and says: "But I mean it. Let me know. And I'll text you our address, in case you change your mind. In case you need some company afterward."

I nod and wrap my hand around his and thank him. We get up to leave, and I head for my car and Karim heads for the shop, where he tells me he is going to buy a bagful of giant Toblerones for his niece and nephews. I can tell that he is both concerned about me and happy at the thought of seeing his family. He has known loss, he has suffered, but he has always had that security, that safety—the certain knowledge that he is loved and wanted. That he could always come home, to a place where he was valued, welcomed, and safe. I fight a pang of unattractive envy as he walks away, and head toward my car.

The rest of the drive is straightforward, down the motorway and toward a hilly city that the map tells me is split into separate towns. Some of it is perched within waving distance of the Peak District National Park, some of it edging toward nearby counties. It is dominated by its industrial heritage, and I see hints of former grandeur in the civic buildings, and signs of both decline and renewal fighting for prominence.

I let my GPS guide me to her address, which is in a town called Hanley. Home of the Potteries Shopping Centre and the Potteries Museum and my long-lost mother.

I drive into a neighborhood that is similar to and yet distinct from the one where I grew up in London. There are tower blocks and maisonettes and flats and bungalows, but also a lot of green space and views of distant countryside roads. Kids are playing football, and older people are standing on corners, chatting, leaning on walking sticks.

It is, without doubt, a housing project—but it is a pleasant one.

I have done my very best not to think too hard about all this on my way here. I pondered buying flowers or chocolates at the service station, decided it wouldn't feel right. That it would add an extra sense of occasion to one that is already heavily laden.

Now, as I sit here in my parked car outside a three-story block of flats built in a squat rectangle, I feel nervous. It reminds me of all those times I avoided going home as a kid, hanging around in the shop or in the dark spaces beneath stairwells. Uncertain of what I was going to find when I opened the door, but never expecting it to be anything good.

Part of me still wants to leave. To drive away. Past Alton Towers. Past Birmingham. On and on to who knows where—a place where nobody knows me and nobody judges me and nobody wants anything from me at all. My hands are still on the steering wheel, as though they might still decide to make a run for it, no matter what I decide.

I breathe deeply and pull down the mirror to check my hair. Heaven forbid I should have one out of place.

It had been a strange meeting to dress for, this—not exactly formal, but hardly the kind of relaxed reunion Karim is heading toward either. In the end I went with my smart skinny jeans and a silky black blouse with floppy sleeves that always makes me feel a bit like a pirate.

As I force myself to finally get out of the car, a woman approaches. I'd noticed her from the corner of my eye, quietly standing in the doorway to the flats, watching me. It wasn't a surprise—I was a stranger, after all, and strangers are always worth keeping an eye on. Maybe especially me, because I look a bit like a pirate.

She is in her fifties, short but solidly built, the kind of woman who looks like she takes no nonsense and gives none in return. Her hair is dyed dark pink at the ends, and she is wearing a top that proudly displays her allegiance to Stoke City Football Club to the world.

"Are you Gemma, duck?" she asks as I lock up the car. I am taken aback and stare at her more closely. I know a lot of time has passed, but there is no way this could be my mother. Also, why is she calling me a duck?

I simply nod, waiting to see what she wants. Maybe, I think, my mum has changed her mind. Maybe she has done her own version of a runner and has sent this person to intercept me, to repel me, to send the pirates packing. Maybe I'd be quite relieved if she had.

The sense of warmth and homecoming I'd felt after that first conversation with my mother has faded in the harsh glare of reality, assaulted by a backlog of feelings that aren't quite as optimistic.

"Right. I'm Sam. Nice to finally meet you. You need to put this in your car." She passes me a small plastic-coated card, and I see that it is to grant me resident parking privileges. I feel very special.

I insert it in the windscreen and turn back to Sam.

"Your mum's waiting for you upstairs," she says. "I'm off to get us some oatcakes. I'll be gone awhile, don't worry."

I thank her and walk toward the doorway. I have no idea who Sam is, or what role she plays in my mother's life, or even what oatcakes are. I am out of my depth here, in so many ways.

I tap in the entry code my mum has given me and enter a concrete lobby with four doors leading off it. Each door is painted the same green, and as I walk up the stairs to the top floor, I know that all the levels will look exactly the same. It is clean, though, and some people have put fake plants outside, or added brass horseshoes to the doors. Taking pride, trying to carve out some individuality amid the uniform face of social housing.

I reach the top floor and see her door. It has been left open, but I linger outside. I feel like I should announce myself somehow, so I rap on the green wood with my knuckles and shout a tentative "Hello!" as I make my way inside.

"Down here, Gems," comes the reply, and I walk on thick carpet down a narrow hallway. There are doors off it, presumably a bedroom, a bathroom, all kinds of rooms. I am tempted to look inside them, but that would be purely to put off the inevitable. Also, weird.

I emerge into a large lounge decorated with chintz-patterned wallpaper. There are pottery ornaments all over the place, on shelves and window ledges and in glass-fronted cabinets. The familiar blue and white of Wedgwood plates, proudly displayed on the walls. Two comfortable-looking sofas, a large-screen TV, an upright unit holding CDs, large windows that give views over the buildings to the hills beyond.

All of this, and her.

My mum, standing in the middle of the room. She is still tiny, still thin, still looks as though an especially sharp wind could sweep her up, up, and away like a plastic bag caught on a current.

She is only in her fifties but could be two decades older. Her cheekbones are raw, her face sunken, as though her demons have eaten her from the inside out. Her skin is pale and tinged with yellow, and her red hair is awash with gray, hanging around frail shoulders.

She stands there holding two steaming mugs of tea, staring at me in the same way that I am staring at her. A squawk interrupts us, and I see a parakeet in a large cage, preening and shaking his tail feathers.

"That's Monty," she says by way of introduction. "I've made you some tea. Lots of milk and sugar, how you like it."

Inside, I grimace, but outside I try to look appreciative. It is how I liked to drink tea when I was seven, but it seems harsh to point that out to her right now.

She puts the mugs down, and we both stand awkwardly, not knowing what to do next. It feels too soon to hug, to chase that distant memory of her embrace. I'm not sure it even really existed.

"You look great, love," she says, reaching out and briefly touching my hair. She snaps her hand back as though she's been shocked, and I know this is as hard for her as it is for me. I was her baby once, and now I am practically a stranger.

"You too, Mum," I lie. In truth she doesn't look well, and it is obvious from the wheeze in her breath that a lifetime of abuse is catching up with her.

She chuckles and answers, "No, I don't!"

"Well, at least you're not dead?" I reply, smiling.

"Ha! Ain't that the truth of it. Better than dead, that's for sure. Sit yourself down now, you're making me nervous, and I think we're both jumpy enough, aren't we?" I sit and find that the sofa is one of those that has no bottom, like the one in Erin's house. I live in a world where I seem destined to be eaten alive by other people's furniture.

I look around at the busy but clean room. At the puzzle books and the small collection of remote controls on the arm of her chair. It reminds me of Margie's place a bit, with its air of clutter and the sense that if you dug deep enough, you'd find traces of prehistoric existence.

"This is nice," I say, and mean it. The fact that she still has a large-screen TV, still has a mobile phone, still has what look like good-quality pieces of pottery, suggests that she is as clean as the room—they'd have been long gone if she was still using.

It is a huge relief, and one that makes me sag as much as the sofa. I hadn't realized how worried I'd been—that part of me half expected her to tap me up for money and make her farewells. That fretting about how she was going to be had dragged me down so much.

"It is, isn't it? Best thing I ever did, getting out of London. Too many bad memories. Too many bad friends."

"What made you do it in the end? Leave, I mean?" I ask as I sip the tea, as much for something to do as from any genuine desire to drink it. "I never knew where you went. Your phone just went dead."

She nods, and I see her fists clench and remember her habit of denting her own flesh with her fingernails when she was upset. I wonder how good for her this meeting is, and hope it doesn't push her back in the direction of bad habits. I know it's not my responsibility to police my own mother, but I also wouldn't want to be a catalyst for a collapse into her old ways.

"You don't have to talk about it," I say quickly. "We can just forget about it, Mum—it's in the past."

She looks up at me, eyes big and face sad, and I get the feeling she knows I am worried, and exactly what I am worried about.

"It's okay, babe. I don't mind . . . except, well, it's a sorry tale and not one I'm fond of recalling, Gems. But ignoring it doesn't mean it didn't happen, and ignoring it also means it might just creep up on me later, so best spit it all out.

"I'm not going to go into too much detail, but basically I hit an all-time low. Even by my standards, which we both know weren't very high. I owed money to some people who weren't fussy about how they got paid back. I was using again, even though I'd cleaned myself up while I was at Her Majesty's Pleasure. You seemed . . . sorted, on your way. You certainly didn't need me. There just didn't seem to be anything worth staying in that life for, and I knew if I did, it'd be the end of me. I suppose I had to make a choice—me or that place, the past. You were . . . part of the past. I thought it was better for both of us."

That jolts, and I feel the familiar stab of rejection that I grew up with. Whatever maternal feelings she had toward me were always so easily overridden by her own needs. I am not in a position to judge—but it still stings.

"And Sam? You met her here?" I say, looking around and seeing clearly that this is a home inhabited by two people, not one. There are coats hanging up that are way too big for my mum, a mug left on the coffee table with a Stoke City emblem, the TV positioned so it can be seen from both sofas.

"I did, not long after I moved up. She used to live in the flat downstairs, but now she lives here. With me. Is that a problem for you?" I see her chin jerk up, a hint of her old defiance showing in her eyes.

"Why would it be?" I reply, smiling. "I'm glad you've found someone you can be happy with." Despite the defiance, I can see that she is relieved at my response. That she has one less battle to fight now.

"I am, I suppose," she says, "happy. Or at least as happy as I can get. I'm on my medication properly; Sam makes sure of that. I don't use anything, other than the cigarettes, obviously—some habits I'll probably take to the grave. I have a nice little life here, Gems. It's more than I expected. More than I deserve. I wasn't much of a mum for you, was I? I'm sorry. Didn't ever feel like I could do anything different. I wasn't ready for a kid, and even now I'm probably stuffing it up."

"It's okay," I say gently, concerned at how quickly she has reached such an emotional point. "I always knew you did your best, Mum."

"Did my best? I suppose I did—but that won't look good on me gravestone, will it? My best was crap, and you should have had better. I was . . . I was a mess. My own childhood was a mess too, even though I never told you about it, and I ran away from home when I was in my teens. I didn't know what a mother was supposed to do. I didn't know anything. I couldn't even look after myself. I should have given you away as soon as you were born; at least then you'd have had a chance."

Her final comment hits me like a punch to the throat. My mother knew I was pregnant. She knew I gave Baby up for adoption. Is this her way of telling me I did the right thing, or has she simply forgotten? Rewritten history?

I don't know the answer but I am hit by a powerful mix of sadness and anger. I put the tea down, the sugar sickening my stomach anyway.

"I turned out all right, Mum," I say simply, chewing my lip to keep the other words inside. The angry ones. The painful ones. The ones that are desperate to lash out but will not help either of us.

"No thanks to me for sure. Anyway—tell me all about it. Your life. Everything I've missed."

"I will," I reply, standing up, "as soon as I've used the loo."

She directs me to the bathroom down the hallway, and as soon as I am inside, I lock the door behind me. I stand in front of the mirror, holding on to the edges of the sink to steady my shaking legs. I splash cold water onto my face and stare at my reflection.

Even now, away from her, I can somehow feel her self-pity. Even as she apologizes, I can feel her self-justification. I can feel her need to be told she was right, she did her best, that everything turned out fine. She was always a black hole of need, and I think I'd somehow buried that memory.

*You are not a little girl anymore*, I tell myself. *You are not weak, or vulnerable, or scared. You do not need to feel threatened. You do not need to give more than you have, in the hope that it will help—in the hope that it will fix her. That didn't work when you were a child, and it will not work now.*

I do a quick and automatic tally of the number of items balanced on the sides of the bath—two shampoos, one conditioner, Tesco own-brand bubble bath, one exfoliating face mask, one rubber duck—before I use the facilities and wash my hands. I give myself another stern look before I leave.

When I go back into the living room, she has obviously just finished a quick cigarette, stubbing it out hastily as I return and then wafting the air to clear it of the smoke. I notice the smell of plug-in air fresheners rising around it but not quite claiming it. Monty squawks away to himself, running up and down his perch as though furiously protesting the presence of a stranger.

"Well," I say, my voice steady as I settle back onto the sofa opposite her, "like I said, I live near Liverpool. I've moved around a lot, done lots of different teaching jobs. Now I am a history teacher. I live in a nice flat right by the beach, and I have a lovely neighbor called Margie. I share her dog, Bill. I've been there awhile now."

She nods and leans forward, her skinny arms wrapped around her body.

"That sounds brilliant, Gems. I know it doesn't mean much, but I was always so proud of you. Despite everything, you've done so well. And what about your love life, eh? Gorgeous girl like you. Any boyfriends?"

"Or girlfriends?" I respond, grinning.

"Fair point. Anyone special?"

I think of Karim, miles down the motorway, probably home by now. Wrapped up in the happy chaos of his family, getting grilled by Asha, playing with the kids.

"I think so," I say. "But it's early days yet. I've not got the best track record on that front; I've managed to mess a lot of stuff up, so I'm just taking it one day at a time."

We share a look, and we both understand what I haven't said—that my track record is poor because I am not good at building and maintaining relationships. That I am scarred and damaged. That I, too, have done my best.

I haven't said it, but she gets it, and I see her lips pinch together in dislike. For a moment, I am seven years old again, seeing the signs of a row brewing and willing to do anything to dissipate it. This is the point at which I would normally sur-render, distract, try to draw her attention away from whatever was irking her.

I don't do that this time. I am too old for such games, and I already know that I cannot win.

"Any photos?" she asks, breaking the moment.

I pull out my phone and sit next to her, realizing as our bodies touch that she is even less solid than she looks. Barely even there.

We sit, and I show her pictures and tell her stories, and she asks questions. We share information about our lives, both of us treading carefully, both of us knowing that there is too much lurking just beneath the surface. Too much between us that could erupt.

I am there for about an hour before Sam returns. She shouts out as she lets herself in, and as she enters the room, I see her worried gaze dart immediately to my mum. Checking for breakages, inside and out. Guarding her, concerned for her.

"Everything all right, duck?" she says, looking from my mum to me and back again.

"Everything's grand," Mum says reassuringly.

Sam has a package in her hands, waves it in the air, declaring that she has oatcakes and will get the kettle on.

"What *are* oatcakes?" I ask, still confused. "And what's with all the ducks?"

My mother laughs, and I remember that sound so well. It is a beautiful laugh, all the more special for its rarity.

"Oatcakes are a big deal around here, babe. Kind of a savory pancake, I suppose, that you make with cheese and bacon and, in some weird cases, jam. And 'duck' is just a term of endearment. It's a strange old place, but I like it."

I can hear Sam clattering around in the kitchen, the sound of cups being washed, of the fridge door opening. It is so simple, this small domestic scene. It is comfortable and calm, the two of them settled in their world.

I am glad that she has found this. For the whole of my life, I have never known her at peace. I have only seen the small spaces between the pain, and then the price she paid for them. This—with her oatcakes and her ducks and her parakeet and her pottery shire horses—is what happiness looks like for her.

I stand up, knowing that it is time to go. We have danced around some things, faced some others head-on. We have tip-toed around the darkness, and I think I now have to leave. This has been big, and now I need to be small.

"I've got to get going, Mum," I say as she gets to her feet. "But it was lovely to see you. I'm glad you're doing well, I really am. The best I've ever seen you."

Sam emerges from the kitchen, a tea towel in her hands, watching us.

Mum initially looks disappointed, her face creased with a small flash of irritation, but she covers it up quickly.

"It was so nice, Gems. I'm glad you're doing okay."

"I am," I reply, not actually sure if I mean it or not.

At the moment I feel raw, like my insides have been scrubbed with a wire brush, but that will pass, I know.

When it does, perhaps I will make this drive again. Perhaps I will invite her to come and meet Margie. Perhaps, one day, this will feel less fraught. We will never be a normal family, but perhaps we can at least be a family—if we both carry on doing our best. And if she even wants to—she has never been an easy woman to predict.

Sam says goodbye, and Mum walks me to the door. She is wearing fluffy slippers with pink bows on them, I notice, her feet tiny, like a ballerina's.

As we stand in the hall, she reaches out, takes hold of my arm with a strength that surprises me.

"Before you go, Gems, I have to say one more thing. I know it won't change anything, but I have to say it. I wish I'd been a better mum for you."

I place my hand on hers, whether to console her or to prize it off, I'm not quite sure, but she isn't finished. "If I'd been a better mum, I could have kept you," she continues, staring at me intently, as though willing me to listen. To hear. "And if I'd been a better mum, then you could have kept *her* . . ."

We have not mentioned the baby I had when I was a child myself. We have not gone down that road, both of us perhaps too scared of where it might lead. My eyes widen, and I have no words to use to tell her how I feel. To tell her that she is right. That if she'd been a better mum, perhaps she'd be known as Grandma now. If she'd been a better mum, maybe we would have raised her together. If she'd been a better mum, perhaps I wouldn't be the way I am. Perhaps my daughter would be here with me now—eighteen years old, by my side. She is right, but it would be wrong for me to say so. Needlessly cruel and pointlessly harsh. What's done is done, and I have no desire to launch some kind of witch hunt, to share blame, to cast around for someone else to carry my pain. But neither can I quite find it within myself to dismiss what she has said, to tell her it is not true, to reassure her that she played no part in how things worked out.

I stay silent, refusing to crack beneath the force of her gaze, the strength of her need. When I was little, I'd have crumbled. Now I am stronger, and I need to remember that. I nod once and smile, letting her interpret that however she wants.

We are at an impasse, looking at each other warily, both weighing up our next moves. I should have left earlier. I should stay longer. Maybe I shouldn't have come at all—none of the options feel right.

Moments pass, and I realize that there is not going to be a neat ending. A warm hug and a promise to stay in touch. A tearful farewell and a lifting of hearts. There is only this—two damaged women circling each other in a dark hallway.

"Take care of yourself, Mum," I say and turn to leave.

# CHAPTER 25

# ONE CANDY NECKLACE AND A HERD OF FLUORESCENT PONIES

**I find myself trapped in** a hellish one-way system as I try to leave, which is perhaps reflective of my state of mind. I did the right thing, going to see her. I know I did.

And she seemed good, really good—yes, she was sad, and nervous, and presented familiar moments of potential confrontation, but all within the loose parameters of "normal" under the circumstances. She hadn't magically transformed into a cartoon mother, but I never expected that. I certainly hadn't magically transformed into the perfect daughter either.

But it was, I decide, positive. I coped. She coped. It didn't feel as though she was going to spin off into oblivion just because she'd had to deal with a difficult situation. Or that I was going to either.

Maybe that's because she is clean and managing her illness, maybe that's because of Sam, I don't know. Either way, I am grateful for that, grateful to have a new memory of my mother—a stabler one, a happier one. At the moment it is too early for that memory, that version, to superimpose itself over the one that lives in a vulnerable corner of my mind—the corner where little-girl me lives.

Yes, it was right to reach out, to see her—but just because something *is* right doesn't mean it *feels* right, and I am hyped up and wired as I drive. Like I've had too much coffee and stayed up for three nights solid.

I find, as I fight my way through traffic to the highway, that I am distracted, on autopilot, not paying anywhere near enough attention to where I am going.

Perhaps that is why I take the wrong turn. Perhaps that is why I find myself on the M6 heading south rather than the M6 heading north. Why I find myself driving toward Birmingham and not toward Liverpool.

Perhaps, though, it is not simply because I am distracted— perhaps I am operating on some kind of instinct, motoring toward Karim and not toward home. I'd told him I wanted to be alone, but now I am not so sure. It is my default setting— but that doesn't mean I can't change. Look at my mum—she's changed, under far more challenging circumstances.

I am upset, and I need comfort, and I am driving toward Karim. It doesn't sound like a big deal, but I feel a sense of mild surprise at my own actions. This by itself may be cause for celebration—hang out the bunting, Gemma, you're actually starting to behave like a human being!

Once I've come to terms with what I'm doing, I call in at a service station near Stafford to get a coffee and pop his address into the GPS. It is not far—less than an hour away now I am on the motorway and away from the sprawl of one city and near to the sprawl of another. As I glance at my phone, I see a glut of messages from Karim. I smile as I open them, feeling a simple thrill of happiness that he is checking up on me.

There are a couple along the lines of "How did it go?" and one with kiss and hug emojis, because he's mature like that.

Next there are lots of photos. They show a large garden in full kids'-party mode—a big table set up with food and drink, a bouncy castle, groups of men and women of all ages, kids in costumes. He has sent close-ups of the popcorn machine and the birthday cake, and I realize that I should eat sometime soon. There is a group shot of his sisters sitting with his dad, who looks like an older version of him, silver threads in his hair.

I smile at the photos of his family, and laugh at his comedic captions, and flick through onto a video that he says one of his sisters took.

It is of the bouncy castle, the low-level hum of the pump almost drowned out by the delighted screams of the children. Shoes and boots are flung far and wide, and about a dozen little ones are leaping around on the purple-and-green plastic, falling over, doing rolls, attempting somersaults. In the middle of them all, looking just as happy to be there, is Karim.

He is bouncing as hard as he can, making them all wobble and shake, the shrieks and laughter equal parts fear and pleasure. A little girl—his niece, I assume—clings to his calves, and he lets out a fake film-villain laugh and shakes her loose before leaning down to tickle her. She clambers back up, scales his body like a climbing frame, and wraps her arms around his head.

It makes me smile to see him like this, at the heart of it all, surrounded by people who love him, and whom he loves in return. But it also makes me realize that today is not the day for me to meet his family. There might be another time when it feels right—there might not. Who knows? But I don't want to go into that garden, into that party, into that scene of communal happiness. I feel too toxic. Too full of my own needs.

Today is not the day to plunge myself into the silliness and purity of a kids' party. Not the day for me to wonder if I am passing muster with his family, with his dad, his sisters, all those cousins and nieces and nephews. Not to mention the strangers, the family friends, the mums and dads of school pals, possibly one of those scary clowns that claim to entertain children but actually only give them nightmares . . .

I feel myself spiraling off into the land of fictional anxieties and walk back to the car. I have made this little detour for nothing, and I need to head home. Before I start the engine I reply to his messages, telling him I am fine, that I will see him tomorrow, that I am glad the party is a raging success. I add four kisses, going crazy.

I am disappointed that I don't feel like I can fit into his world, but I remind myself that this has been a difficult day, and that it has taken its toll.

I feel a sense of distance between myself and Karim, between myself and the rest of the world, but I also know myself well enough to understand that it will pass.

It is a temporary coping mechanism that my psyche has thrown up to help me get through everything—a barrier to protect me from the barbarian hordes. A wall of safety to buy myself the space and time to process what has happened, the way it has affected me.

The thing about walls, though, is that they don't only keep the bad stuff out—they keep the good stuff out as well. I know that, and I am alert to the fact that I need to tear them down again if I want to live the kind of life I am starting to see glimmers of.

That, though, will be a task for tomorrow, I think. I am not superhuman, and I am not perfect, and I am not capable of switching change on and off like a lightbulb. It will take time, and today I need to give myself permission to retreat.

The journey home takes me the best part of three hours, between toilet breaks and traffic snarls, and it is fully dark by the time I park outside my flat.

I sit in the car for a moment, relieved to be here but also emotionally queasy at the thought of heading inside. My flat will be cold, and empty, and bleak. It is what I need, but it is not what I want, and there is a world of difference between the two. I feel heartsick and lonely and utterly incapable of reaching out to any of the people in my life who might make me feel different.

I know that I need to call in and say hi to Margie and let her know I am safely home. I know this because I am very perceptive, and also because of the text she sent me earlier that said, Make sure you call in and say hi and let me know you're home safe.

She's not fooling me—I'm sure she wants to know all about everything, down to the last oatcake, but I am too tired for that. I have driven hundreds of miles and been in a time machine and have eaten nothing but service-station food all day. I can manage "Hello, look, I am alive," but I think that is about all.

I let myself into the communal hallway and hear a welcome-home woof from Bill. Margie has left the door to her flat open again, and I smile as I see he is waiting to greet me just inside as I push it open. I crouch down and let him give me a big slobbery hug with a lot of face licking.

Down the hall and into the lounge, I am greeted by not only Margie but Erin and Katie too. They are all sitting around the TV screen, the lights are off, and whatever they are watching is casting an eyeball-searing neon glow around the room.

I stare at the TV, hearing a mishmash of accents and seeing cupcake-colored characters involved in some kind of dispute— horses, I realize. They're talking horses. It's all very surreal.

"The wanderer returns!" announces Margie when she sees me, pausing the pink horses midsentence.

"Sit down, love!" she says. "We've been watching TV shows we loved as kids. Katie's been finding them on her phone and then throwing them onto the telly—"

"Casting them, Margie!" Katie interrupts, giving me an eye roll as though to say *Old people, huh?* when in reality I have no idea what is even happening.

"I chose *The Flintstones*," declares Margie excitedly. "It made me feel all Yabba Dabba Doo! Erin went for *The A-Team*, because apparently she was once in love with Face. Now here we are . . . *My Little Pony!*"

"This is mine, in case you hadn't guessed," Katie adds. "It's the one where Applejack tries to do the whole harvest on her own, refusing all help until she realizes that she needs her friends . . ."

"I still don't understand," says Erin, who is sitting next to her on the sofa, "why they have farms and harvests. I mean, they're ponies!"

"Yes, but they're anthropomorphic ponies," replies Katie, in the slightly exasperated tone of someone who has had to explain this before, "so they live human-style lives."

Erin winks at me behind her back, and I see it is a running debate between them.

"Well, I'm just glad they didn't take it too far," she adds. "I mean, can you imagine? *My Little Pony: The Slaughterhouse Edition?*"

Katie groans and punches her in the leg, and Margie gestures toward the chair that is going spare.

"Come on, love, we saved you a space . . . and there's an open bottle of Baileys around somewhere—unless Katie's necked it all."

"Yes, that's me," says Katie jauntily, "just turned eighteen and a complete alcoholic! Gemma, sit down, will you, so I can see how Applejack's story ends?" I have not said a word throughout this exchange, this explosion of banter and convivial chat. I have smiled, and nodded at the right places, and absentmindedly scratched Bill behind the ears as he sits next to me.

I don't think it's a coincidence that all three of them are here. That all three of them have obviously been filling in time, waiting for me to come home. They know this might have been a difficult day, and they are, in their own slightly bonkers way, offering me a kind of support group. A soft cushion to land on after any traumas I might have endured.

It is sweet, and I appreciate it, but I still feel the urge to run. To hide away in my own space and lick my wounds.

"Ladies, this all looks wonderful," I say, "and on any other night I'd have an episode of *The Worst Witch* on quicker than you could say abracadabra, but I'm absolutely wiped out. It all went fine, and I'll fill you in tomorrow, but for now I need to crash out. I'm not being an Applejack, my lovely friends, but I hope you'll forgive me if I say good night?"

Katie gets to her feet, clambers over the tangle of dog and human legs, and presents me with a half-empty bottle of Baileys. Aha—she did have it after all.

"There you go," she announces, wrapping my hands around it, "a half-full bottle of Baileys for you."

*Half full*, I tell myself as I prepare to leave. Half full, not half empty. An important distinction.

Katie throws her arms around me and gives me a squeeze. Before I know it, all three of them are surrounding me. I get hugs from them all, Margie tucks my hair behind my ears, and Erin kisses me on the cheek.

I feel overwhelmed, in both good ways and scary ways. These three women have waited up for me. They care about me. They are showing me that so clearly that it almost makes me cry. I know they all want to hear about my day, but I don't have it in me to talk.

Instead, I decide that I can at least stay. I can just sit, and have a drink of Baileys, and let myself be comforted by the sounds of their chatter and their silly TV shows and their simple presence. I am quiet, and none of them try to force anything more from me—they just let me be.

It is soothing, and it calms me more than I ever could have imagined—but I am also genuinely exhausted. At the end of the episode I stand up and tell them all I need to go to bed for a few days.

"Fair enough," says Margie, getting to her feet. "You look knackered, hon. Group hug!"

Before I can dodge out of the way, all three of them descend, laughing as they force me to accept another round of cuddles. We form a kind of rugby pile, Bill jumping up and down at our sides, keen to join in on the silly human fun.

It is silly, and it is fun, and as I make my way up my fourteen stairs, I hope I can hold on to that.

I open the door to my flat and feel both comforted and repelled by the silence. By the emptiness. I am trapped between worlds and worried that I might end up squashed.

There are signs of change all around me—there is extra milk in the fridge, two chairs left outside on the balcony instead of one. Karim's "second-best jacket" is hanging on the peg on the back of the door; a spare toothbrush he uses sits in the bathroom. I am evolving, one inanimate object at a time.

I am also, I think as I crash down onto the sofa, glad to have this time on my own. It occurs to me that everyone I care about is actually happy right now, without me. Karim is with his family. Mum is with Sam. Margie is with Erin and Katie, and I know that Erin is a good person who will stay in Margie's life.

If I were to disappear now, Margie wouldn't be alone— she'd have a replacement me to help her. I could move on without leaving her in the lurch.

My daughter has not been in touch, and I am responsible for nobody else. That brings a sense of guilty relief that I hate. I don't want to be like this, but it feels like an uphill battle to be anything else right now. I can only hope this is a temporary relapse.

I pull off my clothes, climb into pajamas, and lie flat on my bed. I stare at the ceiling, wishing there was something there for me to count. Maybe I should put up some wallpaper with a geometric design that would keep me busy during my idle hours.

I am exhausted but cannot sleep. My eyes are heavy but my mind is circling, leaping from one thing to another, over-wrought and wasted. I am alone. I am safe. I should be content now—it's always worked for me before. Now it is different. I am in limbo—not quite able to fully engage with the world in the way normal people do, but also not quite satisfied to be solitary.

I put the pillow over my face, willing myself to switch off, dreading the night ahead, knowing that I will lie like this for hours and wondering what I can do to avoid it. Every time I close my eyes, they ping back open.

When the knock on the door comes, I groan. I know it will be Erin, or Katie, or both—they will want to check up on me before they leave. They will want to hug me again. They will want to be my friends, my people, my allies. All I want is oblivion and a few hours of peace.

I sit up, drag myself out of bed, and walk toward the door. When I open it, I do a slight double take when I see Karim standing outside.

He looks tired, his hair sticking out at weird angles, and he needs a shave. He is wearing a T-shirt that says "World's No. 1 Uncle," and he is holding a cardboard box full of popcorn.

He smiles at me, sheepish, as though he is embarrassed at being here. Unsure of his reception.

"You're supposed to be in Birmingham," I say, confused. "Are you a mirage?"

"Nope, one hundred percent real. I just came back. I came home. I came here. I had a brilliant day, but—well, I knew you like popcorn. And I knew you had a less brilliant day. And I knew that you'd be up here, on your own, trying to sleep and not being able to . . ."

He hands me the popcorn, and I accept it with uncertain hands. I am baffled and bewildered and wiped out. I need to be alone, but seeing him, with his stubble and his smile and his simple sense of kindness, is undoing me. I am flooded with gratitude, with need, with so many things. I am thrilled and I am terrified at the deluge.

"I also brought you this," he adds, passing me one of those necklaces made of candy on an elasticated string. I've not seen one of those since I was a kid and they used to come in Lucky Bags.

"I thought you could either eat it, or count the sweeties, or whatever."

He drapes it over my neck, and I touch the pink nubs, my fingers tracing their outlines as I do, in fact, automatically start to count them.

"Can I come in?" he says quietly, and I realize that I have been blocking the door, staring at him silently.

"Oh! Of course you can!" I reply, backing up, walking into the kitchen, putting the popcorn down on the table. Popcorn. He brought me popcorn. What a man. He follows me through, and he does not speak. He seems to understand my mood, and he simply takes my hand and leads me through to the bedroom. He pulls back the covers and we climb in, and he pulls me toward him, snuggling me in so my head is resting on his chest and his arms are wrapped around me. I reach up and run my fingers over his jaw.

"I like the stubble," I murmur, and sense his smile. "I like you. All of you. Even if I'm rubbish at saying it."

"I know," he replies. "And I left 'like' behind a long time ago when it comes to you, Gemma. Hush now. We both need some rest. You can explore my stubble in the morning."

I grin, and I close my eyes, and I pull away from my limbo.

This is better, I decide, than being alone. We are better together.

## CHAPTER 26

# ONE MISSING JACKET

**The week after is midterm** exam period, but I go into school on one of the days to run drop-in sessions for students who need some extra help. Only three turn up, but it's better than nothing.

Karim has been decorating his apartment, and I have been helping him. I have been swimming again with Margie, and I have spoken to my mother on the phone to keep the lines of communication open between us. Erin and Katie have gone to Middlesex to visit relatives, and I am calling in to water their plants.

I have, in short, been concentrating on the glass being half full.

Karim has shown me more pictures from the party, pointing out his sisters and his dad and his ex, Zara, with her own kids. She is sleek and beautiful and has a smile that could power the whole of Liverpool. I had a flicker of jealousy when he showed me and obviously didn't hide it well enough—he pounced on it, delighted and gleeful at my reaction.

*"You don't need to worry, babe,"* he said, wrapping his arms around me. *"I only have eyes for you!"*

It was a strange and new emotion, jealousy, and I'm not sure I like it. I do, however, like the fact that it made him so happy. Relationships are mysteries to me. We have even arranged for me to go and meet everyone in Birmingham when we break for the Christmas holidays—which seem far enough away for me to handle the idea calmly.

Again, despite my uneasiness, it made him so happy that I'd agreed to it. Perhaps this is the key to at least one of those mysteries—shelving your own qualms for the sake of someone else. Compromising because you care how they feel. Maybe I've been alone for so long not because I'm broken but because I'm just selfish—and Karim is teaching me the joys of giving. He is so decent, so kind, so thoroughly good that it feels impossible not to respond in kind.

We went to the pub quiz the night before and he stayed over at mine, as usual. It is now one of those rare days when neither of us has a lot to do, and we have luxuriated in bed for way longer than normal.

"I feel like I could stay in bed forever today," he says. "Decorating is harder work than it looks."

"Yeah, you really should work on your fitness levels," I reply, grinning already. Karim is the very picture of fitness, and even though he knows I am winding him up on purpose, I still get a poke in the ribs for it.

"I'm a godlike creature and you know it. You can't get enough of me, woman."

I laugh, and he wraps the covers around us a bit tighter, creating a cocoon of warmth.

"This is nice," I say, "cozy. I feel all snuggly and happy."

He kisses the top of my head and replies, "It is nice. I love waking up with you. And going to sleep with you. And the

things we do before we go to sleep. And pretty much everything in between. Maybe one day we might even be grown-up
enough to move in together . . ."

I tense slightly as he says this and then immediately work
hard to relax my muscles. Karim is finely attuned to my body
and its responses, as well as my mind.

"Maybe," I reply, keeping my tone neutral. I have never
lived with another person as an adult, and I am not sure how
I would cope. I value my privacy, my territory, my own little
kingdom, so much more than other people do—because I
didn't have any as a child. I was always jittery, never safe, and
then when I was in foster care, I always had to share. It's made
me fiercely protective of my living space.

"Wow, don't overwhelm me with your enthusiasm! It was
just an idea, for the future—don't stress about it."

I wriggle around so I am looking up at him, so I can make
eye contact while I talk. He is smiling and does not seem
offended, and that is a good start.

"Karim, if I was ever going to move in with anyone, it
would be you. I can't promise it, and I'd be lying if I said the
idea didn't freak me out a bit, but you know all the reasons for
that. You know what I'm like, and why. I hope you also know
that I'm committed to this. That I'm trying really hard to be
less . . . me."

He strokes my face, and pulls me closer, and tugs the duvet
over our heads so we are in a little cave.

"I know. And I don't ever want you to be less—I just think
that perhaps together we might be more. It's okay. I get it. I'm
happy the way things are, happy to let it all play out the way it
needs to. Happy with you."

"Good," I say firmly, pulling the duvet away. "Now I think you should go and have a shower. Somehow you still smell of paint!"

He sniffs his own skin and wrinkles up his nose before climbing out of the covers. He tucks me in and walks naked and proud toward the bathroom. I lie still and content, telling myself that it will all be fine, that I just need to relax and let life happen. Even as I think it, though, I am staring at my duvet cover, counting up how many times the fleur-de-lis pattern is repeated in different colors.

After a few minutes, Karim walks back into the room. He has a towel tied around his waist, his body damp and glistening. It is a pretty picture, and one I enjoy a great deal.

He raises his eyebrows at me and gives me a half smile, and I know that he knows what I am thinking.

"You're thinking *Damn, what a hot bod; aren't I a lucky woman? Aren't* you?" he says, posing in the doorway, flexing his biceps and grinning.

"No," I lie. "I'm thinking, *I wonder if that strange wet man in the pink towel would mind making me a coffee?* to be honest."

"Fibber! I'd say your pants would be on fire, but I'm pretty sure you're not wearing any . . . So, coffee, or world-beating sex? Your choice!"

I am pretending to debate the two in my mind when the landline rings. Karim pulls a face, and I know he would prefer if I ignored it. So would I, truth be told, but it might be Margie—she is the only person who usually uses that number, and I don't want to be that woman who abandons her pals as soon as a man is on the scene, no matter how hot he is.

"Could you get that on your way to the coffee machine?" I ask pleadingly. "It'll probably be Margie. I'd answer it myself but I'm way too comfortable and warm to move."

He rolls his eyes but walks through to the living room. I hear him pick up the phone and say hello, and then piece together a brief conversation from only his half of it. No, he says, she's not available. Yes, he can take a message. There's a pause, then I hear the phone being put back in place.

I writhe around under the covers, enjoying the sensation, looking forward to our day together. I decide that the coffee can wait, and that I will invite him to come back to bed before he puts his clothes on. Seems like a waste of a naked man not to. Seems like I am very lucky, and I should never allow myself to forget that.

When he doesn't return straightaway, I start to wonder why, and who was on the phone. Not Margie, from the sounds of it, but also nothing important, I assume, as he didn't come and get me. Probably a reminder that my car is due for its servicing or something equally bland.

"Karim?" I shout. "You okay out there? Forget the coffee, come back to bed!"

I am greeted by silence, apart from the vague sound of him moving around in the next room. I frown and climb unwillingly from my cavern of covers. I throw on a robe and walk into the lounge.

He is standing before me fully dressed, a look on his face that I have never seen before—anger. He is avoiding my eyes as he fastens his shirt, but his expression tells me clearly that he is very, very pissed off.

"What is it?" I say, clutching my robe with both hands. "What's wrong? Where are you going?"

"I'm going home," he says simply, grabbing the coat he usually leaves at mine for beach walks from the back of the door.

I stride over to him, hold his arm. He feels tense beneath my touch. "Karim, what's going on?"

"I have no idea, Gemma. I thought things were going well. I thought we were happy, building something together. I believed you when you said you were committed, that you were trying. I thought I understood. But it seems like I was wrong."

"Look, I don't know what you're talking about—who was on the phone?" He stares at me, and I see that beneath the anger there is something else—pain. He is hurting, and somehow, I am responsible for it.

"It was the deputy head at a school in Norwich. She was calling to arrange a preliminary interview for the job you've recently applied for. The job in bloody Norwich!"

For a moment I am confused, befuddled, completely baffled by what is happening. And then I remember. I remember the recruitment agency. I remember the details of the head of history post they sent through to me. I remember that it came on the day my daughter turned eighteen. I remember that I was low, looking for a boost, trying to fill my mind with anything other than waiting for an email that would probably never land.

I agreed for my details to be passed on for that job, but I honestly have not even given it a second thought since. I have been working so hard to fight all my instincts to run, to escape, to evade the web of commitment that is beginning to surround me—but not hard enough, it seems. Even *thinking* about running, apparently, has its consequences.

The timing of this simply couldn't be worse—coming straight after our conversation about moving in together.

"Karim, it's nothing—it's just a misunderstanding. I didn't really apply for a job in Norwich, honestly!"

"Really?" he says, slamming his jacket on angrily. "Because there's a Becky Baker in Norwich who seems to think you did! In fact, she seemed very keen to talk to you about it!"

"Please, Karim, calm down and let me explain!" I sound desperate, and I feel desperate, and I do not like it. I tell myself that I have done nothing wrong, for once. Not intentionally at least.

He pauses, one hand on the door, and I see him make an effort to compose himself. To be fair. To give me a chance.

"Okay," he says slowly. "Go on, then. Explain."

I meet his eyes, and my words rise up and choke me, dying in my throat as they try to escape. How do I explain? How do I get across how hard this all is for me? Anything I say feels like it might make things worse. I take a deep breath and try.

"You know how I am, Karim," I say. "You know I'm . . . not quite right. I was always honest about that. We were literally just talking about it. All of this—us, the job, being here for so long—is harder than it looks for me. That's not your fault, none of it, and I *am* happy! We *are* building something together! This is hard to put into words, but . . . there's part of me, might always be part of me, that needs to feel free. Needs to keep my options open, even if I never plan to use them."

He is silent as he looks at me, then shakes his head sadly.

"I know how you are, Gemma, and I've always accepted it—or at least I thought I had. But hearing you say that hurts. It worries me that this means more to me than it does to you. It worries me that, maybe, I'm just another one of your options."

He gently moves my hand from his arm and opens the door.

"Look, I'm going to go. I need to cool down and think. Maybe I need to consider my options too. I'll speak to you later."

He leaves and closes the door behind him. It slams, even though he probably didn't intend it to—his anger and frustration have spilled over.

I stand there, staring dumbly at the empty peg he has left behind. He has gone, and he has taken his jacket, and that is the jacket that never goes anywhere. It is the jacket that says he is part of my life.

I realize that I am crying. That my cheeks are damp and my bare feet are cold and I feel numb. Not even sad or in pain—just numb.

He has left me, and even though I know I shouldn't over-react, that it isn't final, I can't help but wonder if I will see him again. Apart from at work. Maybe we will become distant acquaintances, avoiding each other in meetings, nodding coldly across corridors, sitting at opposite ends of the staff room. I wonder if it is all over before we even got the chance to see what it would become.

I wonder if I could bear that—to stay here and be near him, but not be with him. I wonder how much of myself I have accidentally given to him. I wonder how this has happened, the good and the bad, so very quickly—the stealthy way it has all snuck up on me.

I go into my bedroom and deal with at least one of the problems I am facing. I put on some fluffy bed socks. The bed socks warm my toes and set me onto autopilot. I head to the bathroom, brush my teeth, knock his toothbrush to one side, and wash away my tears. I make a coffee with the machine. I walk over to the phone, and the notepad beside it.

I see Karim's handwriting, the scrawl of numbers, the place where he has stabbed the notepad with the tip of the pen when he realized what this message he was so innocently taking actually meant. I run my fingers across it, ashamed of the way I have made this good man feel. Ashamed but not surprised.

Maybe it was inevitable. My last boyfriend accused me of being an emotional cripple, and despite my best efforts, perhaps he was right. Perhaps some wounds are impossible to heal. Perhaps I am simply spreading around the pain, and Karim would be better off without me. If I wasn't so selfish, maybe I'd end it right now and give him an escape route.

My phone pings and I glance at it quickly, disappointed when it is Margie.

"You okay?" she says when I answer. "I heard more noise than usual, and a slamming door, and . . . well, I'm nosy. And worried about you."

I feel a sharp sting in my eyes and screw my lids tight to stop myself from crying again. I don't like this new habit.

"I'm all right, Margie. We just . . . we . . . well . . ."

"Had a fight?"

"Yeah. Which makes it sound simple. I know couples have fights, but this feels bigger than that. It feels like it could . . . end things, I think."

"And is that what you want, love?" she replies, and I picture her so clearly, glasses perched on her head, a frown on her face, Bill at her feet.

"No. I don't think so. But I'm also not sure I can do this, Margie. This whole relationship thing. I'm not sure it's fair to him. I feel like I'm going to hurt him and hold him back, and like I should just let him go."

"Oh do shut up, Gem! He's a big boy, and he can make his own choices—sounds to me like you're just being a bit of a wuss, love! Finding excuses to not even fight for it."

I am silent, and taken aback, and hurt, and a tiny bit concerned that she is right. I am so used to Margie supporting me that this new tone is a surprise—even if perhaps I need to hear it. I don't know; I'm a mess.

"Don't go all mysterious on me now—you know I love you, Gemma. But sometimes loving someone means you have to tell them something they don't want to hear."

"I know," I say quickly, not wanting to inflict my mess on one more single person. It is my mess, and I am fed up of splattering everyone else with it, like Karim and his paint.

"Thanks, Margie. Look, I've got to go now. I'll see you later, okay?"

I end the call before she can answer, incapable of becoming embroiled in a longer conversation. I stare again at the message from Norwich and see that its simple line of letters and numbers represents something far more complex.

I chew the end of the pen I am still holding, then sling it viciously across the room. I am so bloody tired of being me. Of never quite being good enough, for myself or for anyone else. It's exhausting.

I pick up the phone, and I dial the number in Norwich.

# CHAPTER 27

# KING I-LOVE-YOU THE FIRST AND A NO TO NORWICH

**I pull up outside Karim's** block an hour later. I have made my phone call, spoken with Mrs. Baker, and the dirty deed is done. Now I just have to tell him face-to-face—I owe him that much at least.

I scamper inside his building, hoodie pulled up against the rain, and consider getting the lift to his flat on the fourth floor. I change my mind and run up the stairs instead, fighting my instinct to count them as I go. My instincts, I decide, are crap.

I am pleasantly warm by the time I find myself outside his home, pulling down my hood and smoothing out my hair. I ring the bell and wait. I know he is here, or at least his car is. I ring again, more insistently, putting an ear to the door and hearing loud music blasting from inside.

I ring once more, holding my finger down until I hear him shouting: "Okay, okay! I'm coming!" He opens the door, and we stare at each other for a moment. He is listening to the Foo Fighters and is holding a paintbrush. There are specks of blue on his T-shirt, and in his dark hair, and also on his face.

"You're covered in paint," I say.

"Yeah. Well. Turns out loud guitar music and decorating don't mix that well."

"Have you been angry painting?"

"Maybe."

"Can I come in?" He is silent for a moment, the roar of "Best of You" sweeping out toward us, and for a split second I think he will say no. That he will turn me away. That I won't even get the chance to say what I have come here to say.

"All right," he replies eventually, moving to one side and ushering me in. He goes over to his phone and speakers, turns the music down. My ears feel relieved, even if nothing else does.

Karim's flat is bigger than mine and, apart from the location, frankly, nicer. It is untidy in a controlled way, filled with sports gear and books and electronics. It is very manlike, apart from the shelf that is covered in framed school pictures of his niece and nephews, all smiling out at us with gapped teeth and smart uniforms. I gaze at the walls we have been painting and see that he has made some progress—if he meant to cover half the floor, that is. He kicks the plastic sheeting he's haphazardly laid down with one foot, actually manages a wry smile as he sees me looking.

"Yeah, well—I was sick of that carpet anyway . . . I'll clear all of that up later. Do you want a drink?"

I don't, but I think we both need something to do to deflate the wall of tension that I can feel between us. I hate it, this new sense of distance. Or maybe I'm just being hypocritical— what I mean is that I hate when the distance is enforced from the other side. I spent long enough keeping him at arm's length, for sure.

"Diet Coke?" I say hopefully. He nods and strides into his kitchen. He comes back with two, and we both pop them open. It is awkward, and nervy, and neither of us seems to know quite what to say. Which is excusable on his part, as I'm the one who turned up unannounced. Not so much for me.

"I spoke to the school in Norwich," I say, deciding to plunge right in.

"Right," he replies, leaving it at that. It seems that he has no intention of making this easy for me.

"And I told them I was no longer interested in the job and they should remove me from the list of candidates." His eyes widen slightly, but still he doesn't speak. I'm going to have to earn this Diet Coke. "I never intended to take it, Karim, honestly," I explain. "It was just—well, a moment of madness, I suppose you might call it. The details came through on the day Katie turned eighteen, and—well, I was a mess. You know I was that day. The recruitment agency asked if I'd be interested, and it all seemed theoretical, and it was for a head-of-department job so maybe I even thought it'd be a good ego boost if they were interested in me . . ."

"And how did that work out for you? The ego boost?" he asks, the words sharp but his tone slightly more mellow.

"Not so well, to be honest. This guy I've been seeing got in a total strop and walked out on me, and then my neighbor told me I was being a wuss and I needed to fight for you."

It is a gamble, trying for light when I can see he still feels dark, but his lips quirk upward in response, almost against his will.

"Well, maybe your neighbor had a point. And this guy, maybe he felt upset," he answers. "Maybe he'd been thinking things were going well. Even imagining a future together. And maybe you're not the only one with insecurities—maybe this guy, despite being a complete Adonis and having amazing skills in every department, felt . . . vulnerable. Perhaps he was hurt at the thought of you being willing to just give it all up and jog off to the other side of the country, without even discussing it with him first."

"Maybe you're right," I say, smiling. "And maybe I'm a complete dick. I'm sorry, Karim—not just for the job thing but for not being able to explain it properly to you this morning. I just felt all tangled up and tongue-tied and shocked. When you went and took your coat I was devastated."

"My coat?"

"Yeah. The one that you leave at mine. It felt . . . so final."

"Ah," he says, shaking his head. "I see. You read too much into the coat, you know. I just needed time to think. And head of department . . . that would have been a good step for you. I think, if I'd known, if you'd told me, I'd have understood. I just felt like a fool, like I'd been investing way too much in all of this. Like it's always me who's pushing for more, you know? And it's always you who's rationing things out."

I reach up, try to wipe paint off his cheek but end up just smearing blue across his skin.

"I hate that I've made you feel that way. And you haven't been investing too much in all of this. You have been investing exactly the right amount—I'm just not sure you're getting enough interest in return."

"Can we stop with the financial analogies? You'll end up doing your human abacus routine and adding up emotional savings rates in your mind if we carry on."

He is, of course, not wrong. I nod.

"I'm not going to Norwich, Karim. I was never going to Norwich, then or now. I'm not going anywhere—and if ever I do plan to, I'll talk to you about it first."

He takes my Diet Coke from my hand and puts both our cans down on the coffee table. Suddenly he grabs hold of me, lifts me off my feet, and hoists me into the air. I let out a scream, and both of us tumble onto the sofa. He tugs me onto his lap, and we end up a laughing heap of limbs. I squirm about and settle, my head resting against his shoulder, his arms around me.

"I mean," he says softly, "Norwich? It's insulting!"

"No, it's not. Norwich is a very interesting place. Boudica was almost from Norwich. It has a fine cathedral dating back to the late eleventh century, and—"

He shuts me up with a kiss, and when finally we pull apart, I am breathless for all the right reasons.

"Ha!" he says, pleased with himself. "I bet an eleventh-century cathedral can't kiss like that!"

"You know that makes no sense, don't you?"

"It makes sense to me, and that's what matters. Look. I overreacted. I know I did. But I also know that this thing, this unexpected thing that's happening with us . . . it's happening fast. Even for me. So maybe I'm a bit unsteady too."

I take his face in both my hands and look straight into his eyes.

"I'm not moving to Norwich, Karim. I'm not moving any-where. I'm not going to leave, because I love you."

He does not reply, and I feel a sense of dread as I wait for him to respond. I knew he might not say it back. I had prepared myself for that, told myself it didn't matter—that it was something I needed to say anyway. That, like Margie said, I had to fight for him. Plus, if his taking his walking coat affected me as badly as it did, it was time to face up to some truths—I am in love, whether I want to be or not.

Still, being prepared for his not saying it back and it actually happening are two different things, and the seconds seem to tick by in slow motion.

I realize, as I bite my lip hard, that I was fooling myself—I wasn't prepared at all. This feels awful.

"You love me?" he says finally.

"Yes. I do. I love you."

"You sound like it actually physically hurts you to say it out loud, you know?"

I laugh, because again he's not wrong.

"Well, cut me some slack. I've never said it before."

"What? You've never told anyone you love them? Ever?"

He is looking at me curiously, obviously intrigued.

"Well, I probably said it to my mum when I was a little kid. And I wrote it in a letter to Baby, but I don't know if that counts. But I've never said it to—"

"A man?"

"No. Not even to my Chris Hemsworth screen saver."

"You don't have a Chris Hemsworth screen saver."

"I know, but I think I might get one."

He pauses, then asks, "So if I were to put this into a historical context—which, as you know, I'm always mad keen to do—I am in fact King I-Love-You the First?"

"Yes, Your Majesty," I reply.

He strokes my disheveled hair back from my face and kisses me lightly on the lips.

"Well, then," he says, smiling, "while we're being honest—I love you too. Absolutely, completely, one hundred percent. Smitten. Gone. All hope is lost."

He follows that up with some more kissing, and then some more cuddling, and all things considered, it is actually one of the happiest moments of my entire life. There are still problems. There are still challenges. But I have to face them—I have to fight for myself as well as Karim. I promised my daughter I would be forever hers, but I have to be forever mine too.

Now I am here, and I am so alive. I took a risk. I pushed myself. I opened up in a way I never thought I could—and it's all thanks to him. The world feels brighter, and warmer, and safer, and I make a mental note: on this day in history, Gemma Jones finally loved someone, and felt loved in return.

I nestle into him, feeling like I never want to move again. He tightens his grip, squeezes me tight, and says: "On a slightly different note, you now have a blue face!" I reach up to feel a glob of damp paint on my face, and find that I am not in the slightest bit bothered. I am exactly where I need to be.

# CHAPTER 28

# SIXTEEN PAIRS OF SPORTS SHOES AND ONE VERY IMPORTANT PING

**I wake up the next** day in the less familiar surroundings of Karim's bedroom. It makes me realize how much time we spend at my place rather than his, and how one-sided at least some of this has been. I make a vow to myself to be more vigilant, to be more even, to be a better girlfriend. Not just for his sake but for my own.

It is also, of course, a room full of things I haven't as yet counted, which is always a fun time for me.

I roll over to his side, already knowing that he has gone. There is a note there, and it makes me smile to see it. I love his little pillow notes.

I pick it up, see that he has gone to get pastries from the Polish bakery. Could he be more perfect? He has, though, signed it "King I-Love-You the First," which balances out the perfection.

I get up and get dressed. I don't keep anything here, at Karim's, and I am punished for that oversight by having to wear yesterday's clothes. It is nothing more than I deserve.

I mooch around his flat, not snooping but examining—the photos of his family, the hardback books that mainly seem to be biographies of sports people. The fridge magnet that says "I Heart Milk," the collection of sneakers all neatly laid out on a shoe rack. Sixteen pairs, to be exact.

It makes me smile, seeing it all. All the tiny pieces of him, the little clues to his personality, the shards of his life all reflected in his home habitat.

I am rooting through his surprisingly large vinyl collection when he appears, wrapped up in a parka and holding a big paper bag.

He puts it down on the table and beats his chest like Tarzan.

"I am hunter-gatherer!" he says in a fake-macho voice. "I bring food for woman in cave!"

"For a hunter-gatherer, there's a lot of Motown in this record collection . . ."

He dumps his coat and sweeps me up into his arms. He starts singing "It Takes Two, Baby" as he spins me around, and I laugh in a way I haven't laughed before. I feel free, and light, and giddy. Like there is fizzy pop running through my veins.

He kisses me and sets me down, disappearing off into the kitchen for plates and coffee. He's a hunter-gatherer with a very evolved coffee machine as well, which is a tribute to humanity's progress.

"What shall we do today, Gemma?" he shouts from the other room. "Go to town? Go to the zoo? Stay in bed and feast? The world is our lobster!"

I am giving this some thought, and coming firmly down on the third option, when my phone calls out for attention. I haven't looked at it since the day before, which is a testament to just how much this being-in-love thing has affected my normal routines.

I pick it up and first see a message from Margie.

Sorry if I was rough on you yesterday, kiddo. It might
have been tough love, but it was still love. Let me know
if you're okay. xxx

I quickly tap a reply assuring her that I am, and see that I
have another notification.

This one is different. This one wipes the silly smile from
my face and demands my full attention. This one is a game
changer.

I am distantly aware of Karim coming back through, of the
clatter of plates and cutlery, of the sight of those mini jars
of jam they always have at hotel breakfasts. Only distantly,
though, because my phone has yet again become the center
of my universe.

He stops, looks at me. Sees my expression.

"What is it?" he asks, suddenly serious. "Are you all right?"

"I think so," I reply, looking up at him, feeling my face drain
of color.

"It's from the Adoption Contact Register," I say, the words
making it real. "She's been in touch. My daughter. Baby. She's
asked for my details, and they've given them to her."

"Okay . . . well, that's a good thing, isn't it? That's what you
wanted?"

I nod, because of course he is right. It is what I wanted,
desperately. And yet now that it has happened, I feel terrified.

# CHAPTER 29

# TWO CHEEKY CORGIS, ONE PEP TALK, AND HAMMERING IT OUT

**I know, of course, exactly** how many weeks, days, minutes, and hours it has been since Baby turned eighteen. I know exactly how long I had been waiting to hear that news—to find out that the process had begun.

Now, I am still waiting. The process has begun, but nothing else has happened. If I'd been a little obsessive about checking my phone before, I am now reaching Olympic gold medal standards. The damn thing is practically glued to my hand, like an extra appendage. Gemma Mobile Hands. Even in lessons, I have it out on the desk, breaking all the rules that I set for the students and usually abide by myself.

Days and nights have passed with no news. Halloween has already come and gone, quickly followed by Bonfire Night, and before it seems feasible, everyone is talking about the staff Christmas party and the shops are all full of boxes of crackers and jumbo tubs of Roses chocolates. Nothing says "birth of our Lord and Savior" quite like a jumbo tub of Roses.

I live my days and nights in a surreal hinterland of actually happening and what-might-happen. I get on with work and I spend time with Karim—or King I-Love-You the First, as he occasionally insists on being called—and I see my friends and I walk Bill and I do yoga and I run and I swim and finally I watch *The Bridge* and I do absolutely everything I can to keep myself busy.

It doesn't work, of course. I seem to have developed a superhuman ability to do one thing perfectly well, while all the time actually being completely focused on something different. The gap between the external and the internal, the surface me and the background me, is widening, and I fear I am going to have some kind of crisis if it continues.

I know it is ridiculous, but I don't seem quite able to end it—to clear my mind, to stop planning for the unplannable, to switch off and relax.

She has my email, my phone numbers, my address. She has had them for over a week, and it feels like the longest week of my life. I am spiraling between certainty that she won't ever get in touch and sheer excitement at the thought of getting to find out about her.

I am made up entirely of questions—what does she look like now? What are her parents like? Does she have any pets? Is she doing exams and planning on going to uni or doing an apprenticeship or something entirely different? What's her favorite food and color and song and book and film? Most important of all, has she been happy?

I have tried, over the years, to keep all of this curiosity under control. There never seemed to be any point in indulging it. Early on, when I was still very young, I seemed to have more resolve—I told myself I didn't deserve to know anything about her, that I had given up all right to know a single solitary fact.

It was brutal, but it also allowed me to go on, to move forward with my own life. In fact, it motivated me—if I didn't make something of myself, if I didn't succeed in dragging myself out of the future that seemed to be mapped out for me, then it would all have been wasted.

As I've aged, it has grown harder—to ignore the questions, the wondering, the way I find myself imagining her and what she is doing and how her world looks. As I've matured, and as she has grown up, it has been almost impossible not to wonder—but I have still tried.

Meeting Katie, though, falling into that rabbit hole that had me convinced she was actually my daughter, showed me that it is not something that is likely to go away. I will always wonder, always imagine. Always yearn. Be forever hers.

Now, as my actual daughter and I make tentative steps toward each other, it is almost unbearable—knowing she is so close but also knowing that I have no way to make her take that final step. To reach out.

It is hard, and it is sucking the life out of me, and I know that I cannot go on like this for any length of time. I will simply burn out, fade away, lose my ability to do all the things I need to do, to be all the people I need to be. I have to find a way to calm down about it all, I know that much—but what I don't know is how to go about that.

It is actually Katie who finally shakes me out of it.

She turns up on my doorstep on a Saturday morning, brandishing her phone and her pink tutu. I groan as I let her in, and say: "Did your mum send you? Is she worried about me? Are you going to try to make me dance it out?"

She pulls a face at me and replies, "No, my mum didn't send me, and yes, she is worried about you, and dancing it out is a tried-and-tested method."

"No. Sorry, Katie, but no. I cannot face another session of K-pop."

"Doesn't have to be K-pop. We can do something from your era, like Bach or Beethoven, if you prefer?"

She grins at me, and it is contagious. Cheeky pup.

"How about a walk instead?" I counter. "There was someone out there with a metal detector earlier. We can laugh when they get a beep and dig up a Guinness can."

"Or look on in absolute astonishment when they find an Anglo-Saxon horde."

"Unlikely, but yeah—that would be good. How are you doing anyway? And if your mum didn't send you, why are you actually here?"

"Because I was worried about you as well," she replies as we troop down the stairs and out again. I have already walked Bill, so I steel myself against the mournful howl he lets out as we walk past. It is almost human, as though he is trying to form the words "Please take me tooooooooo!"

"In class yesterday," she continues, putting her tutu on her hair like some kind of strange ceremonial headdress, "you didn't even line your pens up. And later, you said that Elizabeth the Second made a speech to her troops about the Spanish Armada."

"Gosh—I didn't, did I?"

"You absolutely did. And hardly anyone noticed, and those of us who did probably realized it was a mistake, but you never know . . . A couple of kids might fail their exams because of it. I mean, you could be ruining their lives, you know?"

I laugh at the drama, and as we make our way down onto the sand, reply: "I don't think it'll come to that. But it's not like me, is it? I feel a bit like I'm coming apart at the seams to be honest, Katie."

"I know," she says, her pink tutu streaming behind her in the wind, "and I think you'd better sew yourself back up. She might get in touch, she might not—but whatever she decides, she'll have her reasons. You have to maybe try to trust her a bit."

"You're right," I say, nodding, seeing the corgis run toward us. "But it's hard. She has my details, and I feel like I'm on some kind of countdown. Plus, watch out for one of those corgis; he likes to pee on people's feet."

She nimbly moves her Converse sneaker just in time, and the dog looks up at her, annoyed as he only hits sand. We say hello to their owner—Corgi Man—as we pass him by.

"You're not on a countdown, though, are you?" she asks. "It's not like you're on a time limit. Nobody turns into a pumpkin at midnight. Maybe signing up to the register was a big deal for her. Maybe reaching out and getting your details was even bigger. Maybe she's not quite ready for the next bit yet. You have no idea what's going on in her life outside you either, do you? She might be doing exams and feeling the pressure. She might have a complicated relationship. She might be dealing with stuff with her parents. You're only seeing it from one side, which, as you've always taught us in class, isn't right."

My knee-jerk response to this accusation is to claim it's unfair. To deny it. To say I've always tried to see things from her side. But then I start to wonder if I really have.

Life is complex, for everyone—and especially for a teenage girl making her way in the world. Add in the conflict she might be feeling about me, and it's even more of a mess. I have no idea if her parents know she is thinking of getting in touch with me, and no idea how they might feel about that, but even if they are supportive, there is bound to be part of her that is worried about hurting their feelings as well.

In short, Katie is probably right—this isn't just about what I want, and it's nowhere near as simple as I want it to be. Nothing ever is.

"Okay," I eventually reply, "I see your point." We stop at the edge of the waves, gray and white froth chasing our toes at the shoreline, the wind turbines waving at us in the distance.

"I see your point and you're probably right," I continue. "I need to stop holding on so tightly to it, because apart from anything else, it's not going to change a thing. When—if—she contacts me, it'll be on her schedule, not mine. And in the meantime, I suppose I'd better buck my ideas up. Elizabeth the Second and the Spanish Armada? I'm so ashamed!"

"As you should be. I'll settle for a full apology in writing. But seriously—yeah, maybe you need to just chill out a bit? Because otherwise, if she does want to see you, you'll be a complete wreck by the time it happens, and that won't be a good look on you. Now let's go back to your place and dance it out."

"Do we have to?" I plead, sounding like a teenager myself, I realize.

"We do, but you can choose the track."

We clamber over the dunes on the way back to the flat, and I am grateful to have this young woman in my life. As a student and, it seems, as a teacher—on some things at least. She is not my daughter, but she is important to me.

So important that I plan to completely annihilate her in the dance-off. I decide that we will do "U Can't Touch This" and that we're both going to be MC Hammer—because if you're struggling to move forward, then maybe dancing sideways is the next best option.

CHAPTER 30

# 1,217 WORDS AND EXACTLY THE RIGHT AMOUNT OF FEELINGS

**It is not until the** following week that anything changes. Karim has stayed over, but we are both up bright and early ready to go to work. We are even being daring and going in the same car—we'll be the talk of the staff room if anybody notices us.

We have just come back from taking Bill for a quick run on the beach and are calling in to say good morning to Margie. She flirts shamelessly with Karim, who flirts just as shamelessly back, and by the time we leave he has half persuaded her it might be time to join a dating site.

"Seriously, is that a good idea?" I ask as we walk back around to the front of the building. "She might meet an ax murderer!"

"Bill will protect her," he replies firmly. "Plus, if she goes on a date, we'll go with her and sit at the next table in disguise."

"Why would we need to be in disguise?" I ask as I let us into the lobby. "Her date won't know what we look like."

He pauses and narrows his eyes at me.

"You," he says, pointing one finger, "can be a real killjoy, do you know that?"

"Just being logical."

"I know. That's the problem! I was all set for matching false noses and berets, and now you've taken all the fun out of it!"

"Aah, I'm sorry, baby," I say, checking the mailbox behind the door to see if there is anything I need to drop off for Margie. "Maybe we can do that at home instead?"

He looks interested and replies, "Well, if we're going to do costumes at home, I'll put a bit more thought into it."

I roll my eyes and pull a small pile of envelopes out of the box. A flyer for the local garden center, what looks like a hospital letter for Margie, a phone bill, and an intriguing plain white envelope that is actually handwritten. I drop the others to the floor and stare at this one.

It is postmarked somewhere in Surrey, and there is no return address on the back. No stamp or marker that indicates it is corporate in origin. Just that neat, sloping handwriting in black ink, indicating that it is, in fact, personal in origin.

Somehow, I just know. I don't understand why, but every instinct I have tells me that this is it. This is the moment I have been waiting for. This is from her. That I have been insanely checking my phone all this time, and she has instead gone delightfully old-school.

Karim peers over my shoulder, looks at what I am holding.

"Huh," he says, "weird. Who writes actual letters anymore?" I look up at him, and immediately he sees that I am shaken, stirred, scared, and excited all at once. I don't say a word—there is part of me that even wants to hide it from him. Old habits dying very hard.

"You think it's from her? Your daughter?" he asks, placing a calming hand on my shoulder.

"I think it might be. It looks like it could be. Maybe."

"Well, you could, you know, open it? Or are you planning some kind of full forensic examination first?"

"I know I should open it," I say, stroking the handwriting, knowing that I will feel like such an idiot if it's actually just a cleverly disguised marketing mail-out for memory-foam mattresses or something. "But we've got to go to work."

He ponders this, then replies, "Unless that envelope contains a letter the size of *War and Peace*, we've got time. If not, or if you need longer, then I'm going to call work and say I've got car trouble and we'll both be late. And yes, it's as good a way of outing us as any, I know."

"But I have lessons first thing, and a staff meeting after first period, and—"

"The place will survive without us for an hour, Gemma. This is more important. Come on, let's go inside. I'm going to have a long shower so you can read that in private, but you know where I am if you need me. Then you can tell me about it, if you want to."

He leads me upstairs, and I realize that I have left the other letters on the floor. He sees me looking back and adds, "Don't worry. I'll sort it."

He is, of course, perfect. Kind and calm and take-charge in all the right measures.

"Thank you," I say as we go into the flat. "For being so brilliant. I mean, not many men would be thrilled at the prospect of becoming a kind-of, almost-but-not-quite stepdad to an eighteen-year-old girl . . ."

"Well, I'm not most men, am I? And I know how much this means to you. So sit down, and I'll bring you a coffee."

I do as I am told, and within minutes I am installed on the sofa with a steaming hot mug and a blanket over my legs to keep me warm after my run. Karim kisses me on the top of my head and disappears off to the bathroom.

As soon as he is gone, I realize that I needed the space—this time alone with this shining thing, this feeling as if a bomb is about to go off in my face, this Pandora's envelope. He knew that even before I did. King I-Love-You the First is a mind reader, among his many other talents.

I sip some coffee, the background noise of Karim clanging about in the shower reassuring me, and hold the envelope in both hands as though it is too heavy to support with one. Physically, it weighs next to nothing. Emotionally, it is made of lead.

In this moment, I can imagine anything I want to. A happy ending. An invitation to meet up. A declaration of forgiveness. A description of her perfect life, the life she lived because I didn't raise her. It could even simply be a strict instruction never to contact her. It could break my heart, or make it sing.

In that moment, it could be anything and it could be everything and it could be nothing. I am reminded of that poem again, and know that my dreams are beneath her feet.

I close my eyes, breathe deeply, and take the plunge. I open the envelope, careful not to tear it because every scrap of connection with her is significant and precious. I pull out the contents.

A letter, two sheets filled with the same sloping handwriting as the envelope. Inside the folded pages, dropping out onto my lap, a photograph. I pick it up with trembling hands and look at it, still hardly daring to believe.

I look at it, and I see that she is beautiful. She is perfect. She is magnificent. She is more than I ever could have expected.

Her hair has come in darker than mine, a deep and shining shade of auburn that she probably hates but everyone else will

admire. She wears it short and choppy, a little bit punk. Her eyes
are large and brown, with lashings of black kohl that give her an
exotic look. She has several hoops in her ears, and judging by the
background, she is tall—maybe even taller than me.

The main thing I notice, though, in that picture isn't the
funky clothes or the makeup or the car she's leaning against.
It's the smile. A big, confident, loving-the-moment smile that
seems to beam right through time and space and photographic
paper and into my soul.

It is a smile that says she is happy.

I manage to tear myself away from the photo after a few
moments, reluctant to let it leave my hands, and lay it carefully by my side, scared it might disintegrate like a message in
*Mission Impossible.*

I catch up on the breathing I seem to have been forgetting
to bother with and manage a smile when I hear Karim start to
sing "Bohemian Rhapsody" in the shower. It is, I know, his not-
so-subtle way of reminding me that he is here if I need him.

I unfold the handwritten pages and see an address in the
usual spot. I read it slowly, as I know I will read every single
word slowly. I want to gobble it all down, to inhale it, but I am
making myself take my time. Making myself savor it.

The address tells me she lives in a place called Great Book-
ham in Surrey. I have no idea what that means, or what it's
like, but it makes my heart soar to see it. The fact that she
has put her address on the page means that she wants a reply.
That this isn't just a "please don't bother me anymore" letter.
I hadn't even realized how much I'd been dreading that until
I'm not.

I smooth the paper down on the blanket on my lap, and I
read . . .

*Dear Gemma,*

*It's me—"Baby." Though I go by Beth these days, which is better than being named after someone from Dirty Dancing, isn't it?*

*Thank you for leaving your details on the Adoption Contact Register. It took me a while to decide what to do, and how to get in touch—or even whether I should get in touch.*

*My mum and dad gave me your letter when I was fourteen. Two years earlier than you wanted, but I was a bit of a bitch when I was fourteen, and I think they were worried about it and thought it might help. Plus you'd said that thing about it being good if I had bossy parents, which I think they liked. It didn't stop me being a bitch, but it did maybe make me calm down a bit. Especially your words of warning about the vodka. I think perhaps that came at just the right time, and it was pretty easy to imagine myself in the same position.*

*So, I didn't really know what to write in this—it's a hard situation, and I was worried about upsetting my actual mum and dad as well. They've always been honest with me about being adopted, but still, it must be weird for them, knowing you're out there and knowing I'm sending you a letter. They've never had anything bad to say about you, by the way; they were always just really grateful that I turned up.*

*I talked to them about doing this, and they said they were happy for me to contact you. That doesn't mean they don't have their own doubts and worries about what it might start up, but they're keeping those to themselves for now. If they get any hint that you're bad for me, though, I warn you, they might hire a hit man.*

*I asked Mum what I should write, and she told me some of the things she'd want to know if she was you. She's usually right about stuff, so here goes.*

*Mum is Sue, and she was a nurse in a children's hospital when they adopted me. Dad is Richard—known to everyone as Richie—and he's an electrician. We lived in Watford when I was a baby, but then we moved to Surrey.*

*When I was about four they decided to become foster parents, but they were really rubbish at it because they kept keeping the kids instead—so I have three adopted younger siblings, Irina who is ten, Rory who is eleven, and Isabelle, she's fifteen. It's a bit of a patchwork family and they drive me nuts, but we all love each other really. Deep down!*

*Apart from all that, I suppose I've had a pretty normal childhood. I went to the local school, and now I'm studying psychology, biology, and chemistry before hopefully going to college. I think I want to be a doctor but I'm not totally sure what type yet. I did pretty well in my courses and so far so good with the exams, which is excellent news as I need three As to get into my course.*

*It's weird that you live in Liverpool, because it's my first choice for uni. I came up for an Open Day and loved the place. It's strange to think that you're there too, and we could even have been walking around the same part of the city or eating in the same café or whatever and not even known.*

*Mum says she wonders if I get my academic brains from you, but she's just being daft—it's as much down to them as anything. They always encouraged me to work hard, like they did, and that's just as important as anything genetic, I think, isn't it? I don't mean that to be rude—I just know that they've made me who I am, and I still feel a bit like I'm betraying them by even writing this, no matter what they say.*

*Mum also said you'd probably want to know a bit about me, like everyday stuff. So, I like animals—we have a rescue dog from Romania to add to the chaos. He's a handsome boy called Dax, and a big chocolate lab called Jasper who either eats everything or humps everything. I'm a vegetarian who misses bacon. My best friend is called Poppy, and I have a boyfriend called Nathan—though I'm not sure if that'll last with us both going off to uni, because if we get our grades, I'll be in Liverpool and he'll be in London.*

*I passed my driving test last month, and Dad got me a car for my eighteenth—a fifth-hand bright yellow Nissan Micra that is possibly the least cool car ever, but it is all mine. I like reading fantasy novels, and baking, and I play bass guitar in a band. We're pretty rubbish but it's fun. I'll watch anything with Timothée Chalamet in it, and I love Marvel films, and I like old rom-coms with Hugh Grant in them too.*

*Mainly, Mum said you'd want to know if I've been okay—so yes, I have. I've been happy, even though there was that rough patch when I was younger. I suppose everyone has one, but it could have been worse. (I don't need to tell you that!)*

*I've always felt loved and wanted, and your letter did help with that. I don't blame you, for giving me away—I could tell you didn't want to. I could tell you were in a really crap situation yourself, and some of my sibs have come from difficult homes and I know what an effect that can have. When I was sixteen there was no way I could have raised a baby either. So I suppose what I'm saying is that it's all been fine. You told me to "shine on," and I always loved that—I hope I have.*

*That's pretty much it. I don't know what will happen next, or whether we will stay in touch or whatever. If it's okay with you, I'd like to keep it like this for a while. I wrote this instead of emailing because it seemed right—you sent me a letter, now I'm sending you one. I don't really feel up for phone calls or meeting or anything just yet, but if you want to write to me, that would be fine.*

*If you do, then I suppose I have a lot of questions too. As I said, I think my mum and dad made me—but that doesn't mean I'm not curious about you as well. Like, is it your fault I have this hair? And that I'm as tall as a giraffe? And I suppose I want to know what happened in your life too, after me, and also if you remembered anything more about my biological father.*

*Anyway. This is the longest letter I've ever written. Actually, I think it's the only letter I've ever written outside English lessons—nobody writes letters anymore, do they?*

*So you have my address, and if you want to write back, that'd be good. Just don't turn up on the doorstep or anything!*

*No idea how to sign this one off—so I'll stick with my English lessons.*

*Yours sincerely,*
*Beth*

I finish reading. I read it again. I cannot stop smiling, stroking the paper, staring at that picture. She is here. She is not Baby. She is not Katie. She is Beth. She is in my life, and everything has changed.

# CHAPTER 31

# TWENTY-EIGHT VERY AMUSED PEOPLE AND ONE BIG ANNOUNCEMENT

**We arrive at work in** plenty of time. The drive there has been odd, me sitting next to Karim in the passenger seat, grateful for the belt that kept me tethered in place. I feel as light as a helium balloon, as though I might float away into the autumn sky if I'm not tied down.

He has not quizzed me about the letter's contents, showing self-restraint that I know must be killing him. The very resounding kiss I gave him before we set off, and the smile that has been making my face ache ever since I read the letter, are hopefully enough to reassure him.

"So," he says as he parks the car and switches off the engine, "I assume it was good news?"

"It was, Karim. Really good news. She's happy. She's thriving. She's had a great life. And she doesn't blame me. I feel . . . weightless."

He grins and reaches over to stroke my cheek.

"I'm so glad for you, Gemma. I can only imagine what it feels like, after all these years, knowing that she's safe and well. Letting go of some of that guilt you've been carrying around. So what's the plan? What happens next? And . . . at some point, can I read it? The letter?"

He sounds hesitant as he says this, as though he fears he is pushing some kind of unspoken boundary between us and is uncertain about how I will react.

"Of course you can read it," I reply quickly. "Just as soon as I've had it laminated."

He stares at me for a moment, unsure, until I burst out laughing. I am joking—I think.

"Seriously, yes, you can—let's meet up for lunch to do that," I say.

He is part of my life, and she is part of my life, and I have learned that trying to keep everything separate and safe in its own little box doesn't work so well in the long run.

"And as for what happens next, I suppose I write back to her. And maybe she writes back to me. And we become, I don't know, some kind of heavily emotionally laden pen pals? That's my task for tonight, anyway. Just as soon as I've called an emergency girls' night at Margie's so I can tell them about it as well. All of you have helped get me to this stage, and I can't say how grateful I am. Do you want to see her? Before we go in?"

He nods, and I reach for my bag, carefully pulling out a manila file that I've used to keep the letter and picture in. I suspect I may never let them leave my presence again, that if they are ever more than a couple of feet from my body, some kind of internal alarm will go off.

I pass him the photo, saying, "She's called Beth. Isn't that a lovely name?"

"Yes, but she could have been called Gertrude and you'd still think it was a lovely name," he replies.

He is, of course, not wrong.

"You're right. I think Gertrude is long due for a comeback anyway."

He takes the picture, holding it carefully, his fingers on the edges so he doesn't smudge it. I see his eyes light up as he looks at her, and he is smiling when he passes it back.

"She's beautiful," he says, "and more importantly she looks like one of those kids—the ones who have that confidence, that self-belief. You know the ones."

I know exactly what he means. Doing our job, you work with young people of all different abilities, backgrounds, and types. You do your very best for all of them, try to help them reach their full potential, whatever that is for them. Some are academically gifted, some work hard, some, frankly, will do well to come out of the course with a single pass to their name. But among every group, there are always some that stand out—because they know who they are, and they like who they are, which isn't especially easy in teenager land.

Katie is one of those kids, and I can tell from the photo, from the smile, from the way she has expressed herself so unapologetically in that letter, that Beth is one too. My baby. Beth.

I pack the picture away again, and we walk together toward the staff entrance of the school. There are no students here yet, so when he grabs my hand and swings it, I do not object. It is the kind of day that should be celebrated with a swing.

Katie, of course, knows about me and Karim—but she has vowed not to gossip. It is not forbidden; there are no rules against relationships between staff, but it is also not the kind of thing you want a bunch of seventeen- and eighteen-year-olds giggling about behind your back. It is gold dust for them, the weird concept that teachers—Old People—might have a love life. A potent combination of "yuck" and "ooh." I am pretty sure that Karim has his share of fans as well—the hot PE teacher is a stereotype for a reason—so we might break some hearts once word gets out.

Until now, though, we have been careful in general—neither of us wanted to tell our colleagues that we were a thing until we had a better idea of what kind of thing we actually were. I suppose we wanted to keep it to ourselves for a while, our own delicious secret.

As we enter the staff room, I automatically pull my hand away from his—but he just looks down at me and grins. He strides ahead, right over to the tea and coffee counter, the beating heart of the room.

He picks up a mug and a teaspoon and clangs one against the other, like he's about to make a best-man speech at a wedding. The chatter fades, and everyone turns to look at him. I sense what is coming and have a distinct urge to sneak back out again, to go and hide in the cleaning-supplies cupboard with the bleach and the mops.

"Can I have your attention, please?" says Karim unnecessarily, as he already has the complete attention of every single person in the vicinity.

"I have an announcement to make! You all know me, and you all know our lovely history teacher, Miss Jones. I'm pleased to say that we are officially a couple, and I couldn't be happier!"

He raises the mug, even though it is empty, and adds: "A toast, to me and Miss Jones!"

There is a momentary silence while our colleagues look from him to me and back again, then the room erupts into cheers, laughter, applause, and lots of other teaspoons being banged against the side of other mugs.

I have seen several announcements in staff rooms. I have been in them when people have shared news of their engagements, weddings, pregnancies, new jobs, promotions, and even, on one occasion, a divorce.

I have never, though, been the cause of one myself. I know that I am blushing like a schoolgirl.

People are clapping. People are looking at me. People are patting Karim on the back in congratulations, and others are heading in my direction. I am the absolute center of attention.

I completely hate it, and I also completely love it.

I look over the crowds at Karim, meet his eyes, and give him an "I'll deal with you later" look before I am engulfed by a wave of women who all look as though they have a *lot* of questions for me.

He just winks and gives me a regal bow. I suppose I should be grateful that he didn't call himself King I-Love-You the First.

# CHAPTER 32

# FOUR GLASSES OF BUBBLY, ONE KOOL GANG, AND MY OWN THREE WITCHES

**They are all there by** the time I arrive. I messaged Erin and Katie earlier in the day, asked them to meet me at Margie's at 6:00 p.m., and said that I was bringing champagne.

I am slightly late getting there, because I made the time to call my mother once I finished work. I called her to invite her here, her and Sam, to see my home and my friends and my life. It is a small step, but one I could tell she grabbed at gratefully.

Reading that letter from Beth, seeing that she didn't blame me right there in black and white, made me realize exactly how powerful forgiveness is, and if it is within my power to offer that to my own mum, then I will at least try.

It is a mild evening but full dark by the time I walk through Margie's gate. The chiminea is on, the fairy lights are sparkling, and they are waiting for me, all wrapped up in blankets. I see glasses on the table, and a cake that I can tell Margie has baked herself due to the fact that it is wonky in all the right places. She is many things, my friend, but a world-class baker is not one of them.

Bill wanders over, sniffs my hand, giving me a thorough once-over for any signs of food. He slinks, disappointed, back

STATISTICALLY SPEAKING

under the table, where perhaps he is planning a daring collapsed cake raid.

"Here she is!" announces Margie, struggling to her feet.

All three women crowd around me, and Erin grabs my left hand. She holds it up to the light and they all stare at it intently. I have no idea what is going on.

"Where's the ring?" she says, sounding forlorn.

"What?" I ask, frowning. "What ring?"

"Well, you called an emergency meeting. Told us there would be champagne. We thought Karim had popped the question!"

All I can do is laugh—their expressions are an absolute picture. The more confused and deflated they look, the more I laugh. It is cruel, but I cannot help it.

"Oh God, no," I finally manage to say, feeling a pleasant ache in my sides, "not that! We're not at that stage yet!"

"Yet?" says Margie, leaping upon a morsel of consolation. "Does that mean you've talked about it at least? Do I need to buy a new hat?"

"No! We haven't talked about it. At all. What's the matter with you? Can't a woman celebrate without needing a ring on her finger?"

"Right on, sister!" says Katie, offering me a fist to bump. I oblige, and get the chilled bottle of fizz out of my bag.

I pop the cork as quietly as I can out of respect for the dog lying beneath the table, and pour us all a glass. I don't make a very good job of it, but eventually the deed is done. I grab one of the fleece blankets and wrap it around my shoulders.

"So," says Erin once I'm done, "what's the deal, then? Why are we celebrating? Did you win the lottery?"

"Kind of," I reply, grinning. "In fact, it's better than that. My daughter got in touch."

Margie clasps her hands to her heart and immediately starts to cry. Erin gives me a hug, and Katie says: "Cool. So what's she like? What did she say? Tell me I'm still your honorary long-lost daughter!"

I grin, happy for so many reasons—not least of which is that we have come through that particular hurdle, that we can now joke about what was once a very difficult subject. It is easier to cope with now. Everything feels easier, in fact.

Margie goes off into the flat and puts on some music. I hear the funky riffs and familiar woo-hoos of "Celebration" by Kool and the Gang, and it does indeed make this feel like a party. She probably had it lined up and ready to go for when I showed off my nonexistent diamond, but has decided that this is just as good an occasion.

We settle down around the table, and I pull the precious manila file from my bag.

"Now, I'm going to pass this around so you can all look at it," I announce, "but I am going to insist that there is no cake first!"

"Should we all be wearing white gloves before we touch it?" asks Katie.

Margie and Erin look confused, and she adds: "History joke. You wouldn't get it."

"No white gloves needed, but—well, it is a significant historic document, in its own way. She wrote me a letter!"

"An actual letter?" Katie says, looking impressed. "Wow. I don't think I've done one of those since I was writing to Father Christmas."

"You still write to Father Christmas," says Erin, poking her in the ribs.

"I know, but that's just so you know what to buy me."

They chat among themselves, and first I show them the photo. They consider it very seriously, studying this girl, this mythical creature, this unicorn of my line.

"She's beautiful, Gemma," says Erin, looking a bit teary-eyed herself now.

"Absolute stunner, like her mum," adds Margie, nodding.

"I like her eyeliner," comments Katie. "Makes her look like Cleopatra. It's really weird, seeing her, isn't it? She's the same age as me. And she kind of looks a tiny bit like me. I wonder if she likes K-pop . . ."

The picture is passed back to me with much reverence, and I hand over the letter. Erin takes it, as she is sitting in the middle of the three women, and the other two lean in to read it. It takes them much longer than I want it to take them, as I am desperate to talk about it—to hear what they think, to share their thoughts.

Each of them, I know, will see it from a different perspective, and each will have something to offer.

When they finish and the letter is safely back in its protective cocoon, I look at them eagerly.

"So?" I say. "What do you think? Doesn't she sound amazing? Doesn't she sound happy?"

"She does, love," replies Margie, reaching out across the tabletop to pat my hand. "And I know that's the main thing for you. I know you've always secretly been worried that you gave her up to have a better life, but you've never been convinced that that was what she got. Now you know—she one hundred percent did. She sounds like a bright young woman with the world at her feet, and she's someone you can be very proud of."

"Well, I am proud of her," I say, frowning as I think it through. "But I'm also aware that the pride belongs to her parents, really.

To Sue and Richie. They're the ones who raised her. I just grew her in my belly and donated some genetic material. What do you think, Erin? I'm going to write back to her tonight, and I'm already obsessing about what I should say. I don't want to overwhelm her, or come across as desperate—even though I sort of am!"

Erin smiles gently, and I know that this might be a scenario she has imagined being on the other side of many times. That the whole issue of children, biological or not, might be a bitter-sweet one for her. Katie is not searching for her parents right now, is not looking to be reunited with them, but that might change. Erin, like Beth's family, will be supportive—but she will also be nervous.

"I think she sounds amazing, Gemma. I think her parents sound amazing too, and I know how hard it must have been for her mum to help her write that letter. That took real courage and shows how much they love her. I think they got it just right, don't you? It's early days yet, but the door is open now—it's a beginning. If I was her mum, I'd be proud of her too, and also a bit scared about what all of this means—not just for me but for her. I'd be concerned and have some reservations."

"Like what?" I ask, leaning forward, elbows perched on the table, genuinely keen to know. If there are reservations, I want to address them.

"Well, we know you, Gemma. We know you've gone on to make something of your life. We know you are clever and kind and in your own weird way extremely sorted. But they don't know that yet, do they? For all her mum and dad know, you could be a complete mess. Your life could be a disaster zone, and you could be a bad influence. At worst, you could be someone who might exploit their daughter in some way. Drag her down, emotionally or even financially."

I sit back, horrified at the words, feeling their sting. I have never considered this, but of course she is right. They know nothing about me and must be anxious, waiting to see if I will be an asset to Beth's life or a drain on her emotions.

Their first impressions of me, all that they actually know about me, stem from the fact that I was a sixteen-year-old in care who got pregnant. Not exactly the most inspiring beginning.

Erin looks upset when she sees my reaction and quickly adds: "I know you're not any of those things—I'm not suggesting you are. I'm just telling you how they might feel. How I might feel. Their number one priority will be to protect her, and they don't know yet whether you are someone she will need protecting from. Does that make sense? Please don't hate me. I didn't mean to burst your bubble!"

"No, it's all right," I reply, shaking my head. "It's okay. I asked what you thought, and this is what I needed to hear. I'm sitting here popping champagne corks and they might be sitting at home wondering what kind of threat they might have invited into their daughter's life. It's useful to know, and it will help me write that letter—because I know she will show it to her parents. I'll be writing it as much to her mum as to her. What do you think I should say? What will reassure them?"

Erin looks relieved and gulps down a few mouthfuls from her glass.

"Well, I think you need to write from the heart and not go overboard on the reassurance—it's not like you need to send them a copy of your CV! Just tell them about yourself. Tell them that you're a teacher. Tell them that you have friends. Tell them that you have a partner, and almost a dog—that seems to be a big winner with them. Just make sure they know that this is a good thing, not a scary one."

Katie has been quiet throughout this exchange, and I know she must be soaking it up. It must be odd for her, hearing her mum's views on the issue, and I know she will be storing some of this away in her giant brain.

I glance at her and raise my eyebrows.

"I think," she announces, "that you just need to tell her you've always loved her. That you've never forgotten her or stopped thinking about her. That you know her real mum and dad will always be exactly that—her real mum and dad. That you're not looking to replace them, because you couldn't ever. But that if she wants to, you'd like to stay in touch, take it slowly, and get to know her better. That's what I'd want to hear. You're not that bad, you know, for a grown-up—hey, if you like, I'll write you a reference!"

We all laugh, and the thought of it takes some of the tension away. I dread to think what would constitute a reference from an eighteen-year-old: gives me booze and does dance-offs?

I look around the table at the three of them. One who is old enough to be my mother. One who is young enough to be my daughter. One in the middle, who is my friend. Different ages, different backgrounds, different people—but every single one of them completely perfect in their own way. I feel suddenly weepy, overcome with the realization that for the first time in my life, I have this—I have my own tribe.

I have Karim. I have the Three Witches. I am in touch with my own mother, and with my child. I can feel Bill licking my ankles beneath the table. All is well in the world, and I offer up a silent prayer of gratitude to whoever might be listening.

"Thank you," I say eventually. "All of you. You three, and that PE teacher guy, have changed my life. I couldn't have done any of this without you, without your encouragement and support and without the dancing and the drinking and the laughing. I've gone from being scared of everything to feeling excited about the future. I don't even count as much anymore! Everything has changed, everything—and you are all part of it."

"Are you crying, miss?" asks Katie, calling me "miss" out of school because she knows it will amuse me. Possibly stop me from descending into full-on sobbing.

"I just might be," I say, swiping at my face. "That or I've got something in my eye. Anyway, thank you—I mean it, I really do. And if Beth ever reaches the stage where she wants to meet me, I'll be taking all of you with me. Me, you three, Karim, Bill. Road trip. It's all or nothing."

Margie cackles and replies, "What on earth would she think if she saw all of us trooping around with you like bodyguards? How would you explain that one?"

"It's pretty simple," I answer. "I'd tell her the truth. I'd tell her that you're my family. The one I made for myself."

# CHAPTER 33

# ONE NEW BEGINNING

*Five months later*

**We have been in this** pretty town for hours already, because someone—that would be me—insisted on heading out at five in the morning, "just to be sure." We made the drive down in torrential rain, the same rain that has been battering the land for weeks now, flooding fields and bursting riverbanks and flattening gardens.

As soon as we arrived, it changed—one of those strange moments when the downpour just stopped, sudden and unexpected, as though a giant overhead tap had been switched off. The sun emerged, rainbows appeared, and we all stood in the hotel car park staring up at the dry blue sky as though we'd never seen such a thing before.

It is spring, and we have learned to expect the unexpected. Now we are grateful for the respite, the gentle heat on our skin like a reassuring touch, walking around gloriously unencumbered by raincoats and umbrellas.

The streets of Stratford-upon-Avon have emerged clean and fresh, bright green leaves dripping with liquid, tables and chairs hastily set up outside street cafés. People are laughing and talking to each other, the welcome change in season making friends of strangers.

I am here with Karim and Katie and Erin. Only one of us is missing—two, if you count Bill. The hospital letter that arrived for Margie on the same day as Beth's landed for me was inviting her for a routine mammogram.

She didn't think much of it, and neither did I—it's called "routine" for a reason. The difference this time, though, is that they found a problem. They found breast cancer.

Margie had become such a big part of my life that I think I was more shocked than she was. I simply couldn't imagine my world without her in it and was devastated at the diagnosis. I tried to hide it as well as I could, because I didn't want to end up in the ridiculous situation where she was comforting me instead of the other way around.

It was caught early, before it had a chance to spread, and all the signs are good that the lumpectomy and radiation therapy she had have worked.

We have all rallied around her; Bill moved in with me while she was in hospital, and Margie has dealt with it all in her typical stoic way. She has cried and joked in equal measure, and I am in awe of her resilience, her ability to remain optimistic no matter what is thrown at her.

It was—still is—a huge worry. Even being away from her for one night feels reckless, as though it is inviting disaster. As though the cancer will sneak back if I'm not there to stare it down. Also, I just miss her—we all do. Technically, she is well enough to have come, and we all tried to convince her to. Karim even offered to rent a posh Jeep so we could travel in style. She remained firm, insisting she wanted to stay at home to look after Bill—of course, it was nothing to do with Bill, who would gladly have gone to stay overnight with a sitter.

It was because she didn't want to slow us down, to hold us back in any way.

She is a silly moo, and we all wish she was here, no matter how slowly we'd have needed to take things. We wish she was here, cracking rude jokes and cackling and making us all laugh.

We have compensated for her absence by making constant video calls, giving her a secondhand guided tour of Stratford.

We have taken her on walks around the historic streets, taken her inside the quaint tearooms, held up the screen to show her the Royal Shakespeare Company at the waterside. We have rented a boat, and Karim has rowed us up and down the river, giving Margie a running fake-sports commentary on the way.

We have been on a tour of Shakespeare's birthplace, which sent me and Katie into some kind of history-induced trance. Seeing those higgledy-piggledy rooms, looking through the windows he'd have looked out from as a child, seeing the fireplaces and furniture and beamed ceilings of his home—it was really wonderful.

We have done all of these things, crammed into a blessedly busy day, and now I am here, standing alone outside an art gallery on the amusingly named Sheep Street.

Karim, Katie, and Erin have gone to the nearest pub, after multiple assurances from me that I am going to be fine. I think Karim wanted to hover nearby, waiting to catch me in case of unexpected swooning. It is sweet that he feels like that, but it would be too much for all of us to turn up at once. If this goes well, there will be time for introductions later. For now, I take heart from the fact that I know he is probably watching me from the window. That he cares. That they all do.

I am early, and I decide to give Margie yet another call.

"Hiya, love," she says, her voice amused. "Are you going for the world record on how many phone calls I've had in one day?"

"Sorry, am I interrupting something important?"

"Well, I'm watching *Poldark*, if you must know . . ."

"Ah. Fair enough. Just wanted to check on you."

That, of course, is a lie. I just wanted to hear her voice. I just wanted to hold on to normal for a few more moments.

"So," she says, "are you standing outside the place you're supposed to be meeting her?"

I laugh and reply, "Almost. How did you know?"

"I knew because I know *you*. So, tell me about it—the place where you are right now."

"Well," I say, glancing around. "It's called Sheep Street. There's a really nice town hall, opened by the actor David Garrick in 1769. There are lots of historic buildings—houses, restaurants, a pub. From what I read before we came, there's been property of some kind here since the twelfth century. It apparently has the oldest-surviving cobblestones in Stratford . . . and . . . okay. I feel better now. You really *do* know me, don't you?"

"That I do. So, remind me, then—what is happening on this day in history?"

"I am meeting Beth," I reply, smiling. Even the feel of her name on my lips makes me happy. "I am meeting my daughter."

"You are. So stop blathering and get on with it."

She hangs up, and I smile as I put my phone back into my bag. Margie might not be here in person, but she is making her presence felt. I glance around at the pub across the way, and sure enough, I spot them all in a window seat, Katie waving at me through the glass.

The café is just around the corner, on a cobbled alleyway. I scoped it out earlier, got a quick coffee, counted the tables, the usual me stuff.

Now I have to walk toward it, and toward her. We have written letters, exchanged photos, swapped phone numbers. We have edged into each other's lives carefully and cautiously and, in my case, joyously—but we have never met. Not until today, at this kind-of midway point between her home and mine. Between her people and my people.

I wonder idly if her mum and dad and siblings are lurking somewhere nearby as well—maybe our families are all in the same pub, trying to look out of the same window, all feeling nervous on our behalf.

I take the steps I need to take. I cross the cobbles and close the distance. I stand by the café door.

I look inside, and I see her. I see my daughter, waving at me through the window. I see her smile, her deep red hair, her big brown eyes.

I see my baby girl, all grown up. I see her in all her perfect glory—ten tiny fingers, ten tiny toes.

I open the door. I walk toward her. And I make history.

# ACKNOWLEDGMENTS

Getting to the end of a book is always an achievement, and I would never make it without the help and support of my friends and family.

Thank you to Dom, Keir, Dan, Louisa, Norm, Tara, Dave, and the extended clan for endless chaos, distractions, and inspiration. I love you all billions. Plus, I know they're not reading this, but a big woof to my dogs, who listen to me talk about plots all day long without ever once complaining.

Thank you to my pals—you really are the best. Pamela Hoey, Sandra Shennan, Paula Woosey, Helen Shaw, Ade Blackburn, and everyone from my regular quiz nights—sanity savers every one of you.

My author pals are also fantastic. This can be a strange job, and you do most of it without colleagues by your side. Huge love then to the people who make it feel like I'm not alone—Milly Johnson, Catherine Isaac, Miranda Dickinson, and Carmel Harrington among them.

On the professional front, I'd like to thank my agent, Hayley Steed, and the whole wonderful team at Harper Muse, especially my editor, Lizzie Poteet, Savannah Breedlove, and Kerri Potts.

This is, of course, a work of fiction—but I have tried to root it as much in reality as I could. Thanks to the people who spoke to me about both their personal and professional experiences with care and adoption, including Graeme Harper, whom I have been asked to acknowledge as "the Greatest Man in the World." I have tweaked reality in places where I needed to, because, like I said, fiction.

This book is set in Liverpool, where I live. I loved doing that, and recreating Gemma's little seaside home. I've played slightly fast and loose with some geography, so to my fellow dog walkers—many of whom have their pooches named in this!—forgive me if you find yourself thinking, *Hang on, there are no houses by that second sand dune on the right . . .*

I hope you've enjoyed reading about Gemma and her family—and that you'll join me for the next adventure! Thanks to everyone who has read or written about my books—you really are the vital ingredient.

# DISCUSSION QUESTIONS

1. When we first meet Gemma, she is giving birth to her baby, and afterwards we read a letter that she has written, to be given to her when she is older. What would you include in a letter to your baby, before he or she was born? What would you like to express to them?

2. What advice do you wish you could have given Gemma at that stage in her life?

3. Gemma has built a solitary life as a way of protecting herself from harm. Do you think the trauma of her own childhood explains that, and do you think it worked for her? Did she gain or lose?

4. As a way of coping with her anxieties, Gemma counts and recites facts. What are your coping mechanisms when life starts to feel overwhelming?

5. Was Gemma's assumption about Katie possibly being her daughter understandable, or simply wishful thinking? And what did you think about how she handled the situation?

6. Are the secondary female characters in this book important? What do Margie, Erin and Katie contribute to the story, and to Gemma's journey?

7. What qualities does Karim possess that eventually enable Gemma to take a risk on love?

8. Was Gemma right to reach out to her own mother as well as her daughter, or should she have left that complicated relationship in the past?

9. One of the themes of the book is that you can find a family as well as be born into one—are there any examples of that in your own life?

10. What do you think happens next—do Gemma and Beth become close, do her and Karim stay together? What would you like to see happen?

# ABOUT THE AUTHOR

Debbie Johnson is an award-winning author who lives and works in Liverpool, where she divides her time between writing, caring for a small tribe of children and animals, and not doing the housework. She writes feel-good emotional women's fiction and has sold more than one million books worldwide. She is published in the USA, Canada, Australia, India, Germany, France, Italy, Turkey, and the Ukraine. Her bestsellers include the Comfort Food Café series, *Jenny James Is Not a Disaster*, *Cold Feet at Christmas*, *The A to Z of Everything*, *Maybe One Day*, and *The Moment I Met You*. Her novel *Never Kiss a Man in a Christmas Sweater* was made into a Hallmark movie.

Facebook: @debbiejohnsonauthor
X: @debbiemjohnson

For more from Debbie Johnson, don't miss

*Jenny James Is Not a Disaster*

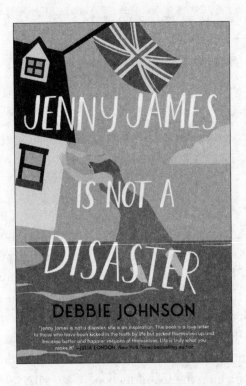

Available in print, e-book, and downloadable audio